STAR WARS
ROMANCE

EYES LIKE STARS

STAR WARS
ROMANCE

EYES LIKE STARS

BY

ASHLEY POSTON

Random House New York

To all of us who played
with lightsabers in the front yard

Random House Books for Young Readers
An imprint of Random House Children's Books
A division of Penguin Random House LLC
1745 Broadway, New York, NY 10019
penguinrandomhouse.com
rhcbooks.com/disney

Cover illustration by Ombretta Tavano
Cover design by Kurt Hartman and Madison Ackerman
Interior design by Madison Ackerman

Library of Congress Cataloging-in-Publication Data is available upon request.
ISBN 978-0-7364-4858-1 (trade pbk.)—ISBN 978-0-7364-4859-8 (ebook)

The text of this book is set in 13-point Mrs Eaves.

Manufactured in the United States of America

1st Printing

The authorized representative in the EU for product safety and compliance is Penguin Random House Ireland, Morrison Chambers, 32 Nassau Street, Dublin D02 YH68, Ireland, https://eu-contact.penguin.ie.

Random House Children's Books supports the First Amendment and celebrates the right to read.

A LONG TIME AGO IN
A GALAXY FAR, FAR AWAY. . . .

Welcome Aboard the Starfarer

PLEASE CHECK THE ITINERARY
FOR YOUR VOYAGE'S UPDATED SCHEDULE

ITINERARY FOR
THE CENTURY OF CHANGE TOUR

DAY ONE—Coruscant

We embark on our tour. All guests are invited to the First Night Soiree to celebrate the CENTURY OF CHANGE tour.

DAY TWO—Alderaan

Upon arrival, guests will embark on a tour of the Monument. There you will learn about the life and culture of the lost planet of Alderaan and how conservation efforts have brought back many agricultural riches thought lost.

DAY THREE—TRAVEL DAY

As we make our way into the Mid Rim, guests are encouraged to explore the Starfarer *and all its amenities. We will serve breakfast, lunch, dinner, and snacks in the mess hall. Entertainment will be provided in the main chamber throughout the day, including a lively historical discussion!*

DAY FOUR—Naboo

Guests are encouraged to meet our special guest in the main chamber before embarking on a tour of a Gungan city and enjoying a rousing lunch with entertainment planetside. (Note the change in excursion details.)

DAY FIVE—TRAVEL DAY

Sit back and relax after a riveting day on Naboo as we venture forth into the Outer Rim with shipside entertainment. Test your mettle in simulated pod racing tournaments, and show off your knowledge during Trivia Hour!

DAY SIX—Tatooine

Stretch your legs as the Starfarer refuels. Visit the markets and taste the local cuisine. Later, attend a tour of a moisture farm like the one Luke Skywalker grew up on!

DAY SEVEN—Geonosis

Embark on a rousing tour of three Clone War battlefields planetside, and then sit back and relax as you taste delicious drinks even a bounty hunter would kill for.

DAY EIGHT—Yavin 4

As you marvel at the lush landscape of Yavin 4, we invite you to hold a vigil with us as we honor all those lost while securing peace through the destruction of the Death Star.

DAY NINE—Kashyyyk

Put on your best shoes; it's time to have a party with some of our furry friends planetside! Shake your cares away as you dance under the stars in an authentic Wookiee celebration.

DAY TEN—Mimban

Journey into the lush forests of this mud planet to learn about the ecological effects of the Imperial occupation and its detrimental mining practices—and meet a real Mud Jumper!

DAY ELEVEN—~~Dantooine~~ Ghorman

Come with us to a city once rich in silk and twill, and learn about the Imperials' slow encroachment into everyday Ghor life, resulting in a massacre of peaceful civilians. A quiet mourning ceremony will take place after.

DAY TWELVE—Endor

On Endor's forest moon, we take our bow. Don't miss this exciting excursion, where we will celebrate the persistence of hope in the galaxy and raise our glasses in a toast to a brighter tomorrow!

DAY THIRTEEN—TRAVEL DAY

Unwind and relax as we ferry you back to where it all began. Make memories in the mess hall, join a sabacc game in the main chamber, or snag a complimentary massage.

DAY FOURTEEN—RETURN to Coruscant

CORUSCANT

CHAPTER ONE

THE DAUGHTER

I was lost.

Frustrated, I checked the directions on my datapad again, turning the minimap around to try to make sense of this maze. It kept freezing, the piece of junk. I'd spent way too long trying to navigate my way through the complicated layers of Coruscant, a planetwide city made like a thousand-tiered cake, to find Baelor's Baubles and Bibelots. I was supposed to be back on the ship by now, before anyone noticed me missing. Kotti could hold off my dad only so long, and I'd already wasted all my time lost in Spindlehub Square, trying to find this place. I was so close—*probably*.

Kotti had warned me that my stubbornness was both endearing and exhausting. "You're like a starving rancor when you're after something," she'd once commented, sore and tired after traipsing through an entire market in Mos Espa on Tatooine, searching for a stall selling the best dustcrepes. "You're either going to get it, or you're going to die trying and bring everyone else down with you."

I had decided to take that as a compliment then, but now I was second-guessing myself. And it made me nervous. On the ship, I knew everything. I knew the routines, I knew the itineraries, I knew every nook and cranny—

Out here, everything was new.

It's good for you to get out and see things, I told myself to quell my anxiety. *You're being silly. What's the worst that can happen?*

My minimap told me I was very close to Baelor's Baubles and Bibelots. It should be right down the next shady alleyway. (It was *always* a shady alleyway.) If Dad knew I was *this* deep in Coruscant, he'd never let me leave the ship again.

A message pinged on my device. It was from Kotti.

Where are *you??*

I decided to call her instead on my comlink and took it out of my oversize leather jacket. "I'm almost there, Ko, no worries."

Static came over the link, and then her voice punched through with sharp panic. "*Almost there?* You've got to be kriffin' *kidding* me, Ardent," she whined.

"The map is really confusing."

She groaned. "Your dad's getting suspicious, and if he finds out that I'm helping you, my job's totally skiffed. I said you were in the 'fresher, but I can't keep him away for much longer."

"I'll be back soon, I promise," I replied, squeezing between two large taupe beings and down the shady alleyway in question. As long as my dad didn't notice me missing, everything would be perfectly fine. "I could be taking a long shower."

"You've already been in there twenty minutes."

I winced. "Then tell him I'm on my cycle."

"*Are* you?"

"I mean"—I thought about the timing—"soon?"

She gave another hard sigh through the comlink. "You owe me."

"I'll buy you a juja-cake from Gharnie's," I promised.

"*Two* of them," she replied, and I agreed because I had a feeling I wasn't as close to the shop as I'd thought I was, judging by the dead end I had just encountered. "Just hurry back. Things feel weird."

I rolled my eyes, because she said that about everything. Coruscant had one of the many ports we frequented, and Dad wouldn't dock at any port in the galaxy that wasn't 100 percent safe. He was allergic to danger. Had been since I was born.

I'd inherited some of that, I thought.

This level made me nervous. If I weren't looking for the shop, I'd *gladly* return to the ship immediately. Who knew what sort of puddles I was stepping in, or people I was brushing up against, or smog I was inhaling—

I tucked my comlink into my jacket pocket again and retraced my steps, setting down the next dark alleyway. This one looked promising. "And once you get this, Ardent, you never have to leave the ship again," I promised myself.

Neon lights blinked above me, their reflections bright in the puddles at my feet. I skipped over the deeper-looking wet spots and side-stepped trash as I followed the directions on my datapad. Was ruining my only good boots worth coming all the way out here to find a romance serial?

Yes—I had it on good authority that Baelor's had the rare last installment of *Under the Tan-Tan Sun*, a serial I'd been looking for the past few years. It was almost impossible to find anymore because the series was close to twenty years old, but a guest last tour had suggested I look at Baelor's.

So here I was.

Something cold dripped on my nose and I shivered, pulling my worn jacket around myself tighter. It was too big for me, but it had belonged to my mom back when she flew freighters for the Republic, and while it didn't smell like her anymore, I felt a little braver with it on.

Besides, it looked cool and vintage and was much better than my tour uniform.

The alley let out into a bustling street in Spindlehub Square, vendors hawking their wares as buskers played outdated glimmik for a few creds, the smell of burning fried mynock making the air smoky and thick. Coruscant had a certain kind of thrill. It was *the* Core World—a hub for hundreds of planets—so cultures and people and stories mingled together like threads twisting into knots.

By the numbers on my datapad, I thought I was finally in the right location. Which meant it was *somewhere* around here. I pushed myself up on my tiptoes to see over the crowd—

And there, nestled between a noodle joint and a clothing store, was a tiny shop with a large front window display showing ancient-looking tomes and strange gadgets from across the galaxy. The hand-lettered sign above the door read: *BAELOR'S*.

Thank the *stars*.

I hurried across the street and ducked into the shop. Inside, every surface was cluttered with . . . *stuff*. Antique knickknacks with notes alleging that they were from far-off places, or originally owned by long-dead Jedi or mercenaries or nightwitches—*Nightsisters*, I corrected the note silently—and Sith. I was quite sure that the Senate insignia ring in the window had *not* belonged to Emperor Palpatine, but of course I couldn't prove it.

This place was tacky and almost certainly pawning off junk, but there was something immediately lovely about it, too.

I loved a good story—a good fairy tale. I was raised on the best of them. I loved how they could transport you to faraway times and faraway places. How they could protect you from heartache and shield you from grief. How they could make you feel understood in a galaxy that often made you feel so incredibly small. And how they sometimes made you care about whether the fictional queen of fictional planet Naroo would be murdered in cold blood by her would-be droid-assassin lover.

Okay, maybe that was just romance serials—but it was still a fun story.

There were shelves and shelves full of old texts and holobooks between old gadgets and half-broken artifacts, and a separate shelf for books on datatape. There must have been hundreds, all stacked on top of each other haphazardly, impossible to look through if you didn't already know what you wanted to find.

As I wandered deeper into the shop, a gadget caught my eye. It was a simple flat plate of copper with rotating disks on top of it that you could spin or flip, and on each circle were different symbols, and on the disk itself was the smallest map of the known galaxy I'd ever seen. The note simply read, *Tool once used by hyperspace prospectors to navigate the stars.*

Something deep inside my chest tugged toward it, like my lungs were caught on a fishhook.

Navigating the stars, huh?

I picked it up. The device was lighter than I thought it'd be, so it couldn't be made out of copper. Whatever it was, though, it was old. My fingers traced the markings on the outer circles. They were worn, almost illegible, but any navigator worth their weight in creds would know what they were.

A star chart.

Was it real?

"You break it, you buy it."

Startled, I jumped and spun toward the checkout counter, where a grumpy reptilian Rodian sat, flipping through a holobook of Alderaanian poetry. I quickly put the device back. "Sorry. I—I was just looking."

"And touching."

"Sorry," I repeated. "It's very pretty."

He inspected me for a long moment and then closed his holobook. "Not many people pay attention to that old thing. It's a celestialabe. You know, before droids charted ships through hyperspace, there were navigators who did that. Some were rumored to have a special knack for it—*astrogating*, they call it."

"Ah." My heart jumped into my throat. I twisted my fingers together, looking down at my filthy boots. "That, um, that sounds dangerous."

"Most things that matter are." The Rodian waved his hand in the air. "But now we've got droids and maps and charts, and the celestialabe is obsolete. Then again," he added, a sparkle in his black eyes, "maybe it'll point you somewhere you've never been. Maybe with it *you* can astrogate, too."

"That's not how astrogating works," I said before I could stop myself.

He narrowed his eyes at me. They were large and buggy. "It's not?"

"I mean, that's what I hear," I quickly amended, and decided to change the subject before I torqued him off further. "Actually, I'm looking for something in particular. The last installment of a serial novel."

The shopkeep sat back on his stool. "Are you now."

"It's kind of rare, but someone told me if anyone would have it, your shop would."

"And they'd be correct." He motioned to the shelves upon shelves of holobooks and datatapes. "Name?"

"*Under the Tan-Tan Sun.*"

The two sucker-like antennae on the top of his head stood up. Then he leaned forward, scrutinizing me, and asked, "By Alkenine Gro'sha?"

I leaned in close, too, holding on to the edge of the counter. "Yes! I'm desperate for it."

The old shopkeep studied me in a new light. He gave a slow nod. "That's an odd serial for someone your age. How'd you hear about it?"

"My mom," I supplied simply. He didn't need to know the rest.

"She's got good taste."

I forced a smile. "Yeah. The last installment ended on a cliffhanger, and this is the only one she didn't have."

The Rodian clicked his tongue. "That's a tough one to leave off on, that's for sure. The Queen should've never left her bedroom. She should've known it was a trap!"

I threw up my hands. "*Especially* after the assassination of Ambassador Naur-Ral!"

He leaned back, waving his hand flippantly. "*Pfff*, I wouldn't be worried about him."

"But she saw his body!"

"Didn't check his pulse."

I gave it a thought. "She didn't, did she?"

"Always check for a pulse," he said solemnly, pushing himself off his stool, and then he shuffled out from behind the counter. He went to the shelf near the celestialabe and started digging through a few bins at the bottom. "I think you might be in luck. I remember seeing one somewhere around here—aha!" He pulled out a small square drive. It was bright blue—like the Crystal of Effervest they were searching for in the serial. The publisher really did know how to market the series way back when.

"If the ambassador is still alive, then who will she choose?" I wondered aloud as he shuffled back behind the counter to make sure the datatape booted up. "The assassin or the ambassador?"

"The assassin droid might still kill her. He *does* need the money."

"The ambassador might backstab her—he wants power!"

We exchanged looks, reader to reader, like to like, before he wrapped the drive in a brown cloth he'd pulled out from under the counter. "You're in luck today, kid. It's the last one I've got."

"Thank you." I took my purse out of my satchel to dig out a few creds and put them on the counter. "Is this enough?"

He didn't even count them as he took the credits and handed over the wrapped datatape. "Happy reading and—may the stars keep you steady," he added with a wink, quoting the infamous goodbye in the serial.

I smiled. It was a real one this time. "And the iron keep you safe."

With a grunt, the Rodian drew on the guise of a curmudgeon again as he sank back onto his stool to pop open his holobook of poetry.

I turned to leave, the package clutched tightly to my chest.

Finally, the last installment. I'd first stumbled on the serial when I found a trunk full of my mom's things in the belly of the ship a few years ago. It was one of the few things Dad had forgotten about, so he'd forgotten to throw it out, too. The serials and old clothes—including this jacket—and star charts were the last possessions I had of Mom's.

And now something of her collection was complete. I had actually *found* it. Maybe escaping the ship every so often wasn't such a bad idea, after all.

Now all I had to do was find my way back to hangar eighty-nine.

As I left the shop, the front door flew open. I collided with a young man hurrying inside. My forehead met his chin, and we both stumbled back, hissing in pain. He was tall, covered in a ratty-looking cloak, hood pulled low.

"Sorry," he murmured, rubbing his chin, already passing me into the shop and heading straight for the old Rodian.

"S'fine," I muttered to myself, because clearly he hadn't stuck around to see if I was, and left. My head hurt. I was sure I had a red mark where his chin had caught me on my forehead. "Ow . . ."

I hoped it wouldn't bruise. I *really* didn't want to think up a lie to Dad. I already had enough going.

Remembering the way I'd come, I started down some steps to a market street lined with shops from different sectors, selling specialties at absurd prices. I was good at navigating places I'd been—it came with the territory, really.

One tended to pick up a few tricks when one was the daughter of Captain Hansifred Quay of the *Starfarer*.

Halfway down the street, I peeked into the package just to make sure I hadn't dreamed up that entire scenario. There it was, the icy-blue datatape and—

There was something lumpy, too. Unwrapping it a little more, I reached inside, my fingers curling around the flat, cold thing beneath the datatape.

The celestialabe.

Had I accidentally snagged it? No, he'd wrapped it in the cloth along with the tape. But I hadn't paid for it, and if my dad saw something like *this*, he'd get suspicious about where I'd gotten it. The trinket was far too expensive. Never mind what the shopkeeper had said—that it was for *astrogating*. Even if that were true, I wanted nothing to do with that.

Nothing at all.

I dropped the celestialabe back into the bag and turned on my heel toward the shop.

I hadn't paid for it.

I didn't want it.

That was exactly what I'd tell the old Rodian when I handed it back to him, but politely. I shouldered open the shop door. "Mr. Baelor—"

"Is this really necessary, friends?" The voice cut through mine, smooth and cool.

As my eyes adjusted to the dark shop, I became keenly aware that it wasn't nearly as empty as it had been a few moments ago. The acrid scent of something burnt—meat? What kind of meat smelled so foul?—filled my nose.

A handful of men surrounded a younger man at the counter. I recognized his filthy cloak, though his hood was pushed back to reveal shimmery silver hair. They hadn't seen me yet, so I ducked behind a half shelf full of pristine creature skulls and peeked out from behind it. I didn't know why my instinct was to hide. It was just a feeling, a shiver up the back of my spine.

Daaric always told me to trust the shiver.

"If we're friends, then hand it over," said one of the men, stepping closer to him. "We tracked you halfway across this blasted galaxy for it."

"Don't look him in the eyes," one of the other men warned. "They're strange."

"That's rude. My mother said I had very pretty eyes," the young man replied with a shrug. His voice had a strange lilt that I didn't expect to hear this far into the Core. It was drawling and lazy, better suited for the Outer Rim—Batuu, maybe. Or an outpost on Bakura. Somewhere in Wild Space.

He was certainly a long way from home.

Where's the shopkeeper? I thought frantically, looking around until I spotted a hand on the ground two aisles across from me. Dread coiled in my belly. *Oh, no.*

I quietly crawled to the shopkeeper and found where the terrible burning smell was coming from. The Rodian had tried to escape and been shot in the back. He lay splayed out, with a smoking blaster wound.

They had killed him. He was dead. I'd just been chatting with him about a serial and now he was *dead.*

I was going to be sick.

Oh, stars, what if they found *me* next?

"Where *is* it, scum?" a man snarled. I heard an altercation and peeked out again from behind the shelves. The apparent leader of the five men had a blaster shoved directly into the Wild Spacer's abdomen. "I won't ask again. Give us the relic and we'll tell you what happened to that teacher of yours."

I fisted my hands. This wasn't good.

"If you're here, I already know," drawled the Wild Spacer. And then a wide smile stretched across his pale face, chaotic and foreboding. "That hotshot new junior officer of yours killed her. What, he couldn't come here himself? Too busy sucking up to your cute little Supreme Leader?"

"Watch your mouth!" the leader sneered, pressing the blaster harder against the Wild Spacer's stomach.

"Aw, sweetheart, did I hit a nerve?"

He had a death wish—that was that—and I was about to be witness to a murder. Would that mean I was an accomplice? How would I be able to sleep at night? These men were really going to shoot him. They were going to murder him right here in a random shop on Coruscant—

No, they won't.

I steeled myself. I liked sleeping at night.

I was about to stand from my hiding spot to do something, *anything*, as a distraction—

The body of the Rodian twitched, and his hand shot up to snag my wrist, keeping me hidden. "Always check for a pulse," he rasped, and from inside his vest he pulled out a blaster.

Oh.

CHAPTER TWO

THE CHASE

To be honest, I panicked.

There really wasn't another explanation for it. One second I was staring down at a not-dead Rodian with a blaster in his hand, the next I was diving for the floor as he roared to his feet, taking shot after shot at the men.

Two went down immediately.

Two more ducked for cover.

Using the commotion, the Wild Spacer slammed his head into the man with the blaster aimed at his stomach, so hard I heard the crack of a broken nose from where I was. The man stumbled back, blood gushing down his face. Then the Wild Spacer kicked a shelf where one of the men had taken cover. It toppled over, spilling holo-books and cheap gadgets onto the ground.

I scrambled to my feet.

Mr. Baelor shouted, *"Run!"*

The leader lifted his blaster and, spinning toward the

shopkeeper, took aim. I shrieked. It was all I could do. I was too far away, and he was too fast with his trigger finger. The Rodian couldn't even aim before the leader shot him square in the chest. He crumpled to the ground.

Then the leader turned his pistol on me.

I was going to die.

Suddenly, a blur dropped from a grate in the ceiling and landed on his head. It was a creature, sort of wide and bulky. It trilled triumphantly as it clawed at the leader's hair and ears, gnawing with angry teeth. The man yelped and tried to throw it off, but every time he grabbed for it, the swift creature dodged to the other side. And then back again. It cackled, like this was a game.

Someone grabbed my wrist. Without thinking, I swung my hand wildly, connecting with their face. The Wild Spacer yelped in pain. I now understood what that man had meant about his eyes being strange. They were disorienting on a human face. Completely black, save for specks of white that gave the illusion of a night sky. He touched his reddening cheek. "You slapped me!"

"Well you startled me!"

"But you—*argh! Chuba*," he cursed, "that *stings*." Shaking it off, he set his mouth into a thin line and took me by the arm as if he wasn't quite sure he wanted to. *"Run,"* he advised, and pulled me away.

I stumbled, catching sight of the Rodian on the ground. *Check for a pulse,* I thought, hoping he was still alive, but with a blaster shot that close . . .

The Wild Spacer tugged me to move, so I did as he'd said.

I ran.

The next few moments were a blur. Leaving the shop. The door slamming behind us. The humid, smoggy market air.

There was one inalienable fact about Coruscant, however: If you wanted to get anywhere fast, you never took your own feet. The market was loud and congested. We wove and bobbed between groups of people, and I remembered reading something about this in one of Mom's serials—

Wasn't it easier to follow people when they tried to claw their way through a crowd, rather than when they tried to get lost in one?

"Slow down!" I cried, pulling at his hand.

He whipped his head back to me, his eyebrows high. He replied, incredulous, *"No?"*

I tugged his hand again. "Slow *down*!"

"If you need me to carry you—"

"Slow down and we'll blend in!" I snapped, and realization dawned on his face.

He slowed his steps—one, two, and then we were in the ebb and flow of the crowd. I forced my body to go slow even as panic clawed up my throat. His shoulders were coiled tight, as if he was also fighting the compulsion to bolt. We were like creatures resisting our base instincts.

Someone hawking pretty beaded bracelets said, "Hey, you with the silver hair! Wanna buy a trinket for your girl?"

He stiffened. "Uh, no, she's not my—"

"I don't do bracelets," I interrupted, and tugged him sharply to the left and between two smoky food stalls. As we went, I pulled the hood of the Wild Spacer's cloak over his head, disguising his hair. He glanced down at me in question, so I explained, "You're too noticeable."

He winked. "Sadly, it's all natural."

I gave him a scandalized look. "Are you flirting with me while we're running for our lives?"

"Is there a better time?"

My stomach did a funny flip. "Yes, *any* other t—*ah!*" I yelped as a red-hot blaster bolt careened over my head and melted the edge of a neon sign above us.

One of the men chasing us shouted, "There they are!"

"Plan failed," he said simply as he grabbed my wrist,

and we were running again, down narrower and narrower alleyways.

I'd taken enough detours on Coruscant to know how to get certifiably lost—and that was exactly what we needed to do. I hoped the alleyways would lead out into a larger street, but instead we found a dead end. So we backtracked to try to find something—anything—but the buildings were squeezed so tightly together there was nothing save for a narrow crevice between two grimy buildings. I could fit, but the Wild Spacer was too broad.

"I'm dead," the Wild Spacer groaned.

Yes, yes, he was. We *both* were. My mind raced.

Wait—

There was a scene like this in the third installment of *Under the Tan-Tan Sun*.

"Try anyway!" I instructed.

He opened his mouth to complain, but the remaining three men were catching up to us through the alleyways, their footsteps growing louder. He muttered something to the sky and squeezed himself sideways into the narrow crevice between the two buildings. I grabbed a large piece of scrap from the ground and shuffled in after him, propping the scrap at the opening to try to hide us.

"This is your best plan?" he hissed. "I can barely breathe in here."

"Then hold your breath," I snapped in a sharp whisper. Then I wiggled my arms up and pulled his hood over his head, hiding his bright hair again. "There."

He narrowed his eyes. "It's the mole on my face, isn't it? Everyone notices it."

I honestly hadn't seen the mole, but now that he mentioned it, there it was—just below the left edge of his mouth.

"And now you're looking at it!" Was he—was he *pouting*?

"It's not the mole," I replied, looking at the mole. It was very close to his mouth, which seemed to always settle into this half grin or half grimace, tucked in at the corner. It was a nice mouth.

I startled myself with that thought—a *nice mouth*? What even did that *mean*?

"Well, it can't possibly be—I think they're coming," he said, his voice going dangerously low. His arm went around my waist almost immediately. I tore my attention away from his mouth, my heart beginning to race in my ears.

The footsteps were close now, the men's voices so loud they reverberated off the metal buildings. They would find us, kill *me*—I'd heard enough stories that I knew exactly how this was going to go, because they were probably syndicate goons or bounty hunters or, or, or some sort of militia—and probably drag this Wild Spacer into an alleyway to torture him for whatever information they must think he had and then—

Stop, I chastised myself. My imagination was getting away from me.

I should've stayed on the ship.

Fear clawed its way up my throat, even as I tried to swallow it down. Was I breathing loud? I felt like I was. What if they found us because of my wheezing? Why was it so hard to breathe? Painful, even? Why was—

Oh, wait.

Something sharp poked into my ribs. It was hidden in the Wild Spacer's cloak. I squirmed, trying to alleviate the pain. "What *is* that?" I hissed.

He hesitated. "What's what?"

"That." And I squeezed my hand between our bodies and moved the object. It was solid and cylindrical.

"Nothing . . ."

"That is *not* nothing."

"It's just—*chess ko!* Watch yourself!" He hissed as I slipped my hand into his gray cloak and pulled it out. At first, it looked like a metal handle to something. The insides rattled. It took a moment for me to realize what exactly I was holding.

A lightsaber.

He tried to grab it back, but I quickly moved out of his reach.

I stared at it, wide-eyed. "Is this yours?"

"Obviously."

"No, it's not."

He turned his face to the sky and took a calm breath. "Then why did you *ask* me?"

"You're not a Jedi. They don't exist. They're gone," I said, and then another thought occurred. "Is *this* what those guys are after?"

His mouth tightened into a thin line. I took that as a yes.

"Are you in trouble?"

He quirked an eyebrow. "How do you know I'm not the one *causing* the trouble?"

"Are you?"

"Do you want me to be?"

I caught his gaze and narrowed my eyes. Looking into his eyes felt like looking into the night sky itself, too large and unfathomable to stare at for very long—though I'd stared into the sky so often, his eyes didn't bother me at all.

He frowned. "Are you all right?"

I cocked my head. "Why wouldn't I be?"

"Because my . . . You know what, never mind." He turned his face away, breaking eye contact.

I asked, "How did you get this l—"

"They're here," he whispered, bending over me and lifting his cloak around us so we were a little more hidden in the gap. The sudden darkness made it intimate, and under *any* other circumstance I would have wondered at our closeness. But my hands were trembling. My heart rattled against my ribcage, so loud I was sure the whole alleyway could hear. We couldn't move. We didn't dare.

And so we waited.

CHAPTER THREE

THE UNFAMILIAR

My mother used to sit me on her lap in the quiet hours all to ourselves on the flight deck, the buttons and knobs on the console blinking and beeping in symphony as she told me, "You can go wherever you want, my heart. The sky is wide."

And I used to believe her. She always looked most at home in the pilot's seat, humming to herself as she flew. Most of the time the *Starfarer* coasted on autopilot—droids and navigational systems were more than enough to accurately take a ship to its destination—but Mom always rechecked the coordinates anyway, and she charted courses, and she dreamed.

My mom dreamed a lot.

She came from a long line of hyperspace prospectors—explorers charting unknown regions of our galaxy and finding safe routes home. That was her magic, I used to think—that wherever she was in the galaxy, she could always find her way home. So whenever she went out on excursions, I never worried. Sometimes she'd be gone for a day or two, sometimes for an entire tour itinerary, but she always came back.

Until she didn't.

I remembered that I had begged her not to go. It was almost my eighth birthday, and she had promised to take me to my favorite restaurant on Naboo. But she went anyway. She took the lander and left on an errand.

On the day she was supposed to come home—my birthday—I stood outside of the cockpit as my father talked with her over the communicator. He sounded worried—no, that wasn't right. He sounded *frightened*.

"Audra, don't. It's too dangerous," my father warned. "Just hide the lander somewhere. Repair the droid. Then come home."

"I can't, Fred," she replied. Her voice was filled with static. She must have been a long way away. "I promised Arie. I'll be fine. You worry too much."

"I worry *just enough*."

She laughed. "I'll see you soon, and Arie will *love* her present. I'll be fine," she added, softer. "I've jumped this a thousand times before."

Dad sounded unsure. "But I was with you."

Mom laughed through the communicator. "You're with me now, silly. Love you wide."

"Audra, love, don't—*Audra!*" Dad's voice broke. He

shouted for our ship's droid, N2-O, to help him get a lock on the shuttle, and for a moment in my memory, he did. Though, that might have just been a haze of my imagination filling in the blurry bits.

She never came home.

I couldn't disappear like Mom. I couldn't do that to Dad. I had to make it out of this alive—no matter what.

I curled my hands tight around the saber hilt, pressing it against my chest. My knuckles were white from gripping it so hard. My heart beat so loud, it thundered in my ears, and I was terrifyingly aware just how screwed we were if they found us—and how much of my body was wedged against this stranger.

When he breathed, I breathed.

In. And out.

In. And. Out.

He was so warm and solid, grounding me in a way that pinned my panic so it couldn't rise any higher. He smelled like the strangest thing—*dust*. Like something older than ships and stars. It made my chest ache in a way I couldn't name—like bittersweet nostalgia, the scent of something I'd never known I lost.

The Wild Spacer's arms wrapped around me tightly.

The side of my face pressed against his chest, and his heart was hammering, and hammering, and hammering.

For all the cool smooth-talking, he was just as scared as I was.

"Do you think they went down that other alley back there?" one of the men asked.

"I think they're still here," said their leader.

Strange—weren't there three of them left? Where had the other one gone?

I heard the Wild Spacer curse under his breath. The next moment happened so quickly. He reached for something on his hip. The men pushed back the scrap of metal blocking the crevice—

The Wild Spacer drew a pistol and fired off two shots. One of the men fired back before both of our hunters went down for the count. White-hot static buzzed over them. Their bodies jerked, eyes rolling into the backs of their heads.

He pried himself out of the crevice first, and numbly I followed suit.

"Did you . . ." My voice wobbled.

"They're only stunned." He glared down at the men in disdain. "But that was probably a mistake."

"Why—" I sucked in a breath as I noticed a blaster hole on the right side of his cloak. "You're hurt!"

Startled, he glanced down and noticed the burn hole, too. He frantically parted his cloak and melted with relief. The shot had missed *him* at least, though it also burned the shoulder of his jacket.

"That could have been worse," he said, more to himself than to me as he took off his cloak. He kicked one of the unconscious men over, turning him on his back, and began patting him down. He found what he was looking for in the man's pockets—a communicator and a small metal cylinder. "Damn. First Order." He scrubbed the top of his head in aggravation and stood. "I was kinda hoping they weren't."

I wasn't sure I'd heard him properly. "I'm sorry—did you just say *First Order*? Like *the* First Order? Like the zealots in the Unknown Regions who want to bring back the Empire *First Order*?"

He stood, tossing his cloak over the men. "Unless there's another one you know of . . ."

"You must be mistaken," I said, shaking my head. "They can't be here—how do you know from that—that *thing*?" I motioned to the metal tube in his hand.

"This," he said patiently, holding up the metal cylinder, "is a code cylinder. They contain coded information about whoever uses them and grant them some sort of security clearance. First Order officers usually carry them."

"How do *you* know?"

He gave me an unreadable look, and his mouth did that peculiar twist again—tucking in at the corner. "This isn't my first time."

If I hadn't been panicking before, I certainly was now. "Oh, stars. Oh, *stars*," I repeated, pulling my hands through my hair. I stepped back. There were two unconscious—perhaps *dead*—fascists on the ground, and despite wanting to kick them *again* for, you know, who they were, the gravity of it all was overwhelming. "This is bad. This is *so* bad. I—I have nothing to do with any of this." I began to tremble. I had done a good thing and helped somebody out, and now I was complicit in a crime. "I just wanted to complete my mom's serial collection."

My voice sounded far away. I sank into a crouch.

"Hey," he said, squatting down beside me. He put a hand on my shoulder. "Breathe, yeah?"

"I'm trying," I replied, realizing that I was still clutching the lightsaber to my chest. I needed to let go of it, but my fingers wouldn't cooperate. They were stuck. The reality of the past ten minutes—the death of the Rodian, the escape, the firefight—came crashing down on me.

I could have *died*.

With a sigh, he sat down beside me. "We can't stay here long. They're gonna wake up soon."

I felt like I was going to vomit. "How are you so calm?"

"Practice," he replied. Then he offered his hand to me. "Sian, by the way."

I looked down at his outstretched hand, then at his face. His strange eyes studied me, dozens of pinholes of white, widening just slightly as he drank me in. "Ardent," I replied, and pried one hand off the saber to shake his hand.

He grinned. "Thanks for helping me back there."

"Yeah . . ." I looked down at the saber.

"I didn't kill anyone, if that's what you're worried about," he added. I *had* been worried about that.

Suddenly, an air vent grate behind us fell with a loud thump, and a creature scuttled out of it. I startled with a yelp as the creature scrambled across the alley and up Sian's body to his shoulder. It nudged its head against his with a purr.

He scrubbed the creature under the chin. "Quick thinking back in the shop, Noola. Were you the one who took care of that last guy?"

The creature chirped in reply. It had three short legs on either side of a long, narrow body, each leg bound with a glossy sort of webbing. Its face was diamond-shaped, with wide gold eyes with a vertical pupil, a forked tongue, and a frame of horns the same deep indigo as the scales on its body. Though the longer I looked, I wasn't sure if it was a trick of the light or if the scales changed colors from purple to green to blue. The only parts of it that didn't shift colors were the tufts of fur on its paws and the tip of its tail.

I recognized the creature from the shop earlier. "That's your pet?"

"She's more like a babysitter," he clarified. "Now. Let's find our way out of here, shall we? But first, can I have that saber back?"

Mortified, I shoved it into his chest. "Yes! Absolutely. It's yours." I looked away, a flush crawling across my cheeks.

He bit back a grin as he returned it to his gray jacket.

Regrettably, when we found our bearings, we were in a *much* seedier area of Coruscant. Dad had warned me to stick to the main streets of Spindlehub Square, because the crime syndicates weren't quite as prevalent there, but here that was quite obviously not the case. Blaster holes marred the buildings, and sparks screeched out of broken tech above. The streets were damp, and the neon lights fizzled. As we made our way toward what looked like the main street, the people mingling there were of a much different crowd, too, and the light that filtered in from above was so removed, it was barely a pale mirror of itself.

We were still in Spindlehub Square, I was sure, but *where* . . . I had no idea.

Neither, it seemed, did my companion.

"We can ask that person where we are," he said, motioning toward what looked like a bar and the bouncer guarding the door.

I hesitated. "Is it safe?"

"I dunno. They look nice though," he added, and waved to the bouncer. I shadowed him, tugging anxiously on my braid.

The bouncer, an incredibly big Houk, eyed Sian. He crossed his massive arms across his barrel-like chest, surveying us with beady eyes set deep in a thick skull decorated with bone ridges. "*Man-tah*. Speak."

Sian perked up. *"Ah'chu apenkee!"* he said with a wave of his hand. Huttese. So he *was* from Wild Space—or at least the Outer Rim. He said something else fast and thick in the language and motioned behind them.

The Houk bouncer narrowed his eyes. Then he said in Basic, "Catch an air taxi at the end of the street."

"*Jupa uba.* Thank you," Sian replied, and tilted his head down the way.

As we followed the bouncer's directions, he touched

his cheek, wincing with a hiss. It was still red, and slightly swollen.

"You have a mean slap, you know," he said. Noola purred again, and he wagged his finger at her. "That's not nice. And you're being dramatic."

Such an odd pair they were.

Luckily, the bouncer had steered us right. There was a taxi call box at the end of the street. Sian dug into his pockets—he had a lot more of them than I would have thought—but when he came up empty, he took a pocket-knife from his boot and crouched down to pop open the money collection bin.

"What are you doing?" I asked in alarm. "You can't just *steal* that!"

He rolled his eyes. "Don't think too hard. I'm just recycling." He pried the door open and took out more than the fare amount, then closed it back up. "How much do you need? Where are you going?"

"A hangar on level five-one-two-seven."

He whistled. "Guess you're a spacer then?"

"My family runs a tour company," I replied. "We embark from there later today—oh, stars," I gasped, realizing, and checked the time on my wrist chrono. "I was supposed to be back almost an hour ago. Dad's going to kill me."

Something over my shoulder caught his eye, but he tried to ignore it. "A tour company—like the Chandrila Star Line or whatever? The really fancy ships?"

I wrinkled my nose. I *wished* we had that kind of money. "We're not so fancy."

His attention flicked again to whatever was behind me. "Ah."

"We're affordable, actually. And we orchestrate visits to historical locations, like battlefields, ancient ruins, and disasters."

"So dark tourism then."

"Just historically significant—what are you looking at?" I added, turning to glance over my shoulder, but he caught my chin to keep me from looking and rubbed a smear of grime off my cheek.

"Keep your eyes on me," he said softly, his voice barely more than a rumble, "and stay calm. There are four people coming toward us with blasters."

My entire body stilled and went cold. "First Order?"

"I don't know. They don't look it. We could have a bounty on us."

Noola chirped to tell us that a taxi hovered over the landing pad, lowering toward us.

Sian said, "We're just going to get in, quickly, and hopefully they won't make a fuss."

"And if they do?"

"You'll be fine. Just do as I say, okay?"

I thought I could hear their footsteps—heavy and urgent—against the movement of the crowd, or that might have just been my imagination.

Either way, it brought the taste of tin to my mouth. "I don't want to die."

He gave me a reassuring smile. "Give me a little more credit, yeah? You're not going to die."

The taxi settled on the platform. It was rusted yellow and long, with a closed cab and tinted windows, looking more like a racing pod than a taxi. I was used to seeing the open-air ones from the higher levels.

He instructed, "Go—*now*."

I did, diving for the door to the air taxi as it arrived. The droid navigating asked, "Where to?"

"Hangar eighty-nine. Eastern spaceport. Topside!"

A blaster bolt pinged off the taxi call box. Sian pulled out his pistol again and fired twice before climbing in beside me. Noola was tucked into his jacket. He slammed the door closed.

"Go!" I cried.

The droid went nowhere. "Fare first."

Sian rolled his eyes. "We'll pay in the air!"

"Request denied," the droid replied.

One of the people after us slammed their fists against the air taxi window, shouting at us to get out. Two others came around the other side. They weren't dressed like the men pursuing us before. They looked a whole lot rougher.

Sian fumbled with the creds he'd stolen from the taxi box and dumped them all into the front. "There! Is that enough?"

"Denied. Too much."

"Keep the change, you hunk of junk!"

The droid debated a moment, earning another dent in its speeder. Then its eyes blinked blue. "Accepted. Taxi en route," it relayed, just as one of our pursuers pressed a blaster to the windshield.

We were *absolutely* going to die.

The air taxi shot into the air, tossing off two of the people, and quickly rose into one of the skylanes.

I bent over, putting my head between my legs. I was going to be sick. "I'm never leaving my ship again," I promised myself.

But I didn't get sick.

"Aw, this was nothing. Just a normal day on Coruscant," Sian said lightly.

I don't know what came over me—I just . . .

I started to *laugh*. I threw my head back, holding my aching sides. The last hour had been so ridiculous, so *impossible*, it was really the only thing my body could do that wasn't crying, and I was terrible at crying, anyway.

I knew he was staring—I could feel it—but I didn't care. The laughter shook all the fear out of me, settled it back in the bottom of my soul like silt in an ocean.

"Oh, yes, that was just a pleasant walk," I gasped between howls of laughter. "A little jaunt around the city, running for our lives!"

He chuckled, unable to hide the smile eating at the corners of his mouth. "We all need a little fresh air and impending doom."

I laughed so hard, it brought tears to my eyes. "I can't believe we survived getting shot at! *Three times!*"

"We're either incredibly lucky," he said, "or incredibly unlucky."

"I almost hate to find out which of us is the unlucky one once we go our separate ways," I replied.

His laughter stopped short. "Ahem. Yeah . . . about that." He rubbed the back of his neck sheepishly. "If those were people looking to collect a bounty . . . then they know you're with me now."

My own laughter caught in my throat. "I am *not* with you."

He leveled a look at me. "You know what I mean."

Wordlessly, I looked between him and his creature, and then at him again. "They think I'm helping you?"

"Well, you kind of did."

"I did," I realized. My thoughts fell on the lightsaber

tucked into his jacket. I remembered what the leader had told him in the shop. "Why's that saber so important?"

"It's not," he replied quickly, looking out the window at the passing speeders.

"Is it yours?"

"No."

"Then whose is it?"

"No one's," he replied, flicking his gaze to me.

A whole lot of helpful answers there.

I studied his easy demeanor. There it was—that strange pulse again in his eyes, white pinpricks widening before retracting again. I made him nervous, or did my questions? "Do you normally lie to people you just met?"

Knowing he was caught, he smoothed an easy smile over his lips. It *almost* made the lie easier to swallow. "I'm usually better at it," he said decisively, "but my charm doesn't seem to work on you."

"And what charm is that?"

His smile widened, and it reached his glittery eyes. "You're fun, Ardent."

"Well, *you're* infuriating."

"I aspire to nothing more."

He laughed again, disarming the tension that had built in the taxi, and we made small talk for the rest of the ride to hangar eighty-nine.

CHAPTER FOUR

THE SMUGGLER

The taxi landed a short walk from the docking bay, and Sian walked me all the way to the entrance. At first I wondered if it was simply because he was invested in my opinion of the most recent galactic pop star who had found themself in another auto-tune scandal or the artificial weather of Coruscant and why it was always so *muggy*, but no. Maybe he was just being chivalrous?

I had my suspicions.

I had my suspicions right up until he cursed and ducked behind a large crate waiting to be moved into the docking bay. He pressed himself flat against it and quickly motioned for me to follow. I didn't see what he was so concerned about until two men emerged from the crowd, heading toward the hangar.

Which sent me quickly behind the crate with him.

He thumped his head against the back of it. Noola chirped inside his jacket. "How does word travel so *fast*?" Then he squeezed his eyes tightly closed and massaged the bridge of his nose. "They're going to be looking for me in every ship out of here," he muttered. "This is *not* my day."

"Well . . ." I glanced around the crate at the men again. "It looks like they didn't see us. They're leaving."

Noola chirped again, and he absently scratched her head as he peeked around the crate with me. "Yeah . . ."

Suddenly, my communicator crackled, making us both jump.

"Hello? Arie? Helloooooo?"

I quickly pulled it out of my leather jacket, about to answer, and then thought better of it and turned it off. I'd see Kotti in a few minutes anyway. "I should get going. I'm sorry I can't be of more help, but I hope everything works out for y—"

"No—wait!" He caught my wrist and then quickly let go of it. A muscle in his jaw throbbed. "Wait," he repeated, as if the words pained him. "I . . . have a favor to ask. I'm not going to get off this planet otherwise."

I pursed my lips, looking down at my wrist, where he'd touched me. "Why is that lightsaber so important?"

"It just is."

Which still wasn't an answer.

"Sorry," I mumbled, and tried to leave again, but with his long legs, he managed to get in front of me and block my way around.

"I just need to get off this planet," he said.

I felt myself tense like a trapped creature. He was tall and broad, a certifiable brick wall I wouldn't be able to budge, but I *could* scream, and that was just as potent. Then everyone in the hangar would come running . . . *including* the people looking for us both.

Which also wasn't great.

"Please," he added, and then seeming to realize he was blocking my way, he agonizingly stepped aside.

I should have fled then. I should have been halfway up the ramp to hangar eighty-nine. Instead, I gave it a thought. I really shouldn't have. But he hadn't lied to me yet, even if he wouldn't answer *all* my questions. He was on the run, and it did make sense that a tour ship was trickier to track than a passenger one. It was like running in a zigzag versus a straight line—harder to hit you if you kept them guessing where you'd turn.

And then there was the whole mess with those First Order goons. . . .

I chewed on my bottom lip as I thought it all through. "You get off at the first stop."

"That's fine."

"Tomorrow."

"Perfect, I hate travel."

This was a terrible idea. I'd already saved him once, but then again he'd saved *me*, too. And if anyone could smuggle him out, it would be me. *Still* . . . I bit the inside of my cheek. "Okay."

Relief flooded his face. "Really? You mean it?"

"Yeah. I'll go tell my dad—"

He gave a start. "*No!* No—the less people who know about me, the better. I promise you that. You saw how those First Order officers hunted me, *and* you. I don't want them after the whole ship."

The chances of someone on the ship finding him were ridiculously high, and what if he did something while on the ship? Stole something? Vandalized? Ate one of Veebee's rare century eggs? I outstretched my hand. "We'll try, but while you're on my ship, I'm holding on to that thing."

His eyes widened. "What? No. Out of the question."

"Then we don't have a deal."

Frustrated, he set his jaw. "You're asking for the moon, Starlight."

My eyelids fluttered at the nickname. It surprised me. "I'm . . . just asking for collateral. You'll get it back when you leave."

"How can I trust you?"

"And how can I trust *you*?" I echoed.

He shifted, muttering to the creature on his shoulder, and then extended the saber to me. "Fine. It doesn't work, anyway. It's broken."

"Even better. We don't usually allow weapons on the *Starfarer*." I put the saber into my leather jacket and then glanced one more time around the crate. It would be hard to smuggle him onto the *Starfarer*—and if we got caught I'd have to explain it all to my father, and I doubted he'd take Sian's dodgy answers in stride like I did. Then there was Kotti, who couldn't keep a secret to save her life, and if anyone else saw him . . .

My attention returned to the crate itself. PERISHABLES, it read, bound for the *Starfarer*, full of food to restock the galley. "I have an idea."

He hesitated. "Will I like it?"

"Depends. Do you like pickled fleek eels?"

He paled, which was answer enough.

Everyone in hangar eighty-nine—in the entire spaceport—knew about the *Starfarer*. If they didn't, then I was pretty sure those people were living under a rock. There were only two reputable tour companies in the known galaxy, and one of them was owned by Captain Hansifred Quay.

(Obviously more companies existed, but none of them were quite as storied as Hyperlight Tours or—sadly—our dreaded rival: the ultra-exclusive luxury cruise company Chandrila Star Line. Though rumor had it that they were about to close up shop due to budget cuts—which was nonsense, but rumors were often more catching than the truth.)

Few people knew the galaxy as well as my family and my family's ancestors. It came with the territory, really. We were descendants of hyperspace prospectors and cartographers who had charted some of the most notorious hyperspace lanes in history. It was said even the famed Plyon cartographers came to the Quays when they needed directions. My great-great-great-grandfather on my mom's side founded the most legendary hyperspace lane of them all. And somehow, while we were swirling through hyperspace across the galaxy, something strange had settled into our bones—something that made us special.

We were exquisite navigators.

Magical, almost.

Or at least that was the rumor.

The Quays never denied it. The rumor was good for business, and it wasn't exactly a *lie*. The actual truth simply stayed in the family, much like our beloved tour ship, the *Starfarer*.

In the docking bay sat the ship, an old CR90 Corellian Corvette, refitted with current tech and refurbished with the kind of painstaking detail only Captain Hansifred Quay could muster, down to the is-that-rust-or-is-that-stormtrooper-blood on the bulkheads. (It wasn't either one. It was paint. Dad just liked to be dramatic. "Everything has to tell a story," he always said, and took it to heart.)

For the nearly three decades since the Galactic Civil War had ended, Dad and his crew had been ferrying daring tourists on journeys to the heart of history itself: to the asteroid field where Alderaan paid the ultimate price in the war, the frigid battlefields of Hoth where the rebels held their ground, Endor's orbit to lay eyes on the carcass of the Death Star II, and countless other scars in recent history—Yavin 4, Naboo, Corellia, Geonosis, Kashyyyk, Coruscant, Ghorman. And those were just the ones we could travel to relatively safely. Sometimes when the stars were quiet, Dad would sneak in a trip to glimpse a dying red giant, or visit a cantina on Batuu, or take a waiver-signed outing to Bakura. History reached across the galaxy, but most stories and their popularity came in lulls and waves, and Dad rode them like the expert historian he had become.

When he finally retired, I would take over the business. No one ever asked if I wanted to. Of course I did.

There *was* no one else.

Besides, people booked travel with Hyperlight Tours solely to say they were on a ship captained by a Quay.

So of course no one blinked an eye when I signed off on the crate hiding the stowaway and sent it off to be loaded onto the ship.

This is a terrible idea, I told myself, because it was.

But what else was I supposed to do?

As I went up the gangway of the *Starfarer*, a Twi'lek stood at the top of it, nose-down in her datapad as she checked off the last bits of her pre-tour checklist. She chewed on her bottom lip worryingly—a habit that was hard to break, even after she made it bleed. Her skin was the color of fresh moss, accented by the golden bands she wore on her forearms and long twin lekku she usually pulled over her shoulders. She rocked back and forth on her heels nervously.

That was never a good sign.

Then she looked up and startled, almost tossing her datapad. "*Ardent Quay!* You're alive!"

"Somehow, I survived," I deadpanned.

"I thought you were *dead*!" she cried, running down the gangway to give me a hug. Her accent was strong, curling at the ends like vines. "I was going to have to tell your *dad*! Then *I* would have been dead!"

"No one's dead," I squeaked as she hugged tighter. Well, *almost* no one. "Can't breathe."

She let go and held me at arm's length. She narrowed her eyes. "Seriously, though, where have you *been*? You were supposed to be back an hour ago!"

I winced. "Did Dad . . . ?"

She waved her hand dismissively. "I'm a professional.

He thinks you were still in the shower. Then you went to your room. Girl stuff. You were right, it worked like a charm."

I groaned. "Great."

"You know, if you'd come back an *hour* ago then I wouldn't have had to lie *to my boss*."

Which was true. "I appreciate it."

If Dad knew I was out on Coruscant, on a level he didn't approve of, *alone*, he'd combust. After Mom died and my brother Valor left, Dad focused on me. I was all he had, so I understood it. Losing Mom was a tragedy, but when my brother left the *Starfarer*, it broke Dad's heart in a way he hadn't recovered from, and ever since it'd been exhausting to try to be both his son *and* his daughter. Kotti told me once that it wasn't my duty to fix everything Val left undone, but she didn't understand. This ship was my dad's entire life—and now so was I.

Kotti twined her arm with mine. "What is your gorgeous best friend for, right? I can lie to my boss *and* haggle down prices for ion chambers to the sublight drive. Truly"—she gave a dramatic sigh—"what *can't* I do?"

"Mmmh, keep a partner for longer than six months?"

"You wound me, Arie. My last partner was at *least* six and a half."

Kotti was five years my senior and one of my favorite people in the whole galaxy. Growing up, I had made friends with other kids during the tours, but it was hard to keep friendships when you kept moving around. Kotti had been the only exception. The first time she came onto the *Starfarer,* she'd been thirteen and with her parents, lovestruck by the grandeur of the ship and its promise of *adventure*. I had been eight and wanted nothing more than a friend.

Ten years later, Kotti was in charge of our guest relations and had become a staple in my life who knew me better than I knew myself most days.

"But seriously," she added, "what happened? I called you and you stopped answering, and then you didn't show up when you said you would. You seriously gave me a heart palpitation."

"I just got lost," I replied quickly, watching two spindly droids behind her tug the crate to the back of the ship and load it into the supply port.

"Liar."

"There was traffic."

"There's *always* traffic. Are you in trouble?"

Not exactly, but it wasn't something I could tell Kotti about—at least not here, out in the open. Besides, I needed to get to the galley before the droids started unpacking the supplies and found my stowaway.

And you'll bring her into all of this if you tell her anything, I thought. *You'll put her in danger.*

And that was the last thing I wanted.

"I thought we didn't lie to each other," she added quietly.

I flinched. "No, that's not—"

From the mouth of the ship, a booming voice cried, "*Daughter!* There you are!"

We jumped, startled, and spun around on the gangway toward the voice.

Standing in the airlock, a middle-aged man crossed his arms over his broad chest and quirked a thick peppery-brown eyebrow. His dark blue uniform was pressed to perfection, not a single golden tassel out of place, with the medals he'd earned from the war pinned to his collar. He must've just gotten out of a meeting with someone important, because he looked quite captain-like at the moment, his deep brown beard braided with souvenir rings and ornaments from faraway planets, his hair pulled into a neat ponytail. His beard had a streak of white, like a vein of silver in clay. He always joked that it was a gift from his children.

I knew he couldn't possibly mean *me*.

Captain Hansifred Quay cut an imposing figure to anyone who didn't know he had a sweet tooth for obessa seeds and a secret love of the opera.

Kotti pushed back her disappointment and called up to the captain, "She finally came out of her room! Yay!"

He studied me, worried. "And everything's sorted?"

"Um—yes." What had Kotti *told* him? "I'm feeling better now."

The worry quickly faded, overcome with excitement. "Grand! Because we need you in tip-top shape for this tour! I have a feeling it's going to be special."

"You say that about *every* tour," I pointed out, and Kotti agreed.

"And I'm right about every tour," he said with a wag of his finger, unable to hide a toothy smile exposing that he was missing his left canine. The way he told it, he had gotten into a fistfight with an Imperial stormtrooper during the war, but I think he lost it in drunk celebration one night just after the fall of the Empire. He tilted his head behind him and said to Kotti, "Speakin' of things that always happen, Veebee needs one of you. She lost her finger again."

Kotti sighed. "*Fine.* I'm done with my precheck, so I'll do it. Where is she? In the galley?"

"Last I saw," Dad said.

The galley? Oh, no. The supply crate. *Sian.*

I jumped. "I'll do it!"

Kotti waved her hand in dismissal. "I really can. I don't mind."

"I know, but—I haven't done anything yet, you know?

I've just been in my room being . . . um . . . *waylaid* . . . and you know Veebee. She always complains."

Kotti eyed me suspiciously. "If you're sure . . ."

"Oh, yeah, take some time off. I got this," I added with a wave of my own hand.

"Perfect," Dad said. "You know, eventually that finger's not fittin' back on. Let me know when you're done?"

Once we agreed, he passed us on the gangway and headed for the hangar bay tech. The lander was acting up again—something about the comms—and Kotti had already tried everything to fix it, so might as well outsource it. While it was technically out of her purview as head of guest relations, she had a knack for engineering in a way that Entoo, regrettably, did not. So she ended up doing a lot of tinkering in her spare time. I think she liked it—she could take out her guest relations frustrations on faulty hardware, and this ship had a lot of that.

While the *Starfarer* was renowned, it was also old as dirt, and with every tour came another thing that broke.

It was only a matter of time before the ship got too expensive to keep in the skies.

Kotti had pulled her arm from mine and climbed the gangway to the open airlock. Even though I couldn't see her face, I knew she was annoyed with me for lying.

I caught up to her in the mouth of the ship and tugged her arm to get her to stop.

"I'm sorry," I whispered to her.

The annoyance on her face softened. She sighed. "It's fine. I was just worried about you."

"I know." I turned my eyes downward so she couldn't see the Sian-sized guilt there.

She studied me for a moment, and I wondered if she knew what I was hiding, though she couldn't possibly.

Then her communicator beeped in her pocket. The garbled voice of Daaric relayed that the ion chamber had been delivered, and she threw back a reply that she'd be right there. Then she said to me, "You're your Dad's heart, you know."

"I know," I replied guiltily, and left for the galley.

CHAPTER FIVE

THE DROIDS

When the *Starfarer* was empty, I could hear it breathe.

Obviously the ship wasn't *really* breathing—it was the ventilation system moving air in and out of the ducts—but there was a sort of life to this place, the kind you could only really hear when its belly emptied of all the tourists it ferried to faraway stars. My footsteps echoed through the corridors, rebounding to me in whispers. Every so often, the ship groaned as it settled its old bones, and electricity whirred through the bulkheads as thumps played through the pipes like a heartbeat.

I knew this ship like a second body. I knew its quirks. I knew its habits.

That was what happened when you spent your entire life on a ship. You figured out all its little nooks and crannies before you ever learned about yourself.

This was my home—the only place I belonged.

I headed down the corridor to the main body of the ship. Since the CR90 was a civilian vessel now, it had been completely refurbished to house guests and keep the crew hidden. The first, or bottom, deck housed the crew quarters, laundry, storage, cargo, maintenance, galley, and launch bay, which fit a lander for excursions.

From the midship turbolift, the next floor up held our guest quarters, with rooms remodeled to add an air of elegance to our hundred-guest tours; three public refreshers; and administrative offices. But it was the third deck that had changed the most from the old CR90 layout. The conference chamber had been turned into the main chamber, and the operations forum became the mess hall. There was also an entertainment room, the med bay, engineering, and the bridge. These two decks were themed to reflect an old warship, complete with blaster holes and fake vents and rust-colored blood splatter, just to sell the story. Dad loved a good story.

The fourth—or top—deck held the captain's quarters, which was once the stateroom suite, and a few operation hubs that kept the ship running, like the power systems, generators, and offline weapons. I rarely went up there. It was always so cold and drafty, anyway.

On the bottom deck, I put my stuff in my room on the way to the galley. It had been my room for as long as I'd been alive, so the bulkheads were pinned with flimsiplast posters and marked up with paint, souvenirs from different places around the galaxy hanging from shelves, fabric draped across the ceiling. I did anything I could to make my room not look like every other one on the ship—honestly, I tried to make it not look like a ship room at all.

I hung my satchel on a hook on the bulkhead and placed the fluorescent blue datatape on the shelf next to the others, an array of jewel-toned colors. Kotti would laugh at me if she knew I wasn't going to read it, but I wasn't sure I wanted to know the ending.

Besides, I had bigger, more distracting things to deal with. Like the saber. It rattled when I picked it up, like something deep inside it was broken. My thumb snuck toward the discolored button on the side. What color was the saber? Did it give off heat? How did it sound?

Sian said it was broken, but that could mean anything, really, and what was the harm in trying to turn it on? I'd never seen one before. I heard that their blades hummed and gave off impressive heat, and I wondered if you could feel the hilt vibrate with the power of the blade, or how it turned all those different colors.

I held out the instrument, saber spout pointing away, and pressed the button.

The saber fizzled.

I frowned, shook it—only for the insides to rattle some more.

I tried again.

Nothing.

I guessed it really *was* broken. What a letdown. It was too worn, too scuffed to be new, and even though the saber didn't activate, something soft and alive was humming inside. I could feel it, gentle and warm, like a heartbeat. It wasn't mine; it didn't belong to me, but it didn't mind me holding it, either.

It just . . .

It wants to go home.

That idea startled me.

Did sabers have *feelings*? Or was it my imagination carrying me away?

A beep sounded somewhere else on the ship, drawing me back to the present. I put the lightsaber in the top drawer of my clothing trunk, underneath my delicates, because it was quite possibly the safest place on the ship.

Then I left for the galley.

It was three doors down the hall, at the very end. I knocked before going inside, more as a courtesy than anything else.

At first glance, the galley looked empty.

VB-35 was usually at the cooktop, magicking up some new recipe. A bolt of dread coursed through me—

Had they found Sian already?

Panicked, I hurried inside, thinking up enough excuses to fill an entire hull.

Luckily, Veebee was sitting at the scratch table, deliberating over a game of holochess. The protocol droid—well, she was part protocol, part security, part whatever I could find on the cheap—slouched in a chair, head in her hand, staring dejectedly down at the game in front of her. Her opponent was the ship's astromech, N2-O.

Veebee had yet to win against N2-O, but as she often put it, "Every droid needs something to aspire to, and I aspire to make them lose."

It was going about as well as it did every other day.

N2-O used a tiny arm to move their piece into position. Then they gave a triumphant bloop.

Veebee frowned. "You cheated."

N2-O beeped accusatorially.

"Fine." Then Veebee turned to me and tilted her head. "Oh, he sent you. Good. Don't look so panicked, it's just a pinky."

Did I look panicked? I cleared my throat and went to the counter, where I unrolled the soldering kit. "It's just been a weird day."

"Oh?" Veebee pushed herself to stand. "Would it have something to do with this?"

And then she tapped the button to the pantry door.

It slid open to reveal a dejected-looking stowaway sitting cross-legged on the floor, his hands tied behind his back with cooking string. He had a dishtowel shoved into his mouth to muffle him.

I stared at him. He stared back.

"I don't know who that is," I lied.

He argued behind his gag.

Veebee tilted her head to the other side.

He argued a little louder, squirming against his bindings.

I wilted. "He already told you I helped him sneak aboard, didn't he?"

"He did, then I gagged him," she confirmed, watching as I went into the pantry to set him free.

Once I pulled the cloth from his mouth, he snapped, "That defective droid said she'd *filet* me!"

Veebee didn't disagree. "I've always wanted to try cooking humanoid meat."

I unbound his wrists. "I told you to stay in the crate."

He winced, rubbing his freed hands. They were a bit red from the string, though it was much easier to see on his pale, pale skin. In the bright, unforgiving light of the galley, he had the coloring of frost on a window, or moonstone. "I was gagging on the smell."

N2-O beeped a question, and Veebee answered, "No, of *course* the captain doesn't know about him. Why else would she have smuggled him in through the pickled fleek eels?"

"And we'll keep it that way?" I suggested.

Veebee debated. "What's in it for me?"

My eyebrows shot up. "*Really?* You're going to resort to blackmail?"

"I could use some new knives," she went on, motioning to her belt of tools.

"So you can just cut off another pinky?" I asked. She inclined her head, and I sighed, motioning for her to go to the counter so I could fix it. "I'll tell you everything while I put your finger back on. C'mon." I pulled the tools from my little work pouch: a soldering iron, a desoldering pump, wire strippers, and tweezers. They gleamed in the harsh galley light.

Being a hodgepodge of droids, Veebee was tall and awkwardly built, so she had to duck in and out of every room, and her limbs were long and scratched from firefights she'd never been in. She grabbed her pinky finger from beside the game board and handed it to me. "It better be a good story."

"It's a great story," Sian suggested, looming over my shoulder as I went to work. "What model are you?"

"Oh? Do my complexities stun you?" Veebee asked.

"I just haven't seen"—he motioned to all of her—"the likes of you before."

"Vee is one-of-a-kind," I said, preparing to solder the wires between her hand and pinky back together. It was a difficult process, and even more so with someone leaning over to watch. I wouldn't normally mind, but for some reason I was all too aware of how he towered over me, which just reminded me about that tiny hiding spot in the alley, pressed against him, our heartbeats too loud and our body heat too warm. I pulled on my glasses, then asked, "Do you mind?"

He blinked at me, confused. "Oh, right." He eased back a little.

That was better. But not by much—especially since he smelled rather strongly of pickled fleek eel. With a little more room, I got started. "When I found Veebs, she was pretty messed up. Her last owners had tossed her into a junk heap, so I patched her up with a weird E-series model I'd never seen before and dragged her out of the junkyard before the Hutts found me."

"It was probably a defective model," VB-35 noted dryly.

"Probably," I agreed.

While Veebee had adapted to her body, it seemed her programming still had issues with physicality in space, so she was all banged and scratched up. Once, she thought she had cleared an airlock but it turned out her right heel hadn't. So I had scooped up the heel of another droid—spare parts really were everywhere—and soldered it on. Standing about as high as Sian, she was just as broad, a mismatch of bronze and scuffed silver parts, with two long tapered antennae on the sides of her head that looked, from a distance, like pointed ears. Veebee was made up like a patchwork quilt, a little bit of all the places we'd been.

I told her that once, and Veebee had gone quiet for a long moment.

"I don't mind that, I don't think," Veebee had replied earnestly. Which would have been a perfectly good answer if she hadn't ruined it a second later with, "But can't you at least *match* my parts?"

Which, you know, *fair.*

Because he was not allowed to hover over my shoulder to watch, Sian wandered the galley instead, poking his head into cupboards and shelves, making himself right at home. He took a handful of nuts from a bag and ate them as he wandered. "So, you really have lived here all your life, huh."

"On this ship? Yeah."

"Sounds awful."

Veebee studied him. "I don't think I like you." His eyebrows shot up, but before he could respond, she asked me, "Why did you smuggle him in?"

I could have either made up another lie or told her

the truth—but frankly, VB-35 and N2-O were two of the most trustworthy people on the ship, and come to think of it, maybe they could help me hide him.

So I told them what had happened. About finding the little shop in Spindlehub Square and finishing Mom's serial collection and meeting the old Rodian shopkeeper. They knew about Mom's trunk. They knew I kept it in the storage room down the corridor, in a crate labeled EXTRA BLANKETS.

Sian commented, surprised, "You were there for an obscure *romance* serial? Then you left?" His eyebrows furrowed in confusion. "What made you go back?"

The celestialabe. I'd never had the chance to return it to the shop, though I had no idea what use it would be at this point. "He accidentally gave me something I didn't pay for, so I went to give it back."

"You wanted to give back something you got for free?"

I fished out the last wire to connect the pinky to Vee's hand. Really, he didn't have to sound so full of disbelief. People had knowingly risked their lives for less, surely. "I know it's silly. You don't have to rub it in."

He must've realized how he sounded, because he quickly shook his head. "I don't think it's silly—"

"I do," Veebee interrupted. She flicked her gaze to Sian and studied him for a long moment. Noola popped her head out of the neckhole of his jacket, blinking sleepily. The droid looked back at me and said, "This is a terrible idea, Ardent."

"I know," I admitted, "but it's just until Alderaan—"

A long low beep sounded over the ship's intercom.

Our guests had arrived.

CHAPTER SIX

THE CREW

Our guests arrived neither late nor early, but exactly at the most inconvenient time.

I quickly finished reattaching Vee's pinky, and warned Sian and his creature not to leave the galley for the rest of the day. "No corridors, no nothing. If you go, get Entoo to disable the cameras first, yeah? They're always fussy on the bottom deck, so no one will think twice. Got it?"

"Yeah, yeah," he replied easily.

"I mean it. If my dad catches you . . ."

"I'll be spaced?" he asked skeptically.

I gave him a level look. "Worse. He knows a few uninhabited moons. No one'll ever know where you went."

He paled. "Um—okay. Heard."

I winked and hurried back to my room to change into my uniform. Did I *actually* think Dad would maroon him on a moon? No, but Sian didn't know that, and I was much better at bluffing than I'd thought I was.

I wished I had time to at least shower, wash the city off of me, but there was no time, so I fixed my braid, tucking in the errant curls so I didn't look like I had run halfway across Coruscant, dodged blaster shots, and found my way onto some weird wanted list.

In the mirror above my dresser, I looked at my reflection and took a deep breath. I was like a ghost of my mom—curly copper hair and pale skin brushed with freckles that grew warmer whenever I was planetside too long. I'd even gotten her hazel eyes.

Audra Quay was beautiful in all the holovids I'd seen of her. She was a descendant of Wild Space cartographers, and it was like the unknown parts of the galaxy had seeped into her skin. She was like a star. She lit up every room she walked into.

Mom had met Dad just before the Galactic Civil War, when the Rebellion was looking for capable pilots and navigators who could run supplies to far-flung bases. They were teamed up, and over near-death experiences and long hours in hyperspace lanes, they fell in love. Dad came up from nothing. His family were merchants on Corellia who disowned him the second he joined the Rebellion. On the other hand, Mom had been the last in a long line of Quays, and so Dad took the name, too. For him, it was like shucking off a coat he didn't need in exchange for his favorite one.

And while Dad didn't have the Quay bloodline, Val and I did.

So it stood to reason that at least one of us would have Mom's skills.

Dad called it lucky that we both did.

Most ships used droids or a navigational computer to calculate the astrogation of a ship through hyperspace, to ensure that it didn't collide with mass shadows—the gravitational wells around massive celestial bodies like planets and stars and rather large asteroids.

But my mom?

She had this intuition—this *sense*—that let her chart the fastest route anywhere. I'd seen her do it a thousand times, disengaging the navicomputer's autopilot to manual mode and programming in data directly off the charts. She could pick a route, and she'd know it was the right one.

Mom had simply called it wayfinding.

She'd taught me a little when I was young. The intuition was hard to explain. It was more a *feeling* than a precise calculation. I imagined it was like how water-seekers knew where to find moisture on desert planets. Sometimes, when I sat on Mom's lap and opened my eyes wide enough and drank in enough of the sky, I could imagine that I saw them—different paths shimmering in and out of my field of vision like ripples in a pond.

"Calm your mind, love," Mom would murmur into my hair. "Let the stars take you."

Sometimes I still widened my eyes and tried to sense the stars, that tug of intuition, but there was too much noise in my head now. Too much anxiety about picking the wrong path and astrogating us into the middle of an asteroid field or the belly of a ship or the side of a moon—

Like Mom had.

One number off, one degree too far, and suddenly you were stardust.

Even if Dad hadn't refused to let me try, I wouldn't have done it.

Mom died astrogating. I might have gotten her hair and her eyes and her gift, but I wasn't going to inherit her fate, too. Closing off a small part of myself was worth the safety it gave me.

With one last look in the mirror, I grabbed my uniform jacket from the hook by the door and hurried to the midship turbolift.

Daaric and Maeve were already there, fixing each other's collars, and Kotti was coming down the opposite corridor with a bag of pipnuts. They crunched satisfyingly between her teeth. She looked refreshed in the starched dark blue uniform of the *Starfarer.* Meanwhile, mine was quite wrinkled.

"Pinky restored?" she asked as the lift arrived.

"Pinky restored," I confirmed, trying to smooth out the front of my uniform jacket at least. "And she didn't even complain."

"Bless the void for that." Maeve shuffled onto the lift first, picking a piece of invisible lint off her sleeve. She was a stout human with grayish-purple hair, fashioned into a tight bun, and calloused hands from a hard life. She had a gravelly voice and the humor of an executioner, and we all loved her for it. "Who wants to bet the first guest here is one of those history buff types?"

The rest of us followed her into the lift.

Daaric put on a snobby accent as he said, "Even though *my* father was part of the Empire, it's still my history and I should *celebrate* it."

Kotti commended him with a polite clap. "Oh! That's really good!"

"Thank you, thank you, I've been practicing." He gave a mock bow. Daaric was a very handsome Zabrak, about fifty, with a crown of six small horns encircling his head and faded tattoos across his cheeks and neck, the design like wispy swirls of smoke. He'd caught the wrong side of a bunch of Corellian smugglers years ago and lost his right eye, so now he wore an eye patch he changed out to match his clothes. He was the ship's bosun and purser, and Dad's most trusted crewmate.

I think if Dad were different, they'd be dating, but he clung to the loss of Mom and Val so blindly that he didn't see Daaric at all. Which, honestly, was a feat, because Daaric was as subtle as a solar flare.

There was something to ponder there, about loving someone unrequitedly, to the ends of the galaxy, without them ever knowing. I would feel bad for Daaric, but he did it willingly. He stuck around because he wanted to, not because Dad pulled him along with the hope of *maybe someday*. Besides, I think Daaric loved the *Starfarer*, too.

I added, "Extra points if they bring up that a Jedi headed the Jedi purge."

"The both-sides-ism is exhausting," Kotti agreed. "Even though it wasn't the Jedi who mass-murdered thousands of civilians and—oh, yeah—blew up a *planet*."

"Almost two," Daaric corrected. "Thank the stars that'll never happen again." He didn't talk much about the war, but most people didn't. It was like this looming shadow they kept facing away from, hoping that if they stopped talking about it long enough, the sun would finally chase the bad memories away.

The main crew all wore deep blue uniforms with our names sewn onto the chests. They had been the same uniforms for the past twenty years—a structured high-collared jacket with gold epaulets and a decorative chain from the right shoulder to the central jacket clasp, high trousers, and a thick black belt at the waist, along with supple boots. The uniform, sewn together with golden thread, always felt angular and sleek, formal and yet well-worn.

There were only eight of us in the main crew. Dad liked to keep a tight ship, and so he hired out seasonal help of about twenty other crew members. Their uniforms, unlike ours, were a warm yellow and didn't have all the decorative elements, but honestly they were *much* more comfortable than our stuffy high-collared prison cells.

We made our way to the main chamber, where my dad was already waiting as the seasonal crew came up from the other turbolift on the dorsal side of the ship, laughing and joking about. They were all young people like me, but I'd learned that in *this* uniform and with *my* dad? Most of the seasonal crew wanted nothing to do with me.

However, that gave me an idea for how to keep Sian hidden. I filed it away for later.

Telly was the last to arrive from the bridge. She was a tall Mon Calamari who as chief officer kept the ship running, and I could count on one hand the number of times she had laughed in the fifteen years she'd been on the ship. She was serious, and quiet, and predictable—the perfect counterbalance for the chaos of Captain Quay.

"Sorry for the tardiness," she said in her deep, melodic voice, "but there was a bit of an issue with the supplies. Rodents got into one, it seems. It's fixed now."

I winced. I bet that was the crate Sian and Noola had broken out of. . . .

"Grand!" Dad clapped his hands as he turned to his entire crew and called everyone to attention. "Now, we're all here, all accounted for?"

The seasonal crew called that they were. Then the main crew. We ran through the current itinerary, the food preparation, the entertainment, the guest list, and any troubleshooting we would need over the next two weeks. Apparently the communications console on the lander, *Starstall*—a modified RY-280 Commuter with a larger passenger capacity for excursions—was still not fixed, so we'd make a brief stop to refuel on Tatooine and drop it off with one of Dad's favored mechanics before heading to Geonosis. We didn't *normally* go to Tatooine, but we had added it to the itinerary to drop off *Starstall*, which caused a little bit of a murmur among the seasonal crew. It couldn't be helped. We needed *Starstall* fixed, and Dad refused to postpone a tour when he could just take a detour.

"As always, like our motto states," Dad added, pointing to the inscription carved above the entryway, "'As long as stories persist . . .'"

"'So do we who champion them,'" we finished, and he smiled proudly.

"Absolutely, friends. Now let's make this a tour to remember!" He clapped his hands in dismissal, and we broke apart to our stations. As one of the main crew—technically Dad's first mate, after Telly, but I did whatever needed to be done on the ship most of the time—I was part of the welcoming party, so I headed toward the docking bay on the bottom deck.

Dad opened the *Starfarer*'s ramp, and it unfolded to the ground, spilling the dusky light of Coruscant into the storied hull of the ship. There were, in fact, at least half a dozen passengers waiting to board, and the moment the ramp touched the ground they started inside, bright-eyed with adventure.

And just like that, the *Starfarer*'s 643rd tour began.

CHAPTER SEVEN

THE GUESTS

The first guests were, unsurprisingly, a four-person group of Galactic Civil War buffs who—the second they stepped onto the ship—commented on how the *Starfarer*, for being a C90 Corellian Corvette from the war, did not look authentic enough. As a military vessel, it looked *too* comfortable. And wasn't having an RY-280 Commuter just impossibly civilian? An RM-09 shuttle would've been much more economical. I resisted the urge to roll my eyes.

After the Buffs—that was what I decided to call them, because I didn't want to expend energy to remember their names—checked in with Daaric on his datapad, they came to me for their room assignments and itinerary. Maeve and the captain were farther down the corridor, well out of earshot, ready to welcome them into the ship with a fresh drink and a chat before they boarded the midship lift.

"No Dantooine? Why *Ghorman*?" one of them complained, scanning the itinerary I had transmitted onto their datapads with a tap from my own. "No one cares about *silks*."

I gave them a tight smile. "As per the notification we sent out a week ago, the captain has decided to forgo Dantooine this tour due to unsafe activity."

"*Unsafe?* You're kidding," another added.

The four of them huddled around me, as if they could bully me into changing it. They were all humans, and by the looks of their clothes, they came from somewhere in the Core. Most war buffs did. Crisp shirts, pressed trousers, and clean-shaven faces. All in their mid-thirties. Clearly used to getting their way with their family names or, alternatively, enough credits.

Usually, I would feel a little unease around them, but after surviving a firefight, these guys seemed . . .

Well, I wasn't very intimidated by them.

"Is it smugglers?" the one with round spectacles asked.

His friend added, "Syndicate?"

"Pirates?" guessed another—a man with a goatee.

"Pirates?" echoed a soft, honeyed voice from the mouth of the open ramp. "If it were pirates, I'm sure Hansifred wouldn't mind."

The Buffs turned to look at the tiny alien woman

standing in the entryway, her goggles making her eyes look wide and bright, as if nothing could get past her. She was dressed in unassuming dark trousers and a coarse-spun blue shirt and vest, her skin the color of warm clay.

Daaric shifted nervously, scratching at the side of his neck. Not like she was dangerous but like . . . he *knew* her and had maybe lost a bet.

That seemed very possible, knowing Daaric.

"Then why can't we go?" the guy in the spectacles asked, and his friends all agreed.

"There are far worse things than pirates," the alien woman replied. Her hands were patiently folded behind her back as she observed them with her magnified eyes. "I'm sure you know whom I mean."

One of the men—Spectacles—sneered. "You can't be talking about those *First Order* rumors, can you?" Then he turned to me. "I thought this was a *reputable* tour. I didn't think Hansifred Quay bought into rumors."

Rumors? Sure, I was shot at today by rumors. But I couldn't exactly say that in front of the crew, so I reined in my annoyance and said instead, "We don't want to take undue risks."

"Sure," scoffed the last man in the group. Tall and gangly, he spoke with bravado, like he was the leader.

Ugh, this tour was going to be *insufferable*.

I gathered four key cards—two to each room—and handed them over. “I’m sorry for the inconvenience, but I promise that we do have a worthwhile experience planned. If not, we would be happy to assist you by refunding your credits before we disembark.”

Grumbling, the men took their room keys and shuffled off into the docking bay toward the lift. The one in the red vest commented enthusiastically that this was the kind of ship Princess Leia Organa used during the war, and my frustration melted.

I wasn’t very good at staying angry, anyway.

Those guys would be a thorn in my side, but at least I knew how to deal with them.

I turned to the alien woman, who barely reached up to my midsection. Her face was welcoming and wise in a comforting sort of way. “Thank you for your help.”

The woman laughed. “Some people thirst for adventure even when they don’t understand the drink. Isn’t that right?” she added with a glance at Daaric.

It was odd to see a fifty-something-year-old pirate go ramrod straight, like he’d just been caught stealing sweets.

Oh, he *did* know her. Ex-lover?

Boss?

The possibilities were endlessly juicy.

I eyed him suspiciously as I pulled up the manifest

on my datapad. "I'm sorry, I didn't get your name before. Who may I welcome aboard?"

"This is Maz," Daaric said, sliding up beside me. Then, a little quieter, he added, "My old boss."

"It's a pleasure to—wait." I paused. "*Just* your boss?"

He gave me a baffled look. "What do you think she was?"

"Uh"—*an ex-lover*—"no one."

The short alien woman laughed. "Oh, I'm not here to steal him back. Don't you worry about that."

"I'm not sure whether to be offended or relieved," he muttered, crossing his arms over his chest. "But what brings you to the Core, boss? Last I heard, you never leave Takodana anymore."

Takodana. A planet somewhere in the Western Reaches, I thought, if I remembered my star chart correctly.

And I usually did.

"We all need a vacation sometime, and you know I love a good history lesson," she replied warmly, though Daaric didn't look convinced. She appraised me with a smile. "You must be Hansifred's child. You look just like him."

I was surprised by that. "I . . . do?"

In the mirror, all I could ever see was my mother.

I didn't quite know what to say, though I'd been

trained to push aside my feelings while talking to guests, so that was what I did and found her name on the manifest. *Maz Kanata.*

I formatted a key card and transferred the itinerary onto her datapad. "If you need anything, please don't hesitate to ask."

"Oh, I'll just annoy Daaric with my requests," she replied with a wink back at her old employee, and shuffled deeper into the docking bay, cooing at the sight of *Starstall*.

When she was gone, I spun to Daaric and asked, "Old boss? Like, *pirate*, old boss?"

He shrugged helplessly. "She might've changed professions."

"Did you lose your eye working for her?"

"Nah. She's the one who shot it."

"What?"

"It was before I went to work for her."

"So she shot you and then employed you," I deadpanned.

He shrugged again. "Lucky break, I guess."

"No, that's not what—you know, never mind." Then I glanced down the ramp to make sure no more guests were currently arriving before I added, "No offense, but why is she here? I doubt she needs a commercial tour to see the galaxy."

He shrugged. "I never understood her when I *worked* for her," he replied helplessly, "so I have no idea. When did she sign up for this tour?"

I read the manifest again. "Last week."

"Huh. I *really* have no idea then."

"Maybe she's just bored," I suggested.

Daaric groaned. "Then I pity us all."

The next guests arrived in taxis, and we went back to work.

This tour had one hundred and seven guests total. It was fewer than we usually had, but at least all the VIP suites were occupied. A lot of older people liked to book with us, so most tours were quiet and cozy, and I really loved wrapping up parties and entertainment programming before midnight. It looked like this tour might be much of the same until three separate large groups of young people checked in, and I began to debate whether to put in my vacation days I never took and commandeer *Starstall* straight to Endor's forest moon to wait for the tour there.

Who was I kidding? I'd never taken a vacation day in my life.

It wasn't until two guests later that I *really* began to debate the idea, when I had to explain—again—why we were not going to Dantooine. I felt bad that Dad had had to change the itinerary at the last minute, but we *did* send out a memo about it, and itineraries changed all the time based on myriad things.

This time, it just happened to be the slow encroachment of fascism.

I checked the guest list after the latest group of tourists, fresh on break from the University of Bar'leth, had come inside. "We still have two guests we're waiting for, right? The Rem'itals?"

"Sadly not," Daaric replied. "They canceled last night. They missed their passenger shuttle from Bestine. Apparently someone stole it."

"That's sad. They're a lovely couple. I remember them from the Corellian Run tour."

"I told them they could rebook without an extra charge. Anyway, that's it. I'll go tell the captain we're ready to shove off." He put his datapad under his arm and started away but then paused and said, "Hey, you okay? You seem kind of . . . frazzled."

I stiffened at the question. Oh, aside from almost getting killed and having to shove a stowaway into a pickled fleek eel container? I was perfect. "I'm . . . fine. Just have a headache, is all."

He rubbed his thumb against my forehead. "Yeah, you've got a red spot."

From where Sian's chin had collided with me in

the shop. I quickly stepped away, rubbing at the bruise. "Yeah. I hit my head this morning."

"You should go to the medbay and get some cream for that," he suggested, patting my shoulder, and retreated into the docking bay, where Dad and Maeve were holding the lift for him. They shouted to ask if I wanted them to wait for me, but I told them to go ahead and I'd retract the ramp.

After the lift door closed, the tension in my chest unwound a little. My fingers still gripped my datapad a little too tightly. I was dizzy from the past few hours and massaged my temples and told myself to breathe.

You look just like him, Maz had said, but when I caught my reflection in the tarnished metal of *Starstall*'s hull, I didn't see my dad at all.

No, Val looked like Dad. Maz was mistaken.

When I looked at myself, I just remembered the way Mom smelled, of ship oil and sweet river roses when they bloomed. If I thought about it too long, I missed her in ways I couldn't describe.

Val did, too, but he'd never understood why Dad refused to let us wayfind. He hated how suffocating Dad was, how restrictive, how like a cage the *Starfarer* had become—

So he'd left.

And when he did, Dad stopped talking about him, too.

As I powered down my datapad, I glanced at the time, wondering if I had a moment to slip to the galley to make sure Sian and his little creature weren't causing chaos. Veebee was right. I *shouldn't* have helped them, but what else could I do? Leave them here?

Yes, my common sense replied.

But no one would guess he'd stowed away on the *Starfarer*. A commercial touring company? It was the last place anyone would look. If you needed to get somewhere fast, stowing away on a cruise ship was the long way around. It was nonsensical.

I went to the control box to close the ramp.

"Steward Quay, do you have room for one more?" came a voice from the mouth of the ramp, drawing me out of my thoughts.

"I'm sorry, but we're . . ." My voice trailed off as one last guest stepped onto the ship, sweat prickling his brow as if he'd run halfway across Coruscant to make it here.

I froze.

Because in front of me, framed by the ever-busy, ever-moving city, was the ghost of someone I thought I'd never see again.

CHAPTER EIGHT

THE SON

I stared.

There was a young man at the top of the docking ramp, a duffel slung over his broad shoulder. His honey-brown hair was pushed back, curling chaotically at the ends, framing a sharp face and sharper hazel eyes. The same eyes I had.

Eyes inherited from our mom.

The world blurred around me, like I was on a ship kicking into hyperdrive.

"Val?" I choked.

Suddenly I wasn't staring at a familiar stranger framed in the open ramp of the *Starfarer*; I was three years in the past on the night he'd left, sitting at that cramped little scratch table in the galley, arguing with him while the rest of the ship slept. I always lied that I didn't remember what the argument was about, but of course I did. I had nightmares about it, because what if I was the reason he left?

We'd been drinking tea late that night, our throats scratchy from our recent tour visit to Hoth, back when Dad deemed Hoth moderately safe (or as safe as an icy-tundra-covered planet in the Outer Rim could be), before the First Order had swooped in. The cup warmed my frigid fingertips. I remembered that the most, how the cup felt searingly hot, like a brand.

Val had sneezed and sniffed, rubbing his nose on the sleeve of his uniform coat.

The entire ship had been in a somber mood since returning from Hoth. Most tours went off without a hitch. We'd land planetside, show where the Rebel Alliance took a stand against the Empire during the Battle of Hoth, and return. It had been a bloody battle, one the rebels had lost, so it was already a hard tour stop.

Still, even without knowing any of that, the remains of Echo Base and the wreckage of Imperial walkers across the tundra made the experience solemn. The tours usually didn't get close to the wreckage—most everything had been picked through, anyway—but that day had been different.

For one, the tour had a group of younger men who had been troublemakers the entire trip, so when Dad found them unaccounted for back on the *Starfarer,* along with Val, he immediately figured out where they'd gone.

"You could have said no," I'd finally said, breaking

the silence. Looking back on it, I wished I hadn't opened my mouth at all. "You didn't have to take them to the ruins."

"I wanted to see them, too," he had replied.

Once Val had returned to the ship with the lander and guests, Dad immediately snatched back the master key he'd given Val just two months before. They had a long talk in his office, and I heard some of the words that were shouted, because ships made of metal carried voices well. Val was going to take over the *Starfarer*. He was going to be captain one day—that was always the plan—so Dad always put more pressure on him.

Val was fiddling with his fingernails. There was still grime under them from exploring the ruins. "You can't say you aren't a *little* curious what's out there."

No, actually, I wasn't. "Dad said they're graves. We don't mess with graves."

Val rolled his eyes. "Nothing was in there."

"You went *inside* one? Val—"

"Why not? As I said, nothing was inside. It was picked clean. Probably by some damn scavengers or something."

I studied him quietly. My fingertips were warm on my cup, and I absently traced my thumbs around the lip of it.

"Don't give me that look," he said. "I know you think all his rules are stupid, too. 'Don't touch anything, don't move it, keep everything exactly as it is.'" He rolled his eyes. "As if the *rest* of the galaxy does that."

"He just thinks things need to be preserved—"

"The galaxy is changing, Arie," he interrupted. He'd just turned eighteen two months earlier, and the itch to break things and smear his name across the galaxy had grown so big, he could barely contain it anymore. "If we don't change with it, *we'll* be relics, too."

"Is that what those weirdos told you on the way down to that Imperial walker?" I asked. "To get you to play along?"

He narrowed his eyes. "They said you wouldn't get it."

"*They* said?" I echoed, eyebrows high. "You talked about me?"

"They asked what you thought about it all."

"Did you tell them that I thought it was reckless?"

He shook his head. "Sure, it was a bad decision to take them down there, okay? Of course it was. But I wanted to see it, too. You can only experience so much by looking out of a viewport, you know. It's like Dad wants to put himself in a bubble and trap *us* there, too." As he said it, I could see the realization begin to flicker across his face. "This ship's a cage, Arie. Can't you see it?"

"It's home," I insisted.

"It's a prison," he snapped, "and I'm *done* telling other people's stories."

"So you want to run away to be in one," I said. My voice was cold, much like my tea was becoming.

He raised his gaze to mine and held it. There was a defiant gleam in his eyes. "I want to do something with my life," he said, seeming to give in to the idea that had wormed into his brain and was now growing, feasting on all the what-ifs the galaxy had to offer. "There's stuff happening out there in the Unknown Regions. There're sightings of stormtroopers more and more often. There're cities getting taken over. The war's not over, no matter what anyone thinks. No matter what Dad thinks. I can do something, Arie. I *want* to do something."

"But what about Dad?" *And me?* I wanted to add, but pursed my lips together so I didn't, afraid the admission would make me feel small.

He turned his head away, quiet. Then he said, "You'll be here."

And that was what made me angry. That he knew he could leave, because I wouldn't—even if I *wanted* to. I had to stay, because Dad would be alone otherwise. Val knew he'd trap me here if he left, just like he was afraid of being trapped himself.

Heat flickered in my middle. I clutched my cup tightly. *"Fine,"* I snapped. "Go. Do your thing. *Whatever!* We'll be fine without you."

"Arie—"

I shoved myself to my feet. My untouched tea sloshed over the lip, but it was cold as I left the galley.

That was the last thing I had ever said to him.

No goodbye.

No "I love you."

Just . . . *Go. We'll be fine without you.*

And we *were* fine; we *would be* fine, but . . .

That didn't mean I felt any less guilty for being the reason he'd left in the first place. Maybe if I hadn't picked a fight, hadn't planted that idea in his head, he'd have cooled off and stayed. It was my fault, I thought.

Just like Mom.

But . . .

But here Valor was, like he'd just popped out for an errand and come back. And for a second, I could trick myself into believing that he had. That I was still that naive fifteen-year-old with my nose buried in serials and my eyes turned to the stars, and I *ached* for that girl.

He grinned in that sheepish way of his that I remembered too fondly, though it looked different on his grown face, so changed from the boy who'd fled three years ago. If it wasn't for the tilt at the corner of his mouth, I wasn't sure I could convince myself that it really was him. He'd grown into his once-awkward height, almost as broad as Dad now. There was a new scar over his left eyebrow, and his skin was a bit darker from some distant planet's hard sun, his freckles deep like ink.

I stood there with my mouth agape. I didn't know what else to do.

"Hey, snotface," he greeted, that familiar grin curling higher into a smile, and it was so familiar that my heart leapt into my throat. The brief shimmer of anger in my belly gave way to joy.

My datapad slid from my hands and clattered to the deck. "It's you."

He grinned, lowering the duffel bag slung over his shoulder to the floor of the ship. "Surprise!"

I—I'd imagined what I would do if I saw him again. In some of my dreams I ran up to him and hugged him tightly, and he smelled exactly the way he always had—like transistor oil and slightly burnt exhaust.

In those dreams, I cried into his jacket, big gulping sobs I didn't even know I'd had in me, trapped down in my belly like a dormant scream. And it just made him hold on tighter. Like Mom used to.

"Hey, hey," he whispered soothingly in those dreams, rubbing circles on my back, "no need for the moisture farm. I've come back."

In other dreams, I punched him so hard he went back in time to the day he'd left, and decided never to leave at all.

But as it stood, I didn't do either.

I just . . . *stared.*

I didn't even hear the lift ding until Dad called, "Daughter? The sensor says the ramp's still open. Is everything . . . ?" His voice trailed off as he recognized the man opposite me. He blinked in the bright orange light of the setting sun, as if he didn't quite believe his eyes.

Valor turned to him with that same smile. I wondered how long he'd had to practice it in the mirror. "Hey, old man."

Unlike me, Dad didn't just stare. "Valor?" he whispered, and lurched past me to grab my brother by the shoulders. *"Val?"* he kept repeating as if he couldn't believe it. Hansifred Quay was an emotional man. He put his heart on his sleeve, and it was one of the many things I loved about him. Another was his hugs—like the one he drew Valor into. Encompassing and warm and tight. It was the kind of hug that made you feel grounded and loved. The kind of hug that made wampas melt—made everything melt, really.

Even Valor.

"You're home!" Dad cried, releasing him, tears running freely down his cheeks. "You're *home*!"

"Yeah," Val replied, his eyes bright with tears. "Sorry it took so long."

CHAPTER NINE

THE SOIREE

There was always a shudder as the *Starfarer* left the atmosphere—a deep groan like a beast shaking off a winter chill—before the ship quieted and the ride smoothed.

With that, the *Starfarer* left Coruscant, bound for Alderaan. Because the planet itself had been destroyed by the Empire during the war, the wreckage the attack left behind was always shifting. The debris field was called the Graveyard of Alderaan. It was a quiet place—not sacred, but sad nonetheless. The graveyard made the approach through hyperspace unpredictable and dangerous, so both Dad and Telly were needed on deck to navigate to it.

It would take about twelve hours to reach a jump point where we could enter a hyperspace lane to Alderaan and avoid, you know, colliding with the debris field that remained of the planet. There was a small space station nestled in the graveyard where we'd stop and take a tour of how different sectors were reviving aspects of Alderaan—agriculture, music, art—for future generations. Though most guests just went onto the space station to get a better view of the graveyard.

In the meantime, I took Val to the crew quarters on the bottom deck and showed him to the room we'd kept for him. The main crew quarters were compact, practical rooms with comfortable beds and personal storage, and shared access to the refreshers and galley with the dorsal side of the ship, where the seasonal crew bunked two to a room. While we could never really afford to keep Val's room unoccupied, Dad did anyway. Val looked around at all the things he'd left behind, perfectly preserved from three years ago. No one ever came into this room, except for Maeve to dust every few months.

"Everything should be where you left it," I said as he opened his standing wardrobe and sifted through his old clothes.

"You all really just *kept* this stuff?" he replied, frowning at his old uniform, probably too small to fit now.

I shrugged. "We didn't have the energy to go through all your junk."

He snorted. "Thanks—and, hey," he added quietly, drawing my attention. He shifted his weight from one foot to the other. It was so very strange to see him after three years, how much he'd changed, what parts of him had grown up and what parts of him were the same. He pulled his hand through his hair nervously, curls catching on his fingers. "It's nice to see you again, sis."

"You too," I replied, and shifted a little in hesitation. "But . . . why *are* you home, Val? Are you just going to disappear again? Dad won't be able to deal with that a second time."

He looked away. "I mean, I'm here now, aren't I?"

"That's not an answer."

He closed the wardrobe and slung his arm around my shoulder. "Since when did you get so pessimistic, sis? I'm back, so let's not get weird about it, yeah?"

As he hung on my shoulder, I wondered if maybe I *was* being too pessimistic. So I shoved those feelings away and put my arm around his shoulder, too. "You're right. And if you leave this time, I'm going to hunt you down and nail you to the deck of this ship."

He barked a laugh. "Now *there's* my sister!"

When he tried to scrub my forehead with his knuckles, I wormed out from under his arm and smoothed down my braid. "Get settled in and then come find me to help set up for the First Night Soiree."

He groaned. "I just got home and I'm *already* being sentenced to servitude?"

"There's no time like the present," I replied, and

kissed him on the cheek. "Welcome home, Val." And I meant it, even though I didn't know why he was here.

"Glad to be home," he replied, and I left him to get his room sorted.

It would be a few hours until First Night started, but guests were already beginning to explore the ship in the meantime. They didn't have access to the maintenance deck, where the crew quarters, galley, cargo, and launch bay were, so at least Sian only had to deal with the crew members. Either way, I popped into the laundry, because I knew Maeve was already in the main chamber setting up for the party, and grabbed a spare seasonal uniform to drop off at the galley.

Sian was sitting at the scratch table, tossing little berries for Noola to catch in her mouth, while Veebee prepared the snacks for the party, with two automated droids that kept getting in her way. She'd shove them out eventually and just do everything herself. She always did.

"Yellow's not really my color. I'm more of a cool-tone kind of guy," he said jokingly when I gave him the spare uniform.

"*Ha.* If you leave the galley, wear this and say you're seasonal in the laundry."

"Laundry?"

"No one ever wants to work in laundry, so no one'll

question it. Vee, the dessert smells amazing!" I added before I left the galley and hurried to the turbolift.

I hated the First Night Soiree.

It was just what it sounded like: a party. Dad always loved a good party. He lived for them. If there was a celebration to be had, Dad was absolutely having it. And because it was the first one with Val back, I was absolutely *dreading* it. Even so, I found myself as I did every single First Night, standing in the main chamber of the *Starfarer*, a sweet drink in hand, chatting with guests against my will.

My uniform felt too tight. My heeled boots were killing me. And if one more guest slid up to me with a hazardous pickup line, failing to see the name sewn on my chest, I was very certain I'd toss myself out of an airlock just to end the agony. I could be compared to a Naboo sunrise only so many times before I began to debate the ethics of murder.

At least the chatter from the guests was all juicy gossip: senators sneaking away together, sabacc championships, planets wanting to join the New Republic, pop stars on the run, who put money on whom in the Canto Bight fathier races . . .

The loudness, the glittering lights, the laughter, it all rebounded off the bulkheads of the ship and burrowed a headache just behind my eyes. In a corner of the main chamber, N2-0 spun bright synths while beeping to the beat. Made to be an R-series astromech only to dream of being a DJ, and not doing a half-bad job of it.

Most of the hundred guests we had on board attended First Night, dancing to the music, orbiting each other like binary stars looking for their other half—or other halves, depending on what they preferred. The green and purple lights painted them in shades of carefree and hungry.

My brother stood on the other side of the dance floor, laughing with one of the guests. They placed a hand on his uniformed chest, much too informally, and leaned closer to him. He bent toward them, easy to flirt with.

It was so strange seeing Val in the crowd—on this ship at all, really—dressed in the dark blue of the *Starfarer*'s crew. Looking at him, I could almost trick myself into thinking he'd never left. Except the uniform was new; if I squinted I could still see the folds in the jacket, and his name wasn't sewn onto the chest.

Why did he have to come back on the *same tour* where I smuggled a man and a lightsaber aboard?

Kotti surfaced from the dance floor, golden bands around her long thin lekku glinting in the light. She was tall and beautiful as always, wide eyes rimmed with sharp eyeliner to match her uniform. She slung her arm over my shoulder and gave me a squeeze.

"You look like you came to your own execution," Kotti shouted into my ear. She looked made for a galaxy full of bright lights and fast music. Her mossy skin glistened with a thin layer of sweat, the brassy bangles on her wrists—*definitely* not uniform-approved—jingling whenever she moved.

"I'm not sure how I feel about this," I observed, watching my brother.

Kotti gasped, oblivious. "What? I *love* this song!"

"No, I mean . . ." I nodded toward Val, flirting with the guest. He laughed and whispered something in their ear, causing them to blush. "Why did he decide to come home *now*?"

"Who cares? I thought you'd be happy."

"I am!"

She eyed me suspiciously.

"Mostly," I admitted, caving like one of Veebee's soufflés. "I just . . . it's going to be weird."

"A little, but he looks *so* good in that uniform," Kotti said, biting her bottom lip. "I remember Val, but you know, I never realized just how hot he is."

I shot her a pleading look. "Don't you dare."

"I mean, you could reintroduce me. . . ."

"Kotti."

She turned away from Val and rolled her eyes. "I'm *kidding*, jeez. We can wait until after the tour."

I really wanted to find that rock to die under now. I squirmed under her sweaty arm. "You're sticky."

"And *you're* haunting this bulkhead like a ghost. C'mon, we're working, we're not *dead*."

I sipped my sweet drink. "Joke's on you. I'm definitely dead inside."

She laughed and unwound her arm from my shoulder. "C'mon. One dance."

"I'm observing," I said.

"Then you can observe from the dance floor." Kotti snatched my drink, drained it, and then deposited it on the table beside us. I made a squawk of anger, but she simply took my hand and pulled me into the crowd of dancers.

I felt a cold sweat break out on my back. "Wait a minute—"

"Life doesn't start in a minute, it starts *now*, Ardent Quay," Kotti chastised, pulling me into the twisting mass of people, to the very center—of *course* she'd drag me to the center—and raising our hands into the air. She shimmied her shoulders, moving back and forth. Kotti was ridiculous, and too loud, and too *much*. She was everything I never was.

"What'll everyone think?" I asked, hugging my arms

to my sides and looking around. "We're supposed to be working—"

Kotti rolled her eyes. "You're not going to get in trouble for one dance, Arie. C'mon, loosen up!" Then she pulled my hand into the air again, smiling so wide her eyes glittered. "Shake off your duty, and forget all the people watching, and celebrate that you are *here*. And how impossible is that?"

That in all the ships in all the worlds in all the galaxy, I had been born into this family, to find this crew, this best friend? I wasn't sure if I believed in fate, or predestiny, but I liked to think that the Force pushed and pulled across space and time, uniting people like stars colliding.

I closed my eyes and let out a long breath.

Okay—if I could go into Coruscant alone and get a serial and run away from First Order goons . . .

I could dance, too.

So I shucked off the mantle of Ardent Quay for a song and danced.

After three songs and a brief musical interlude, Kotti shouted that she was thirsty and left me for the bar. With my eyes closed, I nodded at her to go and kept dancing. The thump of the bass reminded me of the sound of my heart earlier today, pumping through my ears, the shriek of synths like blaster bolts—

I popped my eyes open. My heart beat hard and fearful in my throat.

"I feel silly," I mumbled to myself.

"Allow me to be silly with you then," said a familiar voice before someone placed a hand gently on my lower back and a tall, lanky figure slipped up beside me, yellow seasonal uniform ill-fitting and creased in the wrong places. He smiled. His silver-white hair glimmered with purple and blue hues from the party lights, and his black eyes gleamed.

Trouble, in the flesh.

CHAPTER TEN

THE DANCE

"S*ian!*" I cried, and quickly darted my eyes around, but no one was paying attention. I reined in my surprise and hissed, "What are you doing here?"

In reply, he took one of my hands, his other still steady on my lower back. "Dancing, *obviously*."

"You know what I mean."

"I was bored," he lamented, "and you *did* give me this uniform."

"For emergencies only!"

"Boredom is definitely an emergency," he replied. I assessed the uniform again. He could've used a size larger. It was tight across his shoulders and long torso, showing too much wrist, and his trousers showed too much ankle, but the normal guests would never look that close. "Besides, there's almost two hundred people on this ship, and I'm excellent at slipping away. Don't worry, Entoo disabled the vids on the lower deck. I'll be fine." He spun me around to the music.

I fumbled as I followed him. "Dad will *absolutely* know you aren't crew with those ankles showing."

He lowered an eyebrow. "I don't see him, though. Do you?"

"Not yet . . ."

He sucked in a breath between his teeth. "I think your friend is right, Starlight. You should really let loose a little bit. Undo your braid." To emphasize, he picked up the end of it slung over my shoulder and twirled it through his fingers. "I bet your hair's really pretty down."

Heat crawled across my cheeks. I pulled my braid out of his grip. "You don't know me."

"But we did go through a very traumatic thing together. That must count for something?" He spun me back into him. He was nefariously smooth for a thief. It was hard to keep my guard up. "Besides," he went on in that low voice that was almost a whisper, in a conversation only we could hear, "like I said, I was bored and I could hear the party all the way down in the galley. Veebee said I couldn't miss it."

Skeptically, I eyed him. "She did?"

"Well, she said *she* couldn't miss it," he corrected, "which just means I had to check it out for myself, too!"

I hesitated. Dad hadn't come to the party yet. He wouldn't join until he was sure the ship was in the clear and we were well on our way to Alderaan. "I guess . . ."

"Vee *also* said your brother came back," he added, his voice a little softer. Though his eyes were blankets of black with starry-white motes, I could still feel where he was looking, and at the moment he was most definitely looking at me—studying me. I wondered what I looked like through them. I wondered what kind of girl he saw. "Are you all right?"

My eyes widened at the question. "I—I mean—why wouldn't I be?"

"I dunno. Vee said he left years ago, and she seemed *very* suspicious that he was back."

"Vee sure told you a lot."

"I have a very trustworthy face," he replied.

No, he did not. He had a very handsome face, but trustworthy? I was afraid to trust him with anything I said, though it wasn't for fear that he'd use it against me. It was for fear that he'd learn something I never let anyone find out.

N2-O melted the music down into a slow and sweet beat, and in reply the dance floor ebbed, too. We swayed to the music, turning. He put one hand on my hip and guided my hand to his shoulder, then folded his fingers through my free one. His hand held mine with confidence, warm and calloused where mine was soft—and, oh, the story that told. We were from two different worlds. I bet he had seen enough corners of the galaxy to fill a book, while I . . .

I hadn't seen much of anything at all. The walls of this ship. The itineraries. Countless faces and names.

For a moment I wondered what it would be like out there in the galaxy with him. Outside of these walls.

Dangerous—this boy was dangerous.

So close to him, I felt my heart beating quickly in my throat. I remembered how it had felt being this close to him before, how he smelled like dust and far-off places. I let myself think for a moment that he'd escaped the galley just to come dance with me. That was what would happen to the main character in Mom's favorite serial. If this were *Under the Tan-Tan Sun*, then he'd have snuck into this party just to have a dance, risking the sharp-eyed ambassador and ex-communication from the Assassin's Guild.

But the reality was, when I looked up into his strange and handsome face, he wasn't looking at me at all.

He was watching someone behind me. Something sharp and dangerous flickered through his eyes—barely there and then gone. "Sadly," he said, "I think our dance is cut short."

I didn't understand. "What?"

"Arie!"

I let go of Sian quickly and spun around to my brother. Val dipped through the crowd to me, holding two drinks. One, I guessed, was for me. What happened to that pretty guest he'd been flirting with? "Oh, Val. Hello."

"Who were you dancing with?" he asked suspiciously, glancing around me.

I felt my body stiffen. "Um, this is—" I was about to make up a lie, but when I turned back to Sian to introduce him, he had, in fact, disappeared. He wasn't kidding when he said he was good at slipping away. I hadn't even seen him go. *That* trick would've been useful on Coruscant. "Just a seasonal crew member I know. He—he comes aboard sometimes for work."

"What's his name?" he asked, searching the crowd, but my dance partner had vanished. "He was getting pretty close."

I crossed my arms. Anger lit in my belly. "Well *you* seemed pretty close with that guest earlier. The one with the golden earrings?"

"We were just talking."

"Exactly," I echoed. "We were just talking." Why was I getting so worked up about this? I was sure that if I told Val the truth about Sian, he'd help me. He always hated playing by Dad's rules. "He's just—"

"You know what, you're right. Never mind," he replied dismissively, and offered me one of the drinks. "Thirsty?"

"Thank you." I took the drink, and we excused ourselves from the dance floor and took up residence by the bar. He swirled his drink and took a sip. His was sweet wine. I didn't remember him ever liking wine. I eyed the scar above his left eyebrow and wondered how he'd gotten it. A fight? An adventure?

Where *had* he been?

I asked him as much.

"I've been trying new things," he replied, dodging the question as he leaned his back against the bar, the picture of ease. "You know, different places, different jobs. Sort of trying to see what I like. The ship looks the same," he added.

"We had to replace one of the thruster banks last year," I supplied, "and Dad's thinking about upgrading the navicomputer."

"Of course he is. Whatever he can do to keep you from wayfinding, huh," he replied.

"It's for safety."

He inclined his head. "Have you always been this contrary?"

"Every day of my life," I confirmed. "Have you always been this dodgy?"

"That's new," he replied with a wink.

I smiled, and he mirrored it. It was the closest we ever came to looking like Quay siblings.

We stood there on the edge of the party, not quite sure what to say next, for the rest of the song. Three long years separated us. Three years when he had explored the galaxy while I stayed on this ship of grand tours and distinct itineraries, and he refused to tell me about any of it.

Instead he leaned against the bar and asked, "So what have you done these last three years? Get into any trouble?"

"I don't get into trouble," I replied.

"Any boyfriends? Girlfriends?" He went on digging. "Anyone I need to have a talk with who broke your heart? Say the word, and I can show them exactly what I've learned out there in the galaxy."

"That sounds like a threat."

There was danger in his smile now. "It's more like a promise."

I snorted. "No boyfriends. No girlfriends. No one, really. I've just been here."

To that he sighed and whined, "*Arie*, really? You never escape this cage?"

I stiffened. "It's not a cage."

He scoffed. "Of course it is. He likes to control everything—especially us. Ever since Mom died. Why do you think I left? I don't see how you can stand it."

"Well, one of us had to stay, and you made your choice," I replied coldly. "Unless you've returned to save me from our terrible, awful dad who welcomed you home with open arms? What do you think Dad'd say to that?"

He drained the rest of his wine. "Why don't we ask him ourselves?"

As if on cue, the pulse of music stopped. Then Entoo played a jingle as the captain stepped into the main chamber. He waved at everyone and hurried to the other side of the bar, where he climbed on a stool with one long stride, then onto the counter itself, taking a flute of wine from the bartender.

"Good evening!" he cried, turning to his guests with all the flamboyance of a showman.

I settled back, waiting to hear the same First Night speech I'd heard all eighteen years of my life.

But it was not the same.

CHAPTER ELEVEN

THE DAY

Guests and crew alike raised their drinks.

In his dark blue tour uniform, the gold tassels on his epaulets glinting in the low lights, Dad looked regal and welcoming. He'd braided his dark beard and finished it at the bottom with a golden stud, his hair smoothed away from his face. He looked ever more like the mythological captain of the *Starfarer*. He *was* a storyteller, after all.

Selling the story was half the job.

"Welcome, honored friends, to the *Starfarer*! Some of you I recognize from voyages we've taken before. Thank you for trusting us enough to return for another trip. Nossen Vellur, how's Corellia this time of year?" he asked a family of Sullustans, all wearing matching long-sleeve yellow jumpsuits, and Nossen replied with a wobble of his hand.

Dad barked a laugh. "I hear you! Weather's always

gonna make things hard." Then he turned to a tall wolfish woman. "Yurd, how are your pups?"

To which the Farghul replied, "Perfect, now that I'm away!"

Dad toasted to that. I was never not amazed by his attention to people. He remembered every guest who came through his ship and kept their names with care.

Val was wrong. He wasn't cruel. He didn't trap me here. He didn't lord over me.

Dad was just doing his best, because the galaxy was dangerous, and there were very rarely second chances.

"But I also see a lot of new faces in the crowd," Dad added, motioning to a large majority of the guests, "and it's a pleasure to have you on board. Here on the *Starfarer* we have a tradition. On the first night of every voyage, we raise a toast to all the people who came before us, to help us preserve our past. The good, we celebrate! The bad, we remember so we may never repeat it again. We lose our rights and ourselves when those in power choose to omit or change a narrative, hoping that those of us who lived it will forget. Because of this, we have a saying inscribed in this very chamber, and I would like to toast to it tonight." He turned and raised his drink to the inscription above the doorway into the main corridor, and the rest of the guests echoed his movement.

I raised my drink. Beside me Val patiently ran his

thumb around the lip of his empty glass, not bothering to partake. A flicker of anger bloomed in my chest.

" 'As long as stories persist,' " the captain of the *Starfarer* said, and the crowd echoed the words like a hymn.

" 'As long as stories persist . . .' "

" 'So do we who champion them,' " Dad finished.

The crowd repeated, *" 'So do we who champion them.' "*

Everyone drank. We cheered.

Dad polished off his entire flute in one gulp and raised the empty glass into the light. "This is where I tell you to enjoy the night," he went on, "to dance so hard your feet are sore in the morning—and trust me, you'll do that! But if I may have another moment of your time . . ."

The crowd shifted into silence again, curious. At one of the tables, Maz adjusted her goggles, blinking with those wide, all-seeing eyes of hers. She watched my dad with rapt attention.

I felt dread brewing in my stomach.

Does he know about Sian? I wondered. Was I found out?

"Today I've realized just how thankful I am. Not only is it my daughter's eighteenth birthday, but my only son has come home to help us celebrate it. To Ardent Quay," he said, raising his glass in a toast. Wait—*what*? "May this ship always be your guiding star!"

I froze where I stood. My mouth dropped open. *That*

was why Val was here? For my eighteenth? The shock of it—I'd been worried all evening that he was here for some nefarious purpose, but as it turned out, he was just here for . . . me?

Val elbowed me gently in the side and mouthed, *You forgot?*

He looked as appalled as I felt. A blush cascaded across my cheeks.

To be fair, my birthday wasn't the kind of day I liked remembering all that much. If your fondest memory of your birthday was the hours before your mother died trying to get home to you, I would argue that you wouldn't want to remember it, either.

"To Ardent!" everyone cheered, their drinks high. The colorful lights reflected off of the beautiful glasses, sending sparks chasing across the ceiling.

Daaric sidled up to me, having replaced his dark eye patch with a glittery one for the occasion, and said, "Did you think we *forgot*? It's your eighteenth! A big one!"

I tried to rein in my expression. "Then will you let me try some of your Corellian whiskey?"

Daaric put a hand to his lips. "I'll have to ask your dad."

Dad yelled, *"No!"*

Guests laughed.

"Well, then you'll just have to ask your *other* dad,"

Daaric added with a wink, and finally that made me laugh. I bumped my shoulder against his.

Dad shouted, "I hope everyone's warmed up to sing a rousing birthday song to our favorite navigator?"

The guests cheered.

"Please don't," I begged.

He gasped, acting distraught. "You can't mean that!"

"We *all* mean that," Maeve groused from her spot at the bar, eating a bowl of pipnuts. "I don't have my singing voice on."

Kotti shouted, "Just get to the good part, Captain!"

"Fine, fine," Dad grumbled, and reached into his coat to pull out a box tied with a bow. It was barely larger than his palm and flat enough for me to wonder what could be inside. He walked across the bar, filling up people's glasses with wine as he went, and crouched in front of me, holding out my gift. "For you," he said tenderly. "It's just a small thing. From your family, your crew, to you. Happy birthday, daughter." He bent and kissed my forehead. His beard scratched my skin.

"You better not have bought me anything expensive," I said, hoping I didn't sound too watery.

There were aws and coos.

Dad liked making a spectacle, though I would've preferred to receive this kind of gift in private. Any gift, really.

Telly said, "We would buy you a moon if we could."

"What would she do with a *moon*?" Maeve asked.

Veebee gave a wistful sigh from her station by the buffet. "Never see civilization again."

Entoo chastised her with a bloop from the DJ stand.

I fought off a smile as I peeled back the wrapping. It could be jewelry, but I didn't really wear any. Some sort of holodrama? A chip of artwork? I really couldn't imagine in the least what it might be.

I opened the box. Inside was a rectangular piece of metal with the *Starfarer*'s logo engraved on the front. On the back I knew would be my name—*Ardent Quay*.

It was a master key to the ship, one that opened every door, every locker, every database.

The only other people who had one were my dad and . . . *Val*. Before his was taken away.

My excitement disintegrated.

I stared down at the key for a long time.

Val clapped his hand on my shoulder. "Hey! Look at that. Congrats, snotface!"

I closed the box and held it tightly to my chest. I should have been thankful—*honored*. I needed to be, but I just felt rotten because I wasn't. My bottom lip wobbled, and Dad took that as good emotion. He patted my head and rose to his feet again.

"And now let's get this soiree started! Welcome to the

Century of Change tour!" he roared. Entoo spun a bombastic track, and the party twirled into motion again.

I let my eyes blur and told myself I loved the gift.

That I loved the thought behind the gift.

That, deep down, I wanted it. I had to want it. I *wanted* to want it.

"Excuse me," I murmured, and fled the main chamber as quickly as I could.

Dad called out after me, but I didn't stop. Daaric alleviated the tension by joking that I didn't like to cry in front of strangers, which was true. I didn't remember getting to the lift. I didn't remember taking it down.

I didn't remember anything until I arrived at the door to my room, fumbling for the key in my pocket, but I couldn't get it out.

So I just shoved the box against the keypad.

It unlocked with a *bleep*—

Just as a large crash came from the galley. An intruder? A guest? And I remembered with a bolt of dread—

The stowaway.

CHAPTER TWELVE

THE STOWAWAY

The moment I rounded into the galley, I found what had caused the crash: an overturned shelf, spilling pots, pans, and spices all over the floor. There was a pot boiling on the nanowave stove, giving off a fatty, salty scent, mingling with the yeasty sweetness of something that VB-35 was baking in the oven to serve for breakfast tomorrow morning.

No Sian, though. That was worrying. Where had he disappeared to after our dance?

I righted the shelf and had started to clean up the mess when something sneezed under the cooler. Curious, I bent down to look.

Two wide yellow eyes blinked back.

My tension melted into annoyance. "Lemme guess, this is your mess?"

In reply, the creature hissed.

"Yes, yes, you're very fierce. Hungry?" I added, pushing myself to my feet, and rifled through the cooler for a bit of bone meat Veebee used for stock. I squatted back down and offered it to her.

Noola sniffed, unsure.

I set the snack down in front of her to let her get to it in her own time. "I won't space you."

Noola looked at the meat like it was a trap.

"I won't poison you, either."

The creature decided I was telling the truth—or maybe she was just more hungry than suspicious—and eased out, ears forward, to shove the snack into her mouth whole.

I scrubbed behind her head, and she purred. "Now, where's your owner?"

I checked the pantry, half expecting to see him squeezed between a large sack of topatos and Batuuan clementines, but regrettably no one was there.

Noola chirped, so I asked her, "Where's he staying?"

Her ears pinwheeled to me before she sat back on her haunches and looked toward the corner of the galley on the other side of the scratch table. Right, the preserved goods pantry. Veebee didn't use it often, aside for storing sacks of grain and some freeze-dried jerkies. I went over and pressed the button to open the door. It creaked open.

Most of the grain and jerky had been pushed to the back of the storage room, and a makeshift hammock that looked like one of the tarps we used to cover our supplies in the hangar was slung across the length of the space. His gray jacket was hung on a nail protruding from one of the metal shelves, and his boots slouched by the door. Noola had gathered root vegetable peels Veebee dropped from the cutting board and bits of cloth, making a little nest for herself beneath the hammock.

They'd certainly moved in, hadn't they.

I fingered the hole in his jacket from the blaster on Coruscant, thinking that I could darn that pretty quickly with some thread, but on closer inspection the entire piece of clothing was worse for wear. There was another hole in the sleeve and faded blaster marks on the opposite shoulder, which was threadbare and dusty.

"Who is he?" I asked Noola, just as the door to the galley opened.

Sian stepped inside with a towel draped over his shoulders, wearing clean trousers and a linen shirt with the sleeves rolled up to reveal rather indecent forearms. The attire looked very much like his clothes when we'd met. I guessed he'd worn the seasonal uniform while his own clothes were in the wash. His hair stuck up at odd angles, darker when damp, and droplets of water still clung to the tips from his shower. With the grime of Coruscant washed away, he looked like a new man. Not respectable, but I didn't think I would like him that way—

Like him? Oh, stars. I was in trouble.

I cut my eyes away from him quickly, remembering myself.

"Well, hello there," he greeted happily, the door closing behind him. "Did the rest of your party go well?"

"Fine," I replied, because I didn't want to think about the master key at all. "How did you disappear so quickly at the party?"

He clicked his tongue in admonishment and grabbed a date from a bowl on the scratch table, then popped it into his mouth. "I told you I'm good at slipping away. Not my fault you didn't believe me."

I folded my arms over my chest. "Then why couldn't you slip away from Coruscant without my help?"

"I said I'm good at it, not *great*," he pointed out. "And I was a little frazzled, honestly."

"Right."

"Who was the person who brought you a drink?" he asked, his voice curiously neutral. He picked at a thread on his shirt.

My eyebrows jerked up in surprise. Was he—was he *jealous*? "That was my brother, Val."

"Your brother," he repeated, nodding. "And he . . ."

"Is apparently only here for my birthday. He doesn't visit often." I hesitated and then lied, looking down at my feet. "He works on Corellia. I take it you came to an agreement with Veebs?" I asked, changing the subject.

He gave a one-shouldered shrug. "Yeah, I can stay in the pantry if I become her taster until I get off."

Which was a fate worse than being spaced, but I wasn't about to tell him that.

It was only until tomorrow. No one would find him in the pantry before then. I just had to make sure of it.

"You two should stay in the galley until you leave tomorrow," I said. "Which means no more field trips."

Sian visibly wilted. "You're kidding!"

"No, I'm not," I replied as Noola scurried up my body and perched on my shoulder. I scratched her under her chin, and she began purring. "*Especially* you. You're cute, but that won't save you."

"How dare you. It's saved her every time so far," he replied indignantly, bypassing me to go in his makeshift room and hanging his towel on another protruding piece of metal.

"Well, if Kotti catches her, she might end up on a leash."

He clicked his tongue again, his black eyes gleaming in the low light of his room like far-off solar flares. "Don't tease us with a good time, Starlight."

A flush heated my cheeks again. "No," I said quickly, backing away from him. "No, we're not doing this."

He tilted his head. A smile tugged at his mouth. "Doing what?"

"This." And I motioned to him. And then to me. And then to him again. "This *thing*."

Delighted, he leaned against the doorframe of his new room, a hand on his hip. "*Flirting* isn't a dirty word, Starlight."

Flirting—was that what this was? It felt more like a gauntlet.

"My name is Ardent," I corrected. "Not Starlight. I don't even know how you got Starlight. You're the one who looks like you were made from star stuff."

His eyes widened, and so did his smile. "Is that a compliment, Ardent?"

Come to think of it, I didn't like how he said my name, either, in that Wild Spacer drawl of his, long on the *Aaah*, rumbling on the *r*, the end of it like a soft sigh. No, I would rather not be perceived at all, *thank you*.

And was I blushing harder? Oh, stars, I was.

I turned on my heel and left the galley then, and I suspected he thought he'd run me off, but I went back a few minutes later with an armful of pillows and a thick comforter. "Here. It gets cold down here at night. Tomorrow is Alderaan, and I have an excursion to lead, so I don't think I'll be seeing you off. Your lightsaber will be in the top drawer of my dresser. The door to my room will be unlocked. So—" As I handed him the comforter and pillows, his hands brushed mine. The callouses on his fingertips were hard, his touch light. Gooseflesh prickled across my skin. I glanced up into his star-strewn eyes. They were impossible to look at, beautiful and terrifying, like a night sky cracked open. This would be the last time I'd see him, wouldn't it?

The realization curdled in my chest, tight and horrid. What was wrong with me? I was good at saying goodbye. I'd done it a thousand times. And besides, I barely knew this boy. He barely knew me. Though, what if he got to know me better? What if we'd danced a little longer?

What if he stayed?

With a start I dropped the linens.

"Safe travels, Sian," I forced out. Then I retreated out of the galley again, but not before pausing in the doorway. "I . . ." *I'm glad I met you.* No, no, too familiar. Too raw. "Good night."

"Good night, Ardent," he said. Did he sound like he wanted to say something else, too? But all he said was "Thank you. I owe you my life."

I kept my cool right until I locked myself in my room, and then I slid down my door to puddle on the ground and press my face against my knees. My cheeks burned.

What was *wrong* with me? Every time he spoke, he made me feel things I didn't *want* to feel, and I didn't know what to do about any of it.

And right now?

A crush was the *last* thing I needed.

ALDERAAN SPACE STATION

CHAPTER THIRTEEN

THE GRAVEYARD

As the ship entered the asteroid field that was once the planet Alderaan, the *Starfarer* held a moment of silence.

Outside the viewports, floating chunks of rock drifted, interspersed with bits of glinting metal. When I was little, I thought they were souls that stayed back—fragments of spirits, memories, and what have you.

But as I grew up, I learned the horrible truth:

The glints of metal were remnants of civilization that hadn't been evaporated in the explosion. Billions of people died in an instant, their bodies vaporized. There was nothing left of them when the planet exploded, leaving only scars of rock in space.

A graveyard.

In the middle of that Alderaanian graveyard sat a space station cobbled together from misplaced pieces of junk from across the galaxy, though some of its bigger pieces had been salvaged from what remained of the

Death Star that exploded over Yavin 4. The station was a monstrosity of welded metal and fire-burnt parts, but it was home to the refugees of a planet that no longer existed. And on it was the Monument, an entire floor of the station lined with the names—millions of them—of everyone accounted for who'd died on the planet. It was always a loud level, with music and dance and celebration. Dad said the space station was hope in a bleak part of the galaxy, proving that goodness and life could exist in the darkest of places.

But if that were true, the space station and its monument would have been part of more stories, and not just the graveyard it floated in. No one liked to remember the bad endings. It wasn't a part of history that made heroes, only orphans.

Still, it was a part of history that Dad found essential.

Never mind that it was one of the tour stops that garnered the most interest.

This was one of the optional excursions. Plenty of people thought it was in poor taste to build a space station in the graveyard of Alderaan and refused to be any part of it, but they were few and far between on the *Starfarer*. So we docked with the space station and opened the airlock so most of our guests could leave on the excursion. Luckily, that also meant the *Starfarer* would be a ghost town for the next few hours.

The fewer people on the ship, the less possibility of Sian getting caught as *he* left the ship, so I was thankful for that at least.

I zipped up my uniform and arranged my hair in an Alderaanian mourning braid to pay homage, then met up with Dad on the main deck, just outside the turbolift.

"Here's the list of guests on your tour," he said, handing me a datapad with all the info I needed. "The agricultural center asked us to talk about their harvest, to get people to buy some produce, and remember the gifts at the end."

I skimmed the list quickly. The Galactic Civil War Buffs, a couple of families, a bachelorette party . . . it was an easy group. Kotti must have gone ahead with a much larger one. I asked, "Is Val taking one, too?"

"Your brother hasn't been on a tour in ages. He'd be terrible," Dad said with a laugh.

"He always hated this part," I agreed regretfully.

Dad patted me on the shoulder and handed me a basket full of gifts to give to our guests at the end of the tour. "Have fun, love. And—you're okay? After last night . . ."

"I was just overwhelmed," I replied, not quite a lie. "Thank you. I loved it."

He smiled. "Have fun!"

I left through the airlock and held up a glow rod as guests came out to greet me. I checked their names off the list and decided to wait a few more minutes for the stragglers. The last two off the ship were the droids, who were certifiably not on the list.

"I didn't see you two on the excursion list," I said, pocketing the datapad.

Veebee looked positively appalled—or at least as appalled as a droid without any facial expressions could look. "*Excursion?* Oh no, we are going grocery shopping."

I frowned, moving the basket Dad had given me from one arm to the other. "For what?"

"*Starblossoms!*" VB-35 replied excitedly. Food was the only thing she really *ever* got excited about. "You know I hear the ones on Alderaan were quite sour. They were supposedly all exterminated with the planet—that cannot be helped—but I have it on good authority that this station's agricultural site might have a variation of the fruit. Which is exactly what I am looking for—erm, exactly what *we* are looking for," she added, correcting herself.

N2-O added a tired bloop.

The taller droid threw up her hands. "Yes, yes, I am *dragging* you with me. What else is new? You know it is not safe for rare droids such as myself to go anywhere *alone*. Think of the ruffians who might kidnap me for my heuristic processor and use all five hundred thousand three hundred and twelve original recipes for ill."

The astromech droid chirped in suspicion.

VB-35 gave a start. "*Languages?* Oh, I deleted most of those. Whoever has the space in their databanks for that?"

I rolled my eyes. "Oh, yes, who needs languages? Just be back by the time we leave. Wait," I added, stopping them before they entered the station. "What about the . . ." *The stowaway.*

"Gone. Left with the first group for the tour," Veebee replied.

Disappointment sank like a stone in my gut, but I quickly shoved the feeling away. I didn't *care* that he'd left without saying goodbye. I guessed he would, and last night I hadn't really given him another option. "Ah."

"Come along, Entoo. We are getting rusty just standing here," Veebee added, jostling the metal basket on her arm, and stalked into the space station to find that fruit, her poor astromech partner trailing behind like a dejected companion droid.

After the last of the guests checked in with me, I took a deep breath, slapped my cheeks to wake myself up, and raised my free hand to get everyone's attention.

And my life returned to normal.

I started the tour the same way I had for years. We began on one side of the Monument and slowly made our way through the corridors.

"Alderaan was beautiful," I began, walking backward toward the main hub of the space station. The din of life rebounded through the metal halls, bright music and ringing laughter, the hum of holovids projecting photos of Alderaan throughout the ages. Cities and sunsets, smiling people now dust and star stuff. "Imagine the sunset: evening skies that turned as purple as the crusts of galaxies, inset with stars so bright they shined like jewels, fading into night. Imagine a planet full of lush green trees and alabaster skyscrapers. Imagine Aldera, its capital, built beside a beautiful lake with a backdrop of mountains, a jewel of the Republic—at least, some thought it to be."

I waxed poetic about the art, the culture, the food—the little bits of forgotten memories, of history left to float aimlessly in space—all the things that made a place a home. I knew a little bit about that.

About what made someplace safe and welcoming.

About what made you want to return, again and again.

The Empire hated that. Hated comfort, hated warmth, hated a place that felt so viscerally like *home*—

One of the Civil War Buffs interjected: "The Empire struck Alderaan because it had been without conflict for generations—easy pickings. It had a weak monarch."

I'd stopped the tour group by a museum with a few relics of the monarch in question. "It got worse when they adopted the kid."

"Leia Organa proved herself to be a great leader," I said, gripping the basket tightly out of nerves alone, but was interrupted by his glasses-wearing friend.

"If I were her, I'd have stopped Grand Moff Tarkin then and there. This was her home, and she just *watched*."

Thank the stars no one was around and the lively music covered up most of the Buffs' awful comments. I reined in my annoyance as best I could. "Hindsight makes it easier—"

"Could've been avoided if she was stronger," another guy interrupted me, shaking his head. "Sad, really."

I tried to take control of the conversation. "Leia Organa went on to help defeat the Empire and save the galaxy—"

"Yeah, and Alderaan paid the price. A *good* ruler would've—"

"People do the best they can with the information and resources they have," I said in a tone that I hoped would brook no argument. It was louder and harsher than my usual voice, but it got the point across. "It's easy for us to say we could've done better, but isn't that a little disrespectful to the very real lives that were lost? This isn't a thought exercise. This happened. There is ash mixed into the rock floating out there in space—people. *Billions* of people. You are more than welcome to suppose what Princess Organa *should* have done, but don't do it here. Don't disrespect them here."

The Buffs quieted, looking bashful, like scolded toddlers. I was probably going to get an earful from Dad about this when they complained on their surveys at the end of the tour, but for the first time in a very long time, I found that I didn't care.

What was Dad going to do? *Fire* me?

So I put on a smile and motioned ahead of us, where the station split into four different corridors. The light reflected off of the names on the ground, and they glittered like inlaid crystals. "Anyway, how about we visit the agricultural center?"

As everyone followed me down the corridor, I massaged the back of my neck to ease the tension. Some guests were just *like this*, but they had become more and more frequent as First Order propaganda started circulating more widely in the Core Worlds. I hoped it wasn't a sign of bigger issues.

After the market, we met up with Kotti's group and wrapped up the tour, handing everyone gift bags containing a glittering Piece of Alderaan.

Well, *almost* everyone. One of the Buffs said, "Hey, I didn't get one."

Had I miscounted? Or maybe I lost one somewhere on the station? Just as I began to panic, one of his buddies said, "You can have mine."

"Thanks, man," he replied, miming an explosion. "You rock."

CHAPTER FOURTEEN

THE STARBLOSSOM

That evening after dinner service, I returned to the galley only to find the stowaway sitting at the scratch table, staring down at one of VB-35's new concoctions. My breath caught in my throat. *Sian.* He—he hadn't left? I opened my mouth, then closed it again, because my mind was blank. He was *supposed* to be gone, but he was here. I *should* be angry, but I was . . .

Relieved?

Strangely, terribly, happily *relieved*.

As soon as I went into the galley, he glanced up at me and beamed a wide smile. "Oh, Starlight! I don't suppose you'd fancy saving me?"

It was then I took in his exact predicament, sitting there at the scratch table, some sort of dessert in front of him. It was shaped like a fruit, with some small crystallized bits on top. He looked positively agonized by the turn of events.

I pulled myself together and asked, "What am I saving you from, exactly?"

"His dues," Veebee replied, arms folded over her chest, waiting expectantly for her tester to do the thing he had agreed to do.

I closed the galley door and asked more urgently, "But what's he *still* doing here?"

"Oh, we told him he can get off later," VB-35 dismissed.

"You said he left with the first tour!"

"I thought he did."

Sian said, "I *tried* leaving, but your brother kept snooping around near the airlock. I *couldn't* leave. I don't like this as much as you don't. Trust me."

"He hasn't spotted you, has he?"

He threw up his hands. "I don't know, Starlight! I thought I was careful—"

"You *weren't* very careful," I deadpanned, remembering the party all too well.

He huffed. "I just know that when I tried to leave I found myself diving into a *garbage* chute to keep from getting caught!"

Noola chirped in confirmation, making a disgusted face.

"Even Noola had to go down with me! I had to wash my clothes *again*!"

Veebee waved her hand. "Yes, yes, it was terrible, and you're still here. Now can you taste it?"

The stowaway pursed his lips tightly and eyed the dessert. "That's it? Just . . . taste this? No strings attached?"

"None," Veebee confirmed.

Not that the droid needed strings for this particular favor.

Sian speared the food with a fork. It came away from the plate like marshmallowy slime, smelling strongly saccharine and damp. He sniffed it, shrugged, and took a bite. He chewed it. His already pale skin turned a deathly pallor. He set down his fork.

I asked Veebee, "What *is* it?"

"I call it Starblossom Puget. The fruit might not be ripe, though," she added, watching the stowaway attempt to swallow. "Or it could be the minced raw shaak."

At that, he scrambled away from the scratch table and spit into the sink.

"It's probably the minced raw shaak," Veebee determined.

"You're a menace," I said affectionately.

Sian lamented from the sink, "I should've tried harder to escape."

I rolled my eyes and deposited the dirty plates I'd brought down from dinner service onto the counter, where two other stacks already sat, waiting to be washed.

"I don't know why Val was stalking the airlocks. Maybe Dad asked him to account for the guests who came back on the manifest. The next stop is Naboo, but we won't be landing, so your best bet to leave won't be until Tatooine."

"When's that?" the stowaway asked, and gargled water to get the taste of raw meat out of his mouth.

"A few days," I replied, trying to keep a straight face. "And stop that. You aren't going to die."

"I can feel my will to live perishing," he lamented.

It was *not* funny. It was absolutely not funny at all, I told myself as I bit the inside of my cheek to keep my face neutral and excused myself from the galley. While I doubted anything Vee fed Sian would kill him, a secret little part of me relished the breakdown of his suave persona. It was hard to act cool when you were spitting out raw shaak, anyway.

I was so caught up in trying not to look too delighted by the turn of events that I didn't hear my brother until I had walked past his room. I stopped. He was talking to someone behind his door, and he sounded angry.

I wasn't *nosy*, but he was being very loud. I slipped up to his room and pressed my ear against the door.

". . . and as I've said before," Val went on, "this is my father's ship, sir. I can handle this."

There was static, then a garbled and tinny reply—like someone chatting through a holovid: *"Ambition makes liars out of everyone, Quay."* The speaker's voice was thin and snide, like simply speaking to my brother was beneath him. It made me want to punch whoever it was in the nose. No one talked to my brother that way. *"We have a limited amount of time before his intelligence reports to* him. *The only reason I chose you for this mission was pure happenstance. Don't make a fool of me."*

"No, sir," Val mumbled.

"Good."

The next I knew, I heard footsteps, and suddenly I was backpedaling against Maeve's old laundry buggy that she'd left in the corridor as the door slid open. My brother narrowed his eyes at me.

I feigned innocence, pointing to the laundry buggy. "Just dropping off my dirty towels."

His face pinched, but then he took a towel from his hook. "Thanks for reminding me," he replied, and locked the door after him before he dumped his towel in, as well. "How was the space station?"

"Fine," I replied, wondering if he was angry. He didn't *look* it. Which was way different from the Valor in my memories, who hated when I poked my nose where it didn't belong. We'd gotten into fights more often than not about it, because then I'd go running to tell Dad. "They've started producing starblossoms again, which is really cool."

"Does Dad still do the Piece of Alderaan thing?"

"Yeah."

He snorted. "See? Things really don't change. I should probably go up and help with the cleanup from dinner," he added, zipping up his jacket as he headed for the lift.

"Um—he shouldn't talk to you like that," I called after him, telling him exactly what he wanted to know: how much I'd heard.

Enough, as it turned out.

He glanced over his shoulder, eyebrows furrowing. "How did he sound?"

"Like you were beneath him—like you didn't deserve his time. But you're one of the smartest people I know, Val. If he can't see that, then he's a fool, and *you* deserve better."

His face softened. "Thanks, Arie," he said, and walked onto the lift. I didn't see him again for the rest of the night.

CHAPTER FIFTEEN

THE ARGUMENT

Dad got on the intercom and told everyone to brace themselves as the *Starfarer* jumped into hyperspace to reach our next destination: Naboo.

"Where a very special person is waiting for us!" he teased.

The special person in question had been the ruler of Naboo during the Galactic Civil War. Normally, we took guests on excursions, but construction was going on at the palace, and so Kotti had coordinated a meet and greet instead. Not every day did you come face to face with former royalty, so it was a fair trade-off.

Traveling to Naboo took anywhere between ten and fourteen hours, depending on where we entered the hyperspace lane. I used to wonder if Mom ever used her skills to shorten the distance, astrogating uncharted routes across the galaxy, but every time I asked Dad, he simply shrugged and told me he didn't remember.

He wouldn't even let me *try* to astrogate. He hadn't let Val, either.

The one thing that connected us to our mother was a thing we weren't allowed to explore. I wasn't sure I even wanted to—it *had* cost Mom her life, and so it was frighteningly real, and frighteningly permanent—but Val always took issue with Dad not letting us try. . . . Val called this ship a cage, but . . . it was safe. It was home. I couldn't fault Dad for trying to protect us.

As we eased into hyperspace, the old bones of the *Starfarer* groaned, and the comforting hum of the engine disappeared in the vacuum of sound. It was always a little disorienting at first, when the engines went silent. It unnerved me every time, no matter how many trips I took.

As I clocked out for the night and returned downstairs to go to my room, a tragically familiar face met me in the corridor after I exited the turbolift. A familiar face that was currently trying to break into a room.

A room that was not his.

"What are you doing?" I snapped, stalking past my own room to confront him.

Sian jumped. Noola scuttled between his feet. "I told you to *tell* me if anyone was coming!" he scolded her.

Noola chirped, eyes wide and innocent.

I folded my arms across my chest and narrowed my eyes at them both. "The refreshers are the other way, if that's your excuse."

He sucked a breath between his teeth, starting to pocket the bent fork and the pebble-sized sharp object he was using to pry open the lock. "That *was* what I was looking for, sadly. . . ."

I recognized the other object in his hand. "You're using a *Piece of Alderaan* to try to get into my brother's room?"

"Oh, this?" He tossed the rock into the air and caught it between his first and middle finger. It glinted in the pale lights, looking like a tiny version of the rocks that floated in the Alderaanian graveyard.

Because it was.

That was where the missing souvenir had gone.

"Noola brought me back a souvenir from her excursion. I thought I could put it to use."

"To break into my brother's room?"

"Because he keeps snooping around," he replied simply.

I glowered. "Do you keep giving him reason to? Get away from his door."

"I won't have someone like you judge *me*," he replied.

"What does *that* mean?"

He held up the rock. "Really, Starlight? You profit off of the galaxy's worst moments, and you're trying to make me feel bad about making sure your brother is not a galactic fascist trying to kill me."

I fisted my hands. "You take that back. Val would *never*."

He studied me with those strange, otherworldly eyes. "You're so sure, aren't you?"

"Yes."

"You're naive."

"No, I look at *history*—"

He blinked. "History? Which version of history? Oh, the history where special magical Jedi defeat evil with their special glowing swords? That history? Or the one where normal everyday people quietly fade away until they aren't even echoes of a whisper of a name?"

My mouth dropped open. Eloquent and cutting—if I wasn't so furious I'd be impressed. "Han Solo's a normal guy! He—he wasn't a Jedi or a special person."

Sian rolled his eyes. "Oh, the smuggler who did the Kessel Run in less than twelve parsecs? *That* guy?"

"Fourteen," I murmured.

"Twelve," he argued.

"He was normal—"

"Oh, come *on*, Starlight. You *know* you don't believe that. Normal people don't get stories told about them, because they're the ones who die. They're the thankless ones who let the Han Solos make Kessel Runs, and get picked off in skirmishes, and lose their parents in senseless massacres." He flipped the rock up again and caught it in his hand. And then again. And again. Like a coin. "They're children who become slaves and get brainwashed into being soldiers. They're mentors who die before they ever finish their life's work. You don't talk about *them*. I guess they aren't history, right? They're the fodder."

When I was sure he was done with his rant, I pinned him with my gaze and asked softly, "So which of those happened to you?"

He caught the rock one last time, surprised. "What?"

"Which of those happened to you?" I repeated calmly.

For a moment, hurt fractured his face, and then he quickly schooled it. He barked a laugh. It was strange and sharp. "You're funny."

"If my family's legacy is a *joke* to you, then you can leave. Right now. I'll space you myself."

He held the rock up. It shimmered in the dim lights, with veins of metal melted into it. "*This* makes it a joke, Ardent Quay. These stupid little stones. They're not even useful for picking locks."

Then he dropped it into my hand, turned, and left for the galley again. I saw red. Of all the selfish, awful, *infuriating—*

I threw the rock at him. It hit him square in the back and clattered to the deck.

He stopped in his tracks and spun back to me, looking stricken. "*Really?*"

I pulled myself up to my full height. "Really!"

His eyes glittered with a challenge. "Violence, Starlight, is never the answer."

"I don't know what else'll get through that fat head of yours!"

"My head is *not* fat."

"And these rocks are not *stupid*," I snapped, jabbing a finger at the Piece of Alderaan on the deck. "These pebbles were collected by Alderaanians. Every one of them costs fifty credits. The space station sells them to fund the agriculture center. My father buys *thousands* of them so that you can enjoy the Starblossom Puget Veebee made for you. And if *that's* stupid, then empathy is dead."

Wordlessly, his gaze shifted to the pebble on the deck between us. A muscle in his jaw twitched.

"Empathy doesn't bring people back," he muttered.

"No, but without it, we lose them entirely."

Silence settled between us. Noola looked between the two of us and chirped.

I took a deep breath, cooling my head. "Please go back to the galley. Everyone else will be coming down soon to their rooms, and I don't want you caught. Let me deal with Val, okay? He's *not* a fascist and he probably just thinks you're a stowaway—"

"I *am* a stowaway," he pointed out. Then he smirked,

and it was cunning enough for me to absolutely not like the look of it as he crossed the distance between us. "*Or* he thinks I'm here to steal his pretty little sister away."

Pretty? A heat of anger flickered in my chest. "I'm a little more than that."

"Obviously *I* know that," Sian replied. "I'm talking about your brother."

"He knows that, too," I replied flatly, and put a step between us as I backed away, and then another. "And if he comes around again, tell me. I'll deal with him. Good night, Sian," I added, and quickly turned around on my heel to escape back to my bedroom, but he caught my wrist.

I glanced back, confused and startled. For a brief, hopeful second, I thought he'd apologize. My eyes fell to his lips, and I wondered if they were soft. And then he opened his mouth.

"The *artifact* is still with you, right?" he asked, dropping my hand just as surely as my heart dropped into my stomach like a stone. Oh. It wasn't about me at all.

"It's safe," I assured, staring at the floor.

"Good. I think it's safer there."

"Yeah," I murmured. My voice sounded distant. "I'll keep it safe."

He smiled, reassuring. "Thank you."

I escaped the corridor then and closed my door behind me.

I waited until his footsteps retreated, my back pressed against the door, and then I slid to the ground in relief. The tension unwound from my body.

The overheard conversation with Val earlier, mixed with Sian's sharp critique, began to eat at me from different directions. I felt so silly thinking he'd kiss me in the corridor, *wanting* him to after our argument. How awful. How confusing.

I hated it.

My gaze traveled to the top drawer of my dresser, where the lightsaber was hidden. I had to remember that Sian was only here because I could do something for him. There wasn't another reason. So of course he would be nice and flirt with me as long as I kept him, and this artifact, safe.

It would do me well to remember that.

Quietly, I went to the dresser and took out the lightsaber. The dim light of my room caught in the nicks and scrapes on it. The weapon looked so much older than anything I'd seen before. Whose was it? Where had it come from? Why did the First Order want it? How had Sian gotten it?

Who *died* for it? How many people?

Even though I knew the stories, the whispered histories, it felt silly that something so small could be so important.

My thumb hovered over the button. I knew it didn't work. I knew it wouldn't light up for me. I'd already tried it. I already had my answer, but . . .

Maybe lightsabers had masters. Maybe they chose people who were worthy.

Or maybe they were like any other weapon—like blasters or knives or metal pipes. Anyone could use them, just as anyone could die by them.

I pressed the button, and it sank with a click.

Something inside fizzled. My heart tremored with hope. It could be mine, couldn't it? It could choose me. I could be someone important, someone worthy of a story—

Maybe if I tried it again, it wouldn't be broken anymore. (Maybe *I* wouldn't be broken anymore.)

The barrel sparked with something yellow and bright—like a sunrise—but then it went dark again.

Or, a small voice in my head whispered, *you simply aren't important enough to wield it.*

I put the saber back into its hiding spot in my dresser and covered it with my underwear before I curled up in bed. I lay awake for the next hour, listening to the thumps and groans of the ship, and wondered what it would be like, for once, to be important enough.

CHAPTER SIXTEEN

THE NIGHTMARE

It was a nightmare. I knew it was, but that didn't stop me from feeling afraid. It didn't stop the scream that bubbled up in my throat, the urge to run, to flee, to cry out for help. Something chased me. Something that made me feel like prey. Invisible strings tightened around my throat, like fingers. I couldn't breathe. I couldn't speak.

The lightsaber was in my hand, but it was broken. It couldn't protect me.

It couldn't protect anyone.

A terrible, searing pain sliced through my chest. I glanced down. A red beam speared through me, burning a hole through my heart—

"You are nothing," said a vicious voice beside my ear.

I woke up with a gasp.

My room—it was my room. Alone. I clawed away my covers to sit up, pressing a small soft pillow to my belly.

My heart rushed in my ears, loud and frantic, a scream still lodged in my throat. My chest burned from the pain, even though it wasn't real.

It wasn't real.

I had to keep reminding myself of it.

I smoothed down my wild curly hair and took a few deep breaths. It wasn't real.

You're safe, I told myself.

On the bedside was a datatape reader open to an older serial chapter of *Under the Tan-Tan Sun*. Reading the earlier installments usually calmed me down, but I guessed the scene I had left off on made my dreams weird. The assassin had snuck into the Queen's bedchambers, blade at the ready. That was all my nightmare was—my overactive imagination. But the voice in my dream—

You are nothing, he had said.

It didn't sound like anyone I knew.

But now I was, tragically, too awake to go back to sleep, so I tossed the covers off, pulled on a comfy thick robe, and slipped out into the chilly corridor. The ship hummed gently in hyperspace. There was a certain chill when we were traveling, the kind that ate right down to my bones. I shivered, wrapping the robe tighter around me.

I wondered what it would be like waking up somewhere warm for once.

I didn't know.

Telly was snoring in her room, so Dad must've been at the helm. He'd started to take the late shift more often. He was getting older, so he usually took nights when less risk was involved. It was a pretty easy path from Alderaan to Naboo in the Mid Rim.

I didn't really talk to my dad all that much about my nightmares anymore, but this one clung to my bones, making me feel a little too off-kilter, like a planet knocked off its axis. I needed to talk to someone, and aside from the droids—who were probably recharging—Dad was the only one awake.

"Fine," I murmured to myself, and made my way to the turbolift.

I heard a cacophony of snores as I passed the crew members' doors. The running lights on the floor were dimmed in the night, so I trailed my hand along the bulkhead in the darkness, even though I knew the ship by heart.

It was soothing, the rough metal sliding beneath my fingertips.

There were few things Dad loved more than this ship, and the things he loved he held on to so tightly, he refused to let go. I sometimes wondered if he loved me more than he feared losing me.

Maybe that was what love was.

Lost in thought, I made my way to the bridge and was

about to press the switch to open the door when I heard voices on the other side. Dad and someone else. At first, I thought it might be Val, but when they spoke again I recognized the other voice immediately—

Maz Kanata.

"All I'm saying is that it's a bit too neat, and you are no fool," Maz said.

"Don't say that," Dad replied with a groan. "I'd like to think the galaxy might work in my favor this time."

"The galaxy rarely works like that, friend."

"Then I guess I really am an old fool, eh?"

Maz paused for a long moment. "Yes, but only because you hope. I admire that very much. I wish more people found power in that. We could use you, you know. There aren't many of us old rebels left."

Dad laughed, but it sounded tired. "I'm done with wars, Maz."

She hummed. "You live long enough, and you'll realize that history is simply an echo of itself, and most of us don't listen."

Her soft footsteps came toward the door.

Crap. I reeled back. I didn't want to get caught snooping—*again*. First Val, and now this? I would have made a bad spy. I dove into the utility closet just as the door to the bridge opened, and Maz shuffled out, her hands behind her back in that patient way of hers. I watched through the slats in the door vent as she told Dad good night and shot a pointed look at the utility door.

Yeah, she *definitely* knew I was here.

That was embarrassing.

Maz left, and I counted to ten before I eased out of the closet. By then, Dad had returned to the bridge, and Maz was long gone.

What was *that* about? Was Maz here to recruit my dad for something? That didn't bode well at all. I couldn't think of many things she might be coming to old rebels asking for, and the few I could think of were not good. The Civil War had been over for almost thirty years. We were at peace.

Weren't we?

I knocked on the doorframe before I let myself onto the bridge.

Dad was at the helm, sitting back with one foot propped on his other leg, eating overripe obessa seeds that popped between his teeth like little jelly-filled fruits. The star fields passed outside the flight deck windows in a swirling tunnel of blue light.

He gave a start. "Daughter! What brings you here so late?"

I shuffled over to sit in the copilot's chair and brought my knees to my chest, setting my chin on them. The chairs were soft and well-worn. "I had a nightmare."

"I'm sorry, love." He patted the top of my head like he used to when I was little. "What was it this time? Ewoks chasing you?"

"If only," I muttered, and then lied: "I don't remember."

"You haven't had bad nightmares in a while, not since . . ." *Your mom died.* The words hung in the air, even though he couldn't bring himself to say them. He never could. It was like a part of our lives he just . . . refused to acknowledge, this gaping hole in our hearts he pretended wasn't even there. Instead, he diverted to, "Anything I can do?"

Tell me what Maz Kanata wanted, I thought, but he didn't know I had been eavesdropping. "Nah, I don't think so." I lifted my gaze to the star-streaked viewport. "So how has the night been so far? Uneventful?"

"Eh, mostly." He twisted back and forth in his chair, tugging on his beard. "I can't believe he's home. It feels like a dream."

One that was too good to be true. "Yeah . . . it was really unexpected."

"But it's nice to have the family back together, isn't it? Especially for your birthday tour."

I reached over and grabbed a handful of obessa seeds. "Yeah," I repeated, a little quieter, and ate a few. The stars passed the viewport in long twisting blue ribbons. "What if I want to leave, too?"

Dad paled. "Why would you want to do that?"

I shrugged. "To see what's out there, I guess."

"There's nothin' out there that you can't find here," he replied, and his tone was adamant.

"Yeah, but *I* don't know that. Or what if you're wrong?"

He was shaking his head. "We're not having this discussion tonight, love."

"But, Dad—"

"What would you want out there, anyway?" he asked.

"I don't know! That's the thing. I don't know what I'd want because I don't know what's out there."

"Isn't this good, though? Don't you like this?" he asked, motioning to the ship. "Us here in the *Starfarer*? Kotti and Daaric and Maeve and Telly—aren't we enough?"

I felt a lump in my throat. It was hard to swallow. "Of course you are, Dad! It's not that. Just—just forget about it. I'm sorry." I pulled my knees up to my chest again and wrapped my arms around them. "The nightmare's just got me shaken up, is all," I lied.

He seemed to believe me, at least. He patted my head again and sat back in his chair. I curled my fingers into fists. Val was wrong about me. I *tried* to talk to Dad about leaving, about going on my own adventure, but it never got any further than this, because wasn't Dad right, in the end?

If I was happy here, then what was the point of dreaming of the stars?

We were quiet for a long moment, listening to the quiet rhythm of the ship, but then he stifled a yawn and rubbed his eyes.

I waved my hand at him. "Go to bed. I've got this."

"Nah. I'm fine. You know me. I can run on strong caf and a dream." Even as he said it, he yawned again.

"*Go.* You look like you might fall over at any second, and think of the scandal *that* would be."

"I'm *fine*," he groused. "I don't need—"

Louder, I said, " 'Famed Rebel Pilot Falls Asleep Piloting His Own Tour.' "

"I don't think I'm *famed*. . . ."

"No, but if you fall asleep on your own tour and cause a crash, you'll be famous, and not in a way either of us want. C'mon, I'll be fine up here alone. I've flown this ship a hundred times, and I've been on this route a thousand. It's routine at this point. And besides, I don't think I can fall back asleep, anyway." The nightmare was too fresh in my head, and the lightsaber in my underwear drawer made me nervous even though it was broken. This whole tour did. The lightsaber, the First Order, Val's reappearance, Sian, *Maz* . . .

I didn't believe in coincidences, but I didn't see the connections, either.

He jostled the seeds in his hand, muttering quietly to himself.

"*Dad.* It's dangerous otherwise. That's what you told me, right? A pilot's no good to anyone without proper sleep, food, and company."

Finally, he gave a deep sigh, then pushed himself up to his feet. "Fine. Just remember that the navicomputer's fussy sometimes, and the vids on the crew's deck have been cutting in and out. I'll have to get Entoo on that."

I tried not to wince, because I had a feeling that *was* Entoo doing the cutting. . . . "Noted," I said. "Now *go*."

He scrubbed the top of my head like he had when I was little. "Since when did you grow up, love?"

A long time ago, but you never noticed until now. I returned his smile. "Sweet dreams, old man."

He laughed. Even that sounded tired. I didn't remember him looking so . . . run-down. Was the white streak in his beard wider? Since when did his gaze look so sunken? I had thought the crow's-feet by his eyes were just laughter lines, but they stuck around long after he stopped smiling. "If you need me, I'll be down in a sec, you understand?"

"Aye, Captain." I saluted.

He kissed my forehead with a soft "Love you to the ends of the galaxy."

"Love you all the way back," I replied, and he left the bridge.

The ship sank into quiet, and I was alone at the helm.

Just the hum of the engine, the whir of space outside the viewport, and the endless expanse of sky twisting by in a kaleidoscope of ephemeral blue. I settled into the captain's chair and looked out at the streaks of stars. I tried to concentrate, to find a path—any path—but all I could see were broken roads and dead ends. I couldn't find Naboo. Heck, I couldn't find *anywhere*.

Failure made my chest tight.

I blinked and slouched down in my chair. I remembered bits and pieces of Mom's lessons. She'd taught Val a lot more than she ever did me, and I tried not to feel too bitter about him leaving before he ever taught me anything useful.

"You have to feel it here," Mom had said once, tapping her sternum, "right in the middle. It's a tug. A call, your grandmother always said. You have to want where you're going so badly you can't see anything else."

Maybe that was the problem. I'd never wanted anything that badly before.

Or maybe, because I never used the gift, it had disappeared.

It was a sobering thought.

Unchosen again, like I was to the lightsaber in my underwear drawer.

NABOO

CHAPTER SEVENTEEN

THE COMPANY

The *Starfarer* arrived at Naboo, but because the palace was currently under renovation, we had arranged to have a special guest speaker—Sosha Soruna, the ruler of Naboo during the fall of the Empire—meet us planetside. Instead, she wanted to come up to visit the *Starfarer.* Afterward we would take a shuttle tour down to a Gungan city, enjoy a seafood-heavy lunch, and shuttle the guests back up to the ship for dinner.

Sosha Soruna arrived on the *Starfarer* with little aplomb and even less security, flanked only by an assistant and a single guard. If I hadn't known who the older woman was, in her lovely crimson flying jacket, trousers, and supple boots, I'd have guessed she was a civilian. Her black hair, now peppered gray with age, was pulled back into a simple bun, her face barren except for a thick line of makeup that went from her bottom lip to the tip of her chin.

She smiled when she arrived, and hugged my dad.

"It's so nice to finally meet you in person, Hansifred," she said warmly, "and I'm so glad we could make this work. When Ms. Kotti reached out about this opportunity, I *had* to jump at the chance."

"You honor us with your presence, Lady Sosha," he replied, kissing the back of her hand, and led her to the meet and greet in the main chamber.

It was about thirty minutes of Lady Sosha recounting her days during the war, and her efforts to protect Naboo, and the years that followed. Afterward, quite a few of the Civil War Buffs hung around to ask her more complex questions.

I was posted in the main chamber to help facilitate, stifling a yawn a few times from my long night on the flight deck. When the last of the young men approached her, he came on hard and fast, gushing about some Operation: Cinder military action that happened years ago and how "the passage of time has left you timeless"—which was *such* a smooth line, I had to admit—before he pulled a piece of flimsiplast from his pocket to hand to her.

I intercepted it and politely told Spectacles, "I'll keep it for her."

His shoulders slumped. "O-oh. All right . . ."

Lady Sosha thanked him, and after all the guests had been seen to, she asked to be excused to the refresher.

I escorted her to the closest one and cleared the room before she went in, then guarded the door. When she was done, she washed her hands and inspected her reflection in the mirror.

"The guests on the *Starfarer* are so lovely," she commented. "I appreciate their enthusiasm."

I winced, knowing she was referring to Spectacles. "Sorry about that one guy. He's one of those Galactic Civil War buffs. He sort of is *really* into this part of history."

She didn't seem bothered by him at all. "He was very excited. Let me see the letter?" she added, motioning to the pocket where I'd stowed it.

I handed it to her. The flimsliplast looked familiar—likely from a guest room.

Delightedly, Lady Sosha unfolded the letter, read it, and gave a riotous laugh. "The *bravery* of some men!" she cried.

Alarmed, I looked at the flimsiplast. It was . . . "A *love* letter? I am *so* sorry," I added, mortified. "I promise that will never happen again—"

"No, no, what an honor! Truly, even age doesn't deter some people," she said, and immediately—but not unkindly—ripped the letter up. "What a lovely thing for him to say, even if it's quite absurd."

I realized then that I didn't know much about Sosha

Soruna other than her life as a monarch and her brief time before that as a skilled pilot. After, I had assumed she returned to everyday civilian life, but by the blaster pistol at her hip . . . maybe not so much.

Then she said, as if reading the furrow of my eyebrows as confusion, "I don't quite like men as my paramours."

My eyes widened. "Oh." It didn't help that my voice came out in a squeak. And *that* just made me feel mortified. "Oh, stars, I didn't—did I sound—I didn't mean to—"

She laughed again, tossing the remains of the letter into the trash. "It's fine, my friend. I didn't find out until *much* later in life." She cocked her head. "I was about your age when I assumed the throne of Naboo. It was impossible to think of anything other than saving my people. For *years*, even after the war. I must admit I'm a little jealous of people who found love during it. Leia, and your father, too."

Leia—"As in Leia Organa?" I asked before I could stop myself.

I hadn't realized they knew each other, or were close. My father certainly hadn't met any of the big players in the war, and the way he told it, he was very much a part of it. But the war had been big, with a lot of fronts.

Lady Sosha nodded. "The same. Though most of my ruling years feel transient at this point. I wasn't a part of anyone's life long enough to be anything." A thoughtful look crossed her face. "What's it like living on this ship? You were raised on it, yes?"

"It's . . . nice. I get to see everything. And I'm safe here," I added, because that was what Dad always told me.

You're safe on this ship with me, he assured, as if the rest of the galaxy was full of cruel intentions.

But *safe*, I was beginning to realize, wasn't the same as happy.

"That sounds quiet," she said gently. "I'm glad you can have this kind of life. It's the kind a lot of us worked for, and died for, and yet there is still work to do." She drew a small metal card from her pocket and pressed it into my hand. "If you ever need anything, send a bird."

I frowned. "A . . . bird?"

"A message," she went on. "I'll be more than happy to answer, Ardent Quay. Until then"—she gathered my hands in hers and squeezed them tightly—"may the Force be with you."

She left the refresher and returned to her security and assistant in the main chamber, who walked her back to the shuttle they'd arrived on.

I put the contact card into my uniform jacket, not sure when I would ever call up the ex-ruler of an entire planet, but the thought was nice—almost doting. I bit the inside of my cheek to hide a smile. I wondered if this was, a little, what it felt like to have a mom.

After Lady Sosha left, we gathered the guests who had signed up for the Naboo excursion. Most of the crew—especially Dad—loved going planetside with them, and usually I went, too, but when I saw that Val had elected to stay behind, I volunteered to crew the bridge with Telly. I'd watch the video feeds (and keep our stowaway secret, since he had a penchant for wandering). But really, the goal was to monitor my brother and where, in fact, he was snooping. I didn't exactly think he was worried about Sian taking me away, but if he was poking around, then he was suspicious of something, and I *really* didn't want him finding my stowaway and telling Dad.

For the Naboo excursion, Dad rented a large shuttle and took the guests to tour a Gungan city and have lunch. I situated myself in the copilot's chair and snacked on Dad's secret stash of obessa seeds, thoughtfully flipping Lady Sosha's card over in my hand.

What a strange day.

Telly wasn't the most talkative crew member, but she was most easily the one who could sense my moods from a kilometer away. Maybe she could taste my sourness after years of tenaciously silent observation. Whatever it was, while we sat on the bridge, Telly turned directly to me and said, "Do you want to talk about it?"

I glanced at her, pocketing the card again. "About . . . ?"

Telly blinked slowly. While she wasn't the most talkative, when she *did* talk, it was with purpose. She wasn't about to let this go. "The boy you are keeping in the pantry."

My eyes widened. "I—I don't—who . . . who do you mean?" My voice was a squeak by the end.

She drummed her fingers on the console. "Do you really think you could smuggle an entire man onto the ship without me knowing, Ardent Quay?"

My shoulders slumped. Oh, she'd used my whole name. *That* meant trouble. "Is it that obvious?"

"To me? Yes. Entoo has been very liberal with their video feed disruptions. Who is he?"

"Just . . . a stowaway. He's harmless." I hoped.

"Why didn't you tell us about him, then?"

"Because . . ." I frowned. Honestly, I *could* have told my father and the crew, and I'm sure they would have very happily brought him aboard if they knew the circumstances. No one here was a friend of the First Order.

However . . .

"The First Order was after him on Coruscant, and I was afraid to tell anyone else when I brought him aboard because I didn't want to put them in danger, too," I admitted.

Telly studied me. "And you're sure it was First Order?"

"I think so."

"Do you know what they wanted with him?"

I didn't answer. I had told Sian I wouldn't tell anyone about the lightsaber, and although he'd said *awful* things to me, I wasn't going to betray him. "He needed help. Dad always said to help the people we can, so I did. Would you mind not telling anyone?"

"Not my business," replied Telly, turning back to look out the viewport. "But you *really* need to hide him better." Then she leaned over and pushed a button on the video console. The feeds went dark. "Oh, no," she deadpanned, "whatever will we do? The video feeds are corrupted."

I snorted. "I get it."

She replied, ever monotonous, "Good."

CHAPTER EIGHTEEN

THE APOLOGY

For the second night in a row, I convinced Dad to let me take the night shift. He still looked so tired, and I couldn't figure out why.

We weren't scheduled to leave Naboo's orbit until morning, so all I had to do was keep an eye on the surveillance vids every half hour or so and monitor the incoming comms. Out of the viewport, the wide blue-and-green planet floated like a pearl in deep space. It turned too slow to see, steady and stalwart, a reminder of the passage of time when everything else felt still. The longer I looked, the sleepier I felt.

Tonight would be a hard one to stay awake for.

Then, about halfway through the night, as I tossed sabacc cards into a captain's hat, movement on the surveillance video caught my eye. I pulled it up only to find the stowaway wandering the bottom deck *again*—this time waiting outside of one of the rooms, rocking impatiently back and forth. Noola was sitting on his shoulder, playing with her tail.

I watched him for a while, wondering what the heck he was doing, before I realized he was outside *my* room. And strangely enough, he wasn't trying to pick the lock with a fork and a dream.

I buzzed down to the terminal beside my door. "I'm not there," I informed him.

He jumped, startled, and slapped a hand over his heart. "Warn a guy when you go omnipresent!"

"That's my secret: I'm always a little bit everywhere."

"Frightening," he replied dryly, and raked his fingers through his hair to regain his composure. It was gray in the nighttime lights, floppy and wild, as if it never quite did what he wanted it to do. I'd never met anyone so young with his hair color, and judging by the roots it was natural. I wondered if it was soft—

What was I *thinking*?

Forcing the silly thoughts out of my head, I asked, "What do you want?"

While at the same time he asked, "Can't sleep?"

I frowned. "I could ask the same."

"I'm just stretching my legs. . . ."

"And loitering around my personal quarters?"

His mouth dropped open. Noola squawked, and it sounded a lot like a laugh. "I . . . knocked. A few times."

"Why?"

"Because I can't just barge in?"

I rolled my eyes, even though he couldn't see. "No, I mean *why* are you in front of my room?"

He shifted on his feet, glancing around the corridor even though it was completely empty and, at this time of night, everyone was sound asleep. "Can we talk in person?"

"Why?"

"I think I . . . owe you an apology," he said. "You saw a reprehensible side of me. I don't normally try to break into people's rooms."

"Oh?" I deadpanned.

He winced. "I really don't."

"As far as I can tell, I know exactly who you are. You're cagey, secretive, infuriating—"

"And you're mistrustful and revoltingly moral and stubborn," he batted back, his eyebrows raised high as he turned toward the camera and looked right at it. Then, eyes locked on the lens, he bent toward the comm and added in a softer, growly voice, "Not that I'm complaining."

I stared. My mouth was open, but no words came out. I felt the telltale heat of a blush rushing across my cheeks. "I . . . I am not *mistrustful*! Maybe you're just not very trustworthy."

"Says the mistrustful girl who probably thinks I'm

trying to break into her room to steal something instead of, I don't know, apologizing for being such a rude drydak yesterday."

"You . . . could be," I argued, but it was a weak argument at best.

He scoffed. "Why would I *knock* if I wanted to steal something, Starlight?"

Sadly, he had a good point. "I'm on the bridge for the night shift."

A twitch of a smirk curled at the edges of his mouth. "Is that an invitation up?"

No. It was a risk bringing him up to the main deck. There were plenty more cameras, but I could disable all of them for him to get here. He could help me not fall asleep, if nothing else. "Fine," I caved, "I'll disable the cameras for a minute. But tell Noola to go back to the galley."

He pouted. "And leave her *alone*? Fine. It's her bedtime, anyway. I'll be up soon."

"Be careful," I reminded him, hoping I wasn't about to regret this.

I did, in fact, regret it.

Sian whistled as he stepped onto the flight deck. "Talk about a relic."

I glared at him as I finished my routine hourly checks to make sure the ship was still normal and nothing was out of sorts. Just the normal sort of wrong—a malfunctioning heater, a leak in the air vents, an overheating water pump. "It's an antique."

"I'm just surprised," he added, sensing my annoyance. The door closed behind him, and he made himself right at home in the copilot's chair, stretching out his long legs and crossing them. In the light of the control panel, his hair took on a multicolored hue, reflecting dull shades of green and blue and yellow. He looked out at the blue-green planet of Naboo, reflected in his black eyes. "I'd like to apologize. For yesterday."

I studied him quietly.

He shifted in the chair. "I assumed the worst, and made an ass out of myself. I'm . . . good at that. Assuming. My mentor used to say that I was always too quick to judge, trying to fit something into the narrative I already had in my head. I thought I'd kicked that habit a long time ago, but . . . I did the same with you. I'm sorry," he repeated, and finally turned his strange black eyes to me.

This close, his gaze was mesmerizing. Not quite black at all, but a depthless darkness that seemed to go on and on for eternity. Looking into his eyes reminded me of looking into the galaxy. Silvery-white eyelashes framed them, matching his thick eyebrows, and I distantly wondered if he grew a beard, would it be the same color, too? I resisted the urge to brush back the hair that had fallen into his eyes, just to see them better. He was so earnest right now, it made me want to inspect my earnest feelings, too.

Apologies were hard to come by, and I guessed it took a lot for him to come all the way up here just to say he was wrong. He could've ignored it, but . . . he didn't.

That wasn't nothing.

He tilted his head, waiting.

I quickly looked away, busying myself with checking the coordinates on the navicomputer again. "Apology accepted." I sat back in my chair, pulling my knees to my chest. "But I'm sorry you had to come all the way up here just to say that."

"I felt it was important to do it face to face. Besides," he added, looking around the cockpit again, "I always wondered what the view was like up here."

"It's one of my favorites in the whole galaxy," I admitted.

"I can see why. If I had the choice to do this my whole life, I probably would, too."

My lips pursed tightly together. What did that say if I *didn't* want this? But instead I asked, "What else have you done? I mean, besides being a professional stowaway?"

He arched an eyebrow.

"If you don't mind me asking?"

"Well, let's see . . ." He counted on his fingers. "I've been a smuggler, fathier racer, janitor, Jedi Padawan—"

I rolled my eyes. "*Oh*-kay, you can leave now."

"Sorry, sorry," he quickly backtracked. "I knew what you meant. I'm just . . . shockingly bad at talking about myself."

It was my turn to arch a cryptic eyebrow.

"I was training to be an archeologist," he said.

That surprised me more than anything else. I thought he'd say something along the lines of pilot or courier or info broker. But an *archeologist*? "What part of history?"

"My mentor specialized in lost texts and civilizations. She went to university for High Republic–era politics and discoveries, and was trying to convince me to go, as well, but . . . I don't have the kind of education to get in somewhere like that. She taught me everything she knew, though, so I basically got an education anyway."

"Where did you grow up?"

"A little bit of everywhere."

I frowned. "You're being dodgy again."

He knew he was and winked. "I have to keep *some* allure, Starlight. Or else you won't keep me coming around."

I scoffed. If only he knew. "That's not why I keep you coming around."

He grinned. "So, you admit that you *are* coming around to me."

In more than one way, and in realizing that, I also realized I'd been caught red-handed. My face grew hot, so I scowled and turned back to the navicomputer. "That was a trap."

He grinned. "You like it."

"I despise you."

"Liar."

A smile tugged at the edge of my mouth, and I had to fight it down a little harder than usual. "Maybe a little," I admitted. "I was born here on the ship, somewhere in the Mid Rim but who knows where, really. The *Starfarer* was in hyperspace at the time. I used to wonder what it was like to grow up planetside, you know? Like down there on Naboo."

The glints of ships entering and exiting the atmosphere flared like diamonds. It was one of my favorite planets to watch. There was just something so peaceful about it.

"I'd probably be a different person if I had."

"Right? You could've been like Emperor Palpatine."

I rolled my eyes. *"Ha."*

"But seriously, I don't think so. I don't think where you're born dictates whether you're good or bad. You can be raised in a perfectly lovely family and cause unfathomable amounts of pain." He folded his arms behind his head and leaned back in his seat, closing his eyes. "People aren't born evil, you know? They choose it," he said, his voice carefully neutral, "and it's usually the easier choice. The choice that keeps you in power, the choice that ensures you're comfortable, the choice that never challenges your worldview. Evil is easy."

I scrunched my nose. "I think being good is easy, too. Valuing people, welcoming them, being respectful—"

"Is that being good or being *nice*?" he asked. "Nice is different than good, Starlight."

"Says the man who stole a lightsaber," I replied.

He cracked open an eye.

"You're not correcting me," I pointed out.

"You're right. I did steal it."

"Then are *you* nice or good?"

"I don't know," he admitted. "My mentor—she was good, though she wasn't nice. Not at all. She was crass, and stubborn, and drank too much. She'd never lift a finger for anyone if it wasn't in her best interest."

"Then how was she *good*?"

He sat up in his chair and leaned against the armrest, crooking his finger for me to come closer. I decided to play along and leaned toward him. We were just far enough apart so we weren't touching, but not by much. Close enough to whisper a secret, but far enough that I could deny that I liked this closeness. Though I *did* like it.

I liked that I could count his silver eyelashes, and I liked that I could see a hairline scar across the bridge of his nose. I liked that, this close, in the low light of the flight deck, he could see no one else—as if I was his galaxy.

He put a finger to his lips, and I noticed the beauty mark below them looked indigo in this light. There was a ring on his first finger, made of dark metal and engraved in a language I didn't understand, and his nails were tinted the same bruised color as his beauty mark. "There was once—allegedly—a bas-relief in Palpatine's office when he was in power," he began, his voice barely a rumbling whisper. I felt like he was telling me a forbidden secret, not the history of a piece of art in an office. "It depicted an age-old battle between the Jedi and the Sith. During the end of the Galactic Republic, Jedi would pass it and not think anything of it. They didn't consider it at all, really. But rumor is, the bas-relief was taken from a frieze found in a Sith temple on Malachor. My mentor was obsessed with the relic—didn't care where it came from. She wanted nothing more than to return it to its place of origin."

I was confused. "Sith—aren't they a faction of people who worshiped the dark side?"

"The way my mentor explained, Sith were the antithesis to the Jedi, but we don't know very much about them—who they were, what they wanted."

"But they were bad people."

He shrugged. "My mentor always said that history wasn't a prize to be hung on a wall—for anyone. Good or evil. It wasn't ours to take, but ours to learn from."

"But why not destroy it if it was evil?"

"Because that's how you forget, and if you forget, you repeat the same mistakes over and over. And then, before you know it, the next Palpatine comes along to take power."

"That'll never happen," I said. "We learned."

He shrugged. "So you see, I can't say my mentor was nice, but I do believe that she thought she was good. And so do I." He blew out a breath. "It's exhausting trying to live up to her expectations, though."

"I feel the same way," I mumbled.

He grinned at that, propping his head on his hand, elbow on the console between us. "Look at us, Starlight. We've got similar scars, after all."

"Why do you call me that?"

He blinked in surprise. *"Why?"*

"It doesn't really suit me." I swung my chair toward him. I knew what I looked like—the same reflection stared back at me every morning. Auburn hair more mess than curls, freckles with no discernible pattern, a gap between my front teeth, and thighs that made it hard to fit into most trousers comfortably. I wasn't short and cute or tall and elegant. I was just . . .

His eyebrows furrowed in confusion.

I rolled my eyes. "Come on, I'm not blind *or* fishing for compliments. I know exactly who I am. I'm not pretty like Kotti or elegant like Daaric or striking like you."

At that, he rotated his chair to face me, too. *"Striking?"*

I scoffed, too tired to be coy or embarrassed. "Of course you are."

He scrunched his nose. "It's my hair, isn't it?"

"And your eyes. I've never seen any like yours before."

"Most people haven't," he agreed, before I uncurled my legs and leaned forward, squinting at him. He met my gaze, searching my eyes as I searched his. "And most people can't look at them for long without feeling uneasy."

That surprised me. "Why would people feel *uneasy*?"

He shrugged. "They just do. I think it's the way my eyes look. I can sort of . . . hypnotize people."

"Have you hypnotized me?"

"No," he replied quickly, and then winced. "I mean, I haven't on purpose. Most of the time I can control it, but sometimes it's instinctual. When I'm threatened or nervous or . . ." He pursed his lips. "It's hard to explain. But I don't think I *can* hypnotize you."

I scooted a little closer to him. "Show me?"

He blinked. "What?"

"I'd like to see," I went on.

"You trust me to hypnotize you?"

"You just said you don't think you can."

"Okay. If you're sure." Then he took a deep breath, as if to steady himself, and closed his eyes. When he opened them again, the immovable white specks widened, like pupils—larger and larger, like distant stars coming closer in the viewport.

I did feel a tug of something—a strange fuzziness in my head—but it evaporated just as soon as I started to spin away.

"Oh," I whispered.

He quickly put his hands atop mine, blinking, releasing me from his gaze. "Are you all right?" He sounded concerned. "I'm sorry, I should have warned you—"

"That was beautiful."

He sucked in a sharp breath. Then he looked at me again. *"What?"* Then, a little calmer: "You sure you're okay?"

I nodded. "I felt you beginning to hypnotize me, but you were right. I don't think you can." I searched his eyes still, unable to look away. "They're so lovely. What does the galaxy look like to you?" I mused aloud, and then realized how rude that must have sounded and added, "I mean—there are plenty of different fields of vision and color ranges that different species—"

"I understand what you meant," he interrupted,

not unkindly, and wrapped a piece of my wavy auburn hair around his finger. It had come loose from its braid sometime in the night, and I hadn't noticed. "What color does this look like?"

"Muddy. Not copper, not brown. Kind of . . . not sure what it wants to be."

"Hmm." He played with my hair, unraveling it. "It isn't muddy to me. It's bright. It shines copper." Then he let go of the curl, hand lingering as he studied my face, my mouth. He whispered, "The color suits you." Then he pushed the lock behind my ear. "I call you Starlight because the first time I saw you laugh, after we almost died on Coruscant, you were impossible to tear my eyes away from. Like a flare of light in a sea of darkness. And it was beautiful."

We were so close that I couldn't ignore how intimate this was even if I wanted to. My skin felt electrified, waiting for the moment he would touch me again and spark me to life. Joy trembled in my chest, feeling like firecrackers. Then he took gentle hold of my chin. The tips of his fingers were rough with callouses. What kind of life did he lead to earn hands like that?

Is he going to kiss me? I wondered, my heart beating frantic in my chest, but he seemed patient, measured. So much so that all I could think of was pushing him back into his chair and straddling his thighs so he couldn't escape, then kissing him right here with the glow of Naboo in that lovely silver hair—

Without thinking, I reached up and ran my fingers through the front of his hair, pushing it out of his face. It *was* soft—like how I imagined starlight would feel.

His eyes widened in surprise, and I realized a little too late what, exactly, I'd done.

I quickly retracted my hand and schooled my face. "You should probably go. Veebee is bringing me caf in half an hour—"

"Veebee has brought you caf already, actually," came the voice of VB-35 from the doorway.

Mortified, I whirled around in my chair to find the droid standing there with a cup of steaming-hot caf. Her glowing eyes settled on me, and even though she didn't have an expression, I knew exactly what it would have been: amusement.

"I hope I haven't interrupted anything," Veebee went on casually, letting herself onto the flight deck and bending between us to set down the cup of caf on the control panel. "If I knew you had company, I would have brought two."

I was *never* going to live this down, I could already tell. I blushed and quickly turned to check the navigational console, even though nothing had changed since I last looked. "No, no. He was just leaving."

"I was," he agreed, and pushed himself to his feet. "Good night, Starlight."

I waved my hand in reply and didn't turn back around until I heard him leave.

With VB-35, on the other hand, I wasn't so lucky. If the droid had eyebrows, she would have raised one of them to mock me, but her smugly curious voice had to suffice. "You two looked *awfully* cozy. . . ."

"Please don't," I groaned, and buried my head in my hands. My cheeks were somehow even hotter than they had been a second ago. I wasn't sure what was more embarrassing, the fact that Veebee had caught us so close or that I had wanted to get *closer*.

And that was an awful thing to want in my profession.

Because if I knew anything about star tours, it was that in a job as transient as this, guests came and went like comets. Our tour was just a blip, a passing moment in their lives. We weren't anchors. *I* wasn't an anchor.

Everyone I loved left—even my dad would, eventually. Why would a stowaway who planned to get off when we reached Tatooine be any different?

CHAPTER NINETEEN

THE BAD GUYS

On our travel day to Tatooine, I feared that Sian was evading me. So much so that I began to think I'd done something wrong. Whenever I popped into the galley, he would slip out to the refresher. When I caught him in the corridor, he'd feign looking for Noola. It got to the point where Veebee even asked if I'd said anything to him.

"No!" I cried, stalking to the lift to help Kotti with a holochess tournament in the main chamber. "Nothing!"

I didn't think so, at least. Maybe I had asked too many questions on the flight deck and pried too deeply. I frowned, puzzled. Why did I care so much?

"You're being silly," I mumbled to myself as I made my final rounds in the common areas that night. "He's not evading you."

It *was* a big ship, and it was easy to avoid people, but all day? Never mind he was confined to the pantry and *he wasn't in the pantry*. Maybe I'd find him now, creeping around again while most everyone was asleep, and finally pin him down.

There were some late-night wanderers—a family in the mess hall playing sabacc and a few guests taking showers in the 'freshers, a few in the lounge on the main deck, gossiping about their sleeping friend. There was music in the main chamber and laughter at the tables, but Sian was nowhere to be found.

Well, it couldn't be helped.

With a yawn, I found my way back to my room and opened the door—

There was a shadow near my bed.

"Lights!" I snapped.

The halogens popped on, washing the room in bright, blinding light. I squinted against it, balling my hands into fists—

"Val?"

He stood by my dresser, wide-eyed and frozen, as if he'd just gotten caught. Because he *had* just gotten caught.

Annoyance bolted through me. "What are you doing in *my room*?"

The surprise on his face flickered to confusion. "I'm looking for your master key."

". . . I'm sorry?"

He gave a hard sigh. "So, Maeve locks the supply closet at night and I don't have shampoo. I was going to take a shower," he added, stepping away from my dresser. My underwear drawer was slightly ajar. Had it been knocked open when I'd startled him, or had he been opening it to rifle through? Or had he looked inside already and found the lightsaber?

My heart pounded in my chest.

"This late at night?" I asked, trying to keep my voice calm.

He gave a meandering shrug. "I can't sleep."

"Sure, but you could ask someone for shampoo."

He narrowed his eyes. "C'mon, Ardent, don't make this harder than it needs to be."

"What do you mean?"

He pulled out a holopuck and showed me. WANTED, it read, and showed the likes of Sian and then—regrettably—me.

My throat tightened. "I don't know what that means."

"I thought you were smarter than this, Ardent," he snapped, and kept searching my room, tearing open the cabinets, looking through my jewelry chest. Then he glanced at the box from my birthday and opened it. Inside was the key. Incredulously, he snatched it. "You haven't even taken it out of the box?"

I held up the holopuck. "Is this why you're here?"

He scowled. "Why else do you think I'm here? You're in trouble."

"I don't know, I thought maybe you'd come for my *birthday*? Like you said you did?"

Correctly calling out his drydak crap always made his bad moods fouler. A muscle in his jaw feathered. "I know you're hiding him," he accused sharply, storming out of my room and down the hall to the galley—and straight for Sian's makeshift bedroom.

"Hold on! Wait!" I cried, hurrying after him, but I wasn't fast enough.

He swiped the master key and opened the pantry door. He pulled his shoulders back, triumphant.

But there was nothing in the pantry.

No hammock. No comforter. No pillows. No clothes.

Nothing.

In confusion, I glanced at Veebee, but she simply kept chopping up carrots for the morning's breakfast. "While you're in there, can you grab a bag of rice?" she asked dryly.

Ignoring her, he whirled back around to me and spat, *"Where is he?"* There was a venom in his voice that I didn't recognize. I didn't like it.

"I don't know who you're talking about," I replied levelly.

"That *thief*!" he cried. "The one you helped back on Coruscant!"

My heart leapt into my throat, but I tried to keep my cool. I'd faced guests much more terrifying than my brother. Though my brother had never terrified me before. "I never got his name."

"You *helped* him!"

"They were about to kill him, Val," I batted back. "What was I supposed to do?"

He gritted his teeth. "You don't understand what you've done. I'm trying to help you, do you get that?"

"Funny way of showing it."

With a growl, he threw up his hands. "*Fine!* Whatever. I know he's here. I'm going to find him. And you'll thank me when I do, I promise you that." Then he turned and stalked out of the galley. It took a few deep breaths after the door closed for me to calm down again.

Only then did I realize that he'd taken my master key with him.

I sank into a chair at the scratch table and put my head in my hands. "This is a nightmare."

Veebee kept chopping her vegetables. "I'll say. But you might want to let him out of the cooler," she added, and pointed her knife toward the walk-in cooler in question.

I hopped to my feet and hurried to open it. Sian stood inside, comforter wrapped around his shoulders, shivering. Despite all logic, my anxiety melted the moment I saw him. He might've been cold, but at least he was alive.

"We need to talk," I said to him.

He sneezed. "Y-yeah, you're p-p-probably ri-right."

The galley was no longer safe for him, so when the coast was clear I snuck him into the last bastion of safety—my room.

"Doesn't he have a master key now?" Sian asked, still with the comforter pulled around him, after I'd closed the door. He held a warm cup of tea to thaw his fingertips, and blew on it gently.

I rifled through the junk drawer in my nightstand and pulled out an old slicer, then quickly reprogrammed the door code. "Yeah, but this'll make it a little harder. The master key will still override it, but it'll take a minute—and don't worry, the lightsaber's still in the drawer." At least, the last time I'd checked.

"In the . . . which drawer did you say?" he asked, looking at my dresser.

I froze. "Uh. Just . . . one of them."

He started to open the first one. "This one—"

I quickly lurched over and slammed it closed.

He snapped up his hands. "You almost took my fingers off! Why can't I look in? You didn't mind before."

Because *before* I didn't—I wasn't—

"I'll space you if you look," I said with deadly seriousness.

"Fine, fine. You know, this room looks like you," he added as he poked through all the things I'd collected over the years: the strange bottles and the flimsiplast posters and the souvenirs, the spools of colorful cloth and the knickknacks, and the broken pieces of junk on my shelves. "What makes you collect things?"

I shrugged. "I guess I just like to find some meaning in the junk other people throw away."

He grinned. "You'd make a good archeologist, then, if you ever get tired of this life."

"Ha." I sat down on my bed, folding my legs under me. "You're still leaving tomorrow when we land on Tatooine, right?"

"Yeah," he agreed, staring down into his tea. "That's the plan."

"Good. You can stay here tonight. On the floor. And I'll help you leave tomorrow."

And that was that.

TATOOINE

CHAPTER TWENTY

THE DUST BOWL

Tatooine was no one's vacation destination.

First off, the sand went *everywhere*.

I had learned to wear a shawl over my uniform on the planet because if not I'd have to run my clothes through the wash three times just to get all the dirt off, not to mention all the crevices where the sand hid on *me*. I still sometimes felt the grit between my teeth from the one time Dad got us lost in a sandstorm coming back from a moisture farm, and I rued that day.

Ever since then, when we had to stop on Tatooine, we kept the tour short, to a market day in Mos Espa and then a taxi out to a nearby moisture farm, where Dad would tell the story of young Luke Skywalker and his exploits in blowing up the first Death Star and trying to bring back the Jedi Order—a story most everyone knew.

Most of the guests signed up for the excursion, except for a family who found Mos Espa to be a little too dangerous (though perhaps that was because the family was wanted by one of the factions ruling the city—I didn't judge). Because there was never a good place to drift in orbit and Dad had a friend down in Mos Espa's spaceport who gave him a good docking spot, the *Starfarer* broke through the atmosphere and landed on the same dusty landing pad we had for the past ten years, and the same mechanics came out to refuel the ship.

The boarding ramp lowered with a clank, and guests wandered out into the port. Maeve stayed behind with Telly, because they'd rather watch a fathier race, while Daaric and Kotti split off to find a good deal on a new long-range communicator for the lander. From what I gathered, Dad was still intent on leaving it here until we came back around in a few weeks, when Dad put Tatooine on the itinerary again.

Kotti inclined her head. "Wanna come with?"

"Eh, I think I'm going to stay back," I lied, folding my shawl around my shoulders. I had a stowaway to see off.

Kotti hesitated. "Are you sure? You've been really distant lately. Ever since Coruscant."

I bumped my shoulder against hers. "Yeah, I'm fine. Just a lot on my mind."

"Want to talk about it later? A girls' night after dinner?" she asked.

"I would love that," I replied, because a moment of normalcy sounded intoxicating.

"Good. I'll see you when we get back!" She set off with Daaric toward the markets, counting off on her fingers the list of things she wanted to find. I was so caught up with Kotti, I almost didn't notice Val slipping off in the opposite direction. Where was *he* going? After last night, I didn't trust him—but evidently he sure didn't trust me, either. I needed to make sure he stayed away long enough for me to get Sian off the ship.

I caught VB-35 by the arm as the droid shuffled back up the ramp with N2-0. "Can you two do something for me?"

The droid turned to me, white eyes flickering apprehensively. "Depends."

"Could you follow my brother?"

"Oh, does he need help shopping—"

"No, quietly."

Veebee caught on quickly. Her eyes flickered again. "You know I am not a sneaky droid."

"You don't have to sneak. You can just . . . follow, right? I would," I added, a little quieter, "but I have to see a man about a stowaway."

"Captain Quay does not like Entoo and me to leave the ship on Tatooine. Plenty of droids have gone missing here, and as you know, I am a prized possession—"

"I'll get you whatever ingredient you want. Name it."

Vee didn't even have to think. "Dried woodoo gizzard."

I stared at her.

"You said whatever."

I huffed. *"Fine."*

"Great. Come on, Entoo," she said, turning around to go back down the ramp. N2-O blooped unsurely. "We'll be fine. I need to get some spices anyway, after *someone* knocked them all over."

The droids ambled off in Val's direction. They'd be fine, and if anything happened, I was sure Val would be close enough to help them. He *would* help them. He was still Val.

As I waited for everyone else to leave the port, I found myself picking at my cuticles. Why was I so nervous? It was nonsense. Everything was fine. I would smuggle him out, and no one would be any wiser. So once everyone was gone, I went to the back of the ship, where a crate had been loaded out for new supplies, and pulled the tarp off a short box. It chirped as I pulled open the lid.

Noola jumped out first, and Sian pulled himself up out of the empty crate. "That was much preferable to those pickled whatever-they-weres," he said. "So I take it you're my farewell party?"

"Sorry, stowaways don't get that add-on."

He laughed and climbed out of the crate. He'd taken one last shower, and his hair was pushed back from his face and still damp from the wash, smelling sweet from the ship's complimentary shampoo. His clothes were freshly laundered and gently pressed, though his gray jacket was still regrettably torn. I hadn't gotten the chance to darn it.

It didn't matter now.

I saw him out of the docking port and into the busy streets of Mos Espa. We lingered there for a moment, standing side by side. Then I reached into my pocket and brought out the lightsaber. I'd wrapped it in brown cloth, like a gift.

"Here," I offered. "As promised."

Strangely, he hesitated a moment, as if he didn't want it back, but then he closed the distance between us and gently accepted the relic. He bent toward me. My heart leapt into my throat. His lips brushed against my cheek, light and feathery—barely a touch at all, but a kiss nonetheless. "Thanks, Starlight," he rumbled, and then eased away from me again, and my stomach burned with the space he created between us. He put the saber in his pocket, looking as though it was more a burden than anything else.

"Where are you going to go now?" I asked, trying to keep my head on straight.

He gave another one of his infuriating shrugs, though he was grinning as he did. "I dunno. Guess I'll have to figure it out." He brushed his thumb across my cheek and tucked my hair behind my ear. "You're very pretty when you blush." Then he turned away from me and raised his hand in goodbye. "Be safe."

By the time I found my tongue to reply, I blurted, "Be safe!" but he was already far enough away that I doubted he'd heard me, and then in a blink he was swallowed by the crowded city, and suddenly my stowaway was gone.

CHAPTER TWENTY-ONE

THE JAWAS

Even as I returned to the ship, I could still feel where his thumb had brushed my cheek.

Telly and Maeve were in the mess hall with a few guests, listening intently to a radio station relaying the fathier races. They cheered at the announcers as I passed the open door and made my way toward the main chamber. There, tables had been rolled out and different board games set up.

In the corner of the room, Maz hummed as she played holochess with herself, first moving one side of the board and then spinning it around to move the other. She saw me in the doorway before I could duck away and motioned with her hand for me to come over. I did, pulling up a chair across from her.

"Sit, *sit*!" she welcomed. "It's more fun playing this game with a friend."

"I'm terrible at it," I warned as she reset the board.

I made the first move. "Entoo always wipes the floor with me."

She hummed, studying my play. "That little droid just knows all the good moves." She pushed one of her pieces, and then I pushed another, and she immediately took it. "It's easy to win a game when you know all the good moves."

"I guess you're right," I admitted. "Dad says my mom was also really good at holochess. I can't say, though. I don't remember much about her. But Dad says I look just like her, so when you said I looked like Dad, I was surprised."

"You are the best parts of both of them," Maz said. "You're stalwart and stubborn, like your father, but there's a curiosity in your eyes, too, like there was in hers. While most people looked away, she'd stare directly into the night. She challenged it."

The game was immediately forgotten. "My mom? You knew my mom?"

"She was brilliant in the way only the best of us can be."

Brilliant. Like stars were brilliant. Like glowing homeworlds in the night sky that I kept chasing after, constantly comforted by their light. I blinked back the terrible burn of tears. "I wish I got to know her better," I said, and made my next move to distract myself so I wouldn't cry. It was sloppy, so she took that piece, too, and then clicked her tongue in disappointment. The move put her k'lor'slug in line with my Mantellian Savrip, which could take it. I didn't, though, and moved to claim a different piece instead.

She hummed again. "You are so very like her."

"I just know that trap," I said with a grin. "Entoo *loves* that one—"

There was a beep from my communicator.

"Oh! Speaking of which . . ." I dug into my pocket for it. It couldn't be Kotti or Daaric; they'd call Telly directly if anything was wrong, so it had to be one of the droids. "Veebee? Is everything—"

"Not all right," the tinny voice of VB-35 replied.

A cold sweat chilled my spine. "What do you mean?"

"I have gotten into a bit of a—" The staticky voices of other people interrupted her. I froze. It was the unmistakable chatter of Jawa Trade Talk.

I quickly asked, "Veebee, where are you?"

Above the din in the background, N2-O gave a pitiful bloop.

"I tried offering them credits, Entoo," Veebee stated, *"but the only currency they want is my body. My gloriously rare—wait, unhand me! Get your hands off! Entoo! Resist!"*

N2-O shrieked a war cry.

Uh-oh.

"Where are you?" I insisted. "What's happening? How did—"

The communicator went dead. I tried to reach them again, but the call went unanswered. Oh, no. Oh, *no.* I had sent them on a recon mission, and they had somehow ended up being kidnapped by Jawas. I just got *rid* of trouble. I didn't need more. With a groan, I scrubbed my face with my free hand.

Think.

How the heck had Veebee crossed *Jawa traders*? Everyone knew they operated on Tatooine, so Dad had always been insistent that neither of the droids leave the ship. But I'd asked them to follow Val, and now—

Val.

This was my fault.

Maz tapped her finger to her chin thoughtfully. "Trouble afoot?"

"I'll be back. I'm so sorry to cut this short!" I popped to my feet, careful not to jostle the holochess table. My head was scrambled. I didn't know what to do, where to go—wait. I did. Maz wordlessly held up my satchel, and I took it, digging out my datapad. We'd put a tracker in Entoo a few years ago when their directional programming got damaged and they'd been losing themself in weird places on the ship. We'd fixed them, but I'd never taken out the tracker *just in case*. I still had their location code, so I found it and memorized the readings. Though once I had, I realized I didn't know what to do with them.

It wasn't like I carried a compass with me.

Maz hummed to herself as she dug into her vest pockets and pulled out a small square. "Here. Catch!" She tossed it to me.

I fumbled to catch it. The square was about the size of my palm. It was a compass. The arrow on the dial spun and settled due north.

"It won't point you to the coordinates, but it should help."

"Thank you," I said earnestly, slinging my satchel over my shoulder. "If my dad comes asking where I am, tell him I'll be back soon?"

Maz made a gentle shooing motion. "You should get going. And, Ardent?"

I was already halfway out of the mess hall, but I spun back to her frantically. "Yeah?"

"Your mother always trusted herself," she said softly, slowly blinking her eyes behind her goggles. "She'd tell you to do the same."

"Right," I whispered, then turned and ran out of the mess hall. My droids were in trouble, and it was my fault.

I was sure my mother would've never done something so careless.

I hurried down the ramp of the *Starfarer* and out into

the market, using the compass to guide me. I cut down streets and squeezed past stalls and shoved through groups of people, all the while trying not to get trampled or hit by speeders.

By the time I hit the edge of town, gasping for breath, I realized they were long gone. I put my hands on my knees. I had thought at least I would see the Jawa caravan leaving, but there was nothing but dusty roads and traffic cresting the hill in the distance. This was the only main road into the town from this direction—or at least that was what my map said.

And there was no sign of them anywhere.

"Crap," I murmured, trying to catch my breath. "If I were Jawas, where would I go?"

"That way."

Startled, I looked toward the voice.

Lanky build, threadbare gray jacket, dust-covered dark trousers, scuffed boots, a shock of silver-white hair. *Sian.* Pointing with a half-eaten meat skewer into the desert, following the main road.

I righted myself, not quite trusting my eyes.

"At least, that's the direction their caravan went," he added, and pulled another piece of meat off the skewer. Noola, on his shoulder, purred. "That the direction you're going?"

I looked at the compass again. "Yes. I think."

He finished the skewer. "Perfect," he said with a mouth full of food. "Let's go."

"But . . ."

"I know." He sighed dramatically. "I have great timing."

"And you're very modest about it," I said.

He smiled and dug into his jacket, pulling out a ticket-chip. "*Jee riqsi*. I know. You think I can convince the Advozse over there to exchange this ticket for his speeder?"

A ticket off-world? I had begun to tell him that I could do it myself, that he didn't need to change his plans for me, when he gave me a knowing look. So I settled for, "You don't have to."

"You helped me on Coruscant," he replied, pulling a small satchel with food and supplies over his head. A present from Veebee, no doubt. He must've grown on her like a wart. "Let me repay the favor."

I just hoped he wouldn't end up regretting it.

CHAPTER TWENTY-TWO

THE INCIDENT

Turned out, the Advozse refused to trade a few hours on their speeder for a ticket off-world, so Sian put a hand on their shoulder and looked them in the eye. The Advozse tensed, brows wrinkling all the way up to their cranial horn. I couldn't see their eyes—Advozse had very sensitive vision, so this one wore goggles—but the rest of their face cracked with abject horror, and then . . .

Nothing.

Their shoulders slumped. Their arms went lax.

Sian patted their shoulder and muttered, *"Aplot, ma bukee,"* and shoved the ticket into their pocket anyway. Then he motioned for me to follow him to the speeder.

"What did you do to them?" I asked, worried, as he climbed onto the vehicle and Noola scrambled into his jacket. He fastened her in to make sure she was safe and secure.

"You know when I asked if you were okay looking

into my eyes, when I tried to hypnotize you?" he replied, flicking a switch to turn over the engine. It sputtered to life, levitating the speeder off the ground. "That's kinda what's supposed to happen. People normally get disoriented. Confused, sometimes. Or worse . . ."

I glanced back at the Advozse, who had pushed up their goggles and was rubbing their eyes. "Will they be okay?"

"Yeah, it'll wear off. They'll just have a headache for a minute. We'll bring their speeder back," he promised, and told me to get on.

I motioned for him to scoot back. "No, I'm driving."

"You?"

"I promise I'm a better driver than you," I replied, and it didn't even take him a second to think about it before he scooted back in the seat. I climbed up front. I tested the brakes and the acceleration, revving the engine to get a feel for the speeder, and then I told him to hang on. He wrapped his arms around my middle tightly, and I ignored the way my stomach flipped at his touch as I whipped the speeder around and set off down the dusty main road into nowhere.

The sandcrawlers couldn't have been too far ahead.

And luckily, they weren't.

The problem was, however, getting them to stop.

"Get out in front of them!" Sian yelled above the

wind. "And park sideways! They won't want to run you over!"

"You sure?" I shouted back.

"Probably!"

Well, that was a better idea than nothing. So I sped ahead of the caravan. About two hundred meters away, I parked horizontal in the road and waited.

The vehicle had kicked a dirt cloud high into the afternoon sky. The sandcrawlers chugged along quickly. There were three of them in a V formation, and as they came up to me and the speeder horizontal in the road, their flotilla slowed to a stop. The dust cloud drifted past us, and as it dissipated into the sky, Sian snuck away from the speeder. We had cobbled together some semblance of a plan while waiting for the caravan to catch up, though I was only half sure it would work. It'd worked in *Under the Tan-Tan Sun*, but asteroids never struck the same planet twice.

From an open hatch of the closest sandcrawler, a Jawa shouted something. I squinted, wishing I had a translator, but my only translator was currently being held captive by the same Jawas I was trying to reason with. I knew enough Trade Talk to get the gist of what they'd said, though: "Get out of the way or we'll run you over."

"I just want to talk!" I shouted back. "I think you've got something of mine!"

The Jawa chattered, and I picked out enough words to roughly translate it to, "We don't have anything of yours!"

"Two droids! I don't remember selling them to you!"

The Jawa in question slammed the hatch shut, and through the metal hull of the sandcrawler I heard them shouting back and forth to each other. Bickering, much like a disgruntled family. I steeled myself, hoping I wasn't about to find myself in the middle of a firefight—or worse, *bartering*.

Then the sandcrawler gave an exhausted sigh, the loading ramp fell to the ground with a clang, and three Jawas shuffled out. They came up to my elbows at best and were dressed in dark brown robes with munition strapped to their chests, yellow eyes glowing brightly like twin moons under their dark hoods.

I met them, twisting my fingers. Why did Sian get the easy job? "I'd like my droids back," I repeated. "Please."

The first Jawa folded their arms across their chest and chattered. I made that out to be something like, "What'll you give us?"

Oh, no. Bartering it was.

"I won't give you anything," I argued, crossing my arms over my chest to mirror their stance. This one was clearly the leader. "They're *my* droids. You stole them."

The second one said in a high voice, "We *traded* for them."

"*Traded?* I didn't trade anything," I challenged, and the three Jawas exchanged confused chatter. Apparently, they didn't care *who* had traded the droids. I sighed and said, "Fine, let's trade for them. *Again.*"

The third Jawa muttered something to the first two, but I couldn't make it out. It didn't matter. I just had to keep them talking until Sian scaled the side of the closest sandcrawler and got the droids. Entoo's signal was coming from the first one, so I knew at least the astromech was there. Veebee was probably with them.

At least, that was my hope.

The three Jawas discussed among themselves quietly before one signaled to the other two. With a loud sigh of exhaust, the other two crawlers in the caravan started moving again, giving us a wide berth, and left for the canyon in the distance. I hoped that meant the Jawas were willing to hear me out or, better yet, just give me my friends back.

Finally, the first Jawa asked, "What'll you give us? Something good."

"Something better," the second one corrected.

My communicator crackled as Sian radioed in, quiet enough so only I heard. *"Found them. Erm, parts of them."*

I curled my hands into fists. These guys really did work fast, didn't they? They had a reputation for a reason. I just had to stall them long enough for Sian to get my droids out of there. Neither of us had weapons, and I had a feeling the munition on the Jawas' chests wasn't just for decoration. Sweat prickled on the back of my neck.

"Well?" the third Jawa asked. "What to trade?"

From my communicator, Sian said, *"Keep them talking. I can't seem to find the astromech's head—*chuba."

Chuba? What did *chuba* mean?

There was a thunk from inside the sandcrawler and then a flash of electricity. Sian flew backward out of the transport and landed hard on the ramp. He rolled over himself and stopped, blessedly face up. "Ow," he croaked.

A fourth Jawa marched onto the ramp, shaking an electrified baton, their voice loud and accusing.

I winced. I didn't need to understand the words to get the gist this time.

Things were about to go very, very badly.

"You're stealing!" cried the first Jawa, taking an angry-looking ion blaster from their robes. "We don't like stealers!"

Think, I told myself, mind scrambling for something—*anything.* So I gasped in offense, slapping my hand to my chest, and feigned naivety. "I am *not* a stealer!"

"Aren't you with this?" The fourth Jawa jabbed their electrified baton into Sian again as he got to his feet.

There was a *pssst*, and he jerked in pain—with a yelp—and dropped to his knees.

I winced. "I . . . don't know him?"

Sian gave me a tortured look.

The fourth Jawa prepared to strike him again.

"Well!" I quickly added. "I don't know him *well*! He just wanted to . . . um, to make sure the droids were intact. You stopped, so we figured . . ."

"He *snuck* on," the fourth accused.

I blinked slowly. "No, he didn't," I said, my voice strangled yet calm. "He walked up the ramp. Didn't he," I added as a not-question to the Jawa's three friends. They'd all had their backs to the ramp the entire time, so they couldn't say and ended up shrugging in answer. "See? He just wanted to see the droids."

The fourth Jawa narrowed their eyes. "You could ask."

Then they marched back up the ramp, grabbed a rope, and tugged at it. The arm of a crane swung out, and strung upside down from it was Veebee, an arm missing and one eye cracked. From here, I could also see Entoo inside the crawler, already half stripped of their exoskeleton, hood completely gone.

Oh, poor things.

VB-35 saw me and limply hung there, as if she'd lost

the will to live. "Oh, take your time," she commented dully. "I will just be here, hanging around."

"Trade?" asked one of the Jawas. "Big trade."

Right. Big trade, and I didn't have *anything* on me to do that with. Jawas were scavengers, so I was sure the rarer the haul, the better. So what was rarer than a cobbled-together junk droid and an astromech?

I wrinkled my nose. "You know, I think I changed my mind. They aren't worth much."

Veebee stared at me. "Thank you. I will remember this."

I ignored her and cleared my throat. "Sian, don't you have the—the—" I had to stall while I thought about what to *actually* do. "The *thing*?"

He stared at me from where he knelt, crispy from being shocked and dusty from being sent rolling across the ground. At that moment I could see all hope leave his eyes. "The thing," he repeated like a dead man.

I bet he was regretting not taking that shuttle off-world instead.

"Yes, the *thing*. The *thing* we're going to trade. The *thing* that's really valuable," I insisted, trying to clue him in to play along. I didn't care what he had—a knife, a belt buckle, *something*. As long as it was a *thing*.

He gave me a long, steady look and then took a deep

breath through his nose. "Right. The *thing*." He held up his hands to show the Jawas that he was going to reach for something and slipped his hand into his pocket.

Stars, I hoped it was something good and not—

Oh, void take me.

He held up the lightsaber, still wrapped in brown cloth.

"This what you were thinking?" he asked.

"Yes?" I squeaked. *No*. No it *absolutely* was *not*. He wasn't actually going to trade *that*, was he? The same thing we'd almost been killed over on Coruscant?

The Jawas all exchanged looks. One of them grabbed for the lightsaber, but Sian held it high above his head, which was a *little* mean, but then again so was stealing two droids and disassembling them within the span of, like, an hour.

"What is it?" one of the Jawas asked.

"Junk," spat another.

From the sandcrawler, Veebee said, "We are doomed."

Sian clicked his tongue in admonishment. "This is a famed and terrifying artifact from a long-extinct era," he began dramatically. The Jawas seemed very dubious. "I spent the better part of my life trying to acquire it. Countless people have died for it and by it—including my own mentor. It is a cursed and terrible thing, and it's wanted by some of the most nefarious people in the galaxy!"

"Droids can't be worth that much to trade. You lie," said the third Jawa as their buddy switched on the electric baton again to give Sian another zap.

I quickly added, "He isn't!"

The Jawas exchanged looks again. Then the third one asked, "Then why trade?"

"Because . . ." I racked my brain. Sian motioned for me to keep going, so I did. "Because . . . what could we do with a relic? My d—my *captain*—needs those droids for his ship, but we're too novice to know what to do with a relic. But you guys? I'm sure you'll know immediately."

"But what *is* it?" asked the first Jawa, and the others chattered in agreement.

Sian and I exchanged looks, and then he held out the package. "Why don't you see for yourself?"

The first Jawa took it and undid the string, rolling the saber out into their other hand. The old metal flashed in the afternoon suns like a flare. The Jawa said something to their friends, too fast for me to figure out, and handed it to the second one.

The second Jawa pressed the button. There was a satisfying click and then—

Nothing.

The Jawa shook it. The saber's insides rattled.

The first one jabbed a finger at me and accused, "You lie!"

I winced. "We never said it worked?"

The fourth Jawa, the one with the baton, gave an enraged cry that in any language sounded like death, and the other Jawas reached for weapons in their robes.

Oh, no.

"Noola! *Now!*" Sian cried.

Suddenly, a loud thunk came from the sandcrawler again, and then it shivered and slowly began to ease forward. The Jawas looked at each other, counted four, and realized no one was left on the crawler. So there was no one to drive it. And it was currently gathering speed *away* from them.

Regrettably, with both my droids still on it.

With shouts of surprise, the Jawas abandoned us completely. They tossed the lightsaber away and ran after the crawler. Sian stumbled to his feet and caught it as I lurched after my droids.

"Vee!" I cried.

VB-35 turned her head just enough to watch me dodge between the scrambling Jawas and make it to the crawler first. "This your plan?" she asked as I passed her going into the vehicle, found N2-O's head on a workbench, and shoved it back onto the rest of the droid.

Entoo gave a war cry, popping out a small arm with a blowtorch attached. I shoved them off the ramp, and they smacked against the hard ground and rolled to a stop, almost knocking Sian down in his rush to follow me.

The Jawas had caught up to the crawler, though it had begun to pick up even more speed.

Suddenly, something small and scaly darted between my legs and scrambled up the side of the crane. Noola bit into the wires and chewed through them.

"Well, sh—" Vee crashed onto the ramp and, with agonizing slowness, slid off into the sand with a screech of metal on metal.

Noola jumped onto my shoulder and purred.

"Thanks, friend," I whispered, scrubbing the top of her head, and grabbed Veebee's missing arm from the nearby workbench. A moment later, the Jawa with the baton smacked it against the bench, electrifying it. I jumped away and slowly sidled toward the edge of the ramp, the angry Jawas cornering me. I held Veebee's arm tightly to my chest. "But how are *we* supposed to get out of this?"

The Jawa with the electric baton crept closer. I shuffled backward until my heels dipped off the edge of the ramp. The crawler was going fast enough that if I jumped, I'd get hurt. I'd get hurt very, very badly.

"Thief!" the Jawa cried, jabbing the baton at me.

"You stole my droids!" I argued.

"You stole them back!" one of the other Jawas argued, shaking their fist.

Honestly, maybe I *should* just jump—

"Starlight!" Sian cried.

I glanced behind me.

To my surprise, Sian had hopped on the speeder and come after me. As the crawler picked up speed, so did he. He pushed the speeder parallel to the ramp and threw out his hand. "Jump!"

Noola had no qualms about those instructions, and she scurried to my other shoulder and took a flying leap, catching herself on the speeder.

He held his hand out to me. "C'mon!"

I couldn't make that. He kept having to dodge around rocks and debris in the road. Then again, on the other side, the Jawas came closer. The electric baton sizzled.

I squeezed my eyes closed.

Maz had said that my mom would tell me to trust myself.

So I opened my eyes and turned around, and when Sian dipped in close again, I jumped. I felt the swing of the electrified baton just miss me as I leapt. Sian grabbed my arm tightly as I crashed onto the seat, still clutching Vee's arm, and he pulled away from the crawler quickly—too quickly. The speeder spun. I curled my hands around his middle, Veebee's missing arm securely between us, and pressed my face into his back.

Wind whipped around us. The speeder whined.

Then, suddenly, it came to a stop against an orange rock. The cloud of dust we'd kicked up swamped over us. We coughed, and he pulled his arm over his mouth. I pressed my face into his back, choking back gasps.

It was so quiet, all I could hear was my thrumming, frantic heart in my ears.

Finally, as the dust began to settle, he asked me, hoarsely, "Are you hurt?" His hands went down to mine around his waist and squeezed them tightly. "We're alive. We're okay."

And we were.

He kept a tight, solid grip on my hands, letting me gather myself a little while longer, until I finally pried my arms from around his waist and eased back. I swallowed the knot in my throat and whispered, "We really need to stop almost dying together."

"Hey, I'd rather almost die with you than the alternative," he replied with a wink.

I was too dazed to blush, so I shoved his shoulder and muttered that this wasn't the time for jokes. We needed to go back and get the droids. "Do you still have the lightsaber?"

He patted the inside of his jacket. "*Soong eniki*. I have the *thing* right here."

I snorted. "That was quick thinking on your part."

"Yours too. I've got to *hand* it to you"—and he motioned to Vee's arm, which was still lodged between us—"we make a pretty good team."

"A team of liars," I pointed out wryly, remembering VB-35 and N2-0, "who probably need to go pick up their droids. Do you think those Jawas will be okay?"

Sian started up the speeder again. "They'll be fine. But *we* should probably get out of here before they turn around and come back."

So we picked up Veebee, who was still lying on the ground exactly where she'd slid off the ramp. With a little coaxing and a promise that I would buy her whatever ingredients she wanted—on top of that dried woodoo gizzard—for the next month, I gave her her arm back and put her onto the speeder before going to look for Entoo. The astromech droid was still on their side, blowtorch lit, livid as a gundark. We managed to calm them down enough to strap them to the back of the speeder and return to Mos Espa.

As we entered town, I dug my communicator out of my jacket to radio the ship. "Kotti, we're on our way back," I said, but all I got in reply was static. "Kotti?"

Veebee said, "Perhaps they're all busy?"

"Maybe, but—oh, no."

As we parked the speeder, a large ship rose from the spaceport into the sky. By the shape, it looked like a CR-90 Corellian Corvette. There weren't many of those still flying, and a terrible feeling cemented in the middle of my gut.

"Is that . . . ?" I ventured.

"Yes," Veebee confirmed, "I believe that is our ship leaving."

The thrusters lit and propelled the starship into the sky, through the clouds, going, going—

"No," I whispered, pressing the button on my communicator again. "Kotti! Anyone! I'm not on the ship! *Hello!*"

The ship rose higher in the sky, barely a pinprick, almost nothing at all.

"*Starfarer*!" I called. "You're missing—"

One moment the ship was there, and then its light streaked across the sky . . . and it was gone.

"—me."

The *Starfarer* had left.

It had actually left.

And I was still on Tatooine.

CHAPTER TWENTY-THREE

THE MISTAKE

Sian came up beside me, accompanied by VB-35 and N2-0, as if together they could ferry me through what was quickly becoming a nervous breakdown. The astromech beeped a word of encouragement, but Sian sighed and shifted his weight from one foot to the other. "I think you're stranded, buddy."

Stranded.

A strange tightness constricted my chest. I'd never been this far from the ship before. I'd never been this far from home—

With no way back.

"I'm sure someone can help us out," he went on, rubbing the back of his neck, not quite convinced himself. "I don't know anyone, but if we ask around . . ."

I didn't need help. What I needed was a time machine. What I needed was some way to go back a few hours so I could comm my dad and tell him about the droids. If I'd done that—told him about the Jawas—then things would've turned out differently, I was sure. I just . . . I'd thought I could handle it. It had been my mess to begin with.

And now the ship was gone. *Without* me.

"Well, at least Captain Quay *has* to come back," VB-35 said, "to pick up the lander—"

"*Starstall*!" I cried, jumping to my feet. "We can use *Starstall* to contact the ship!"

Veebee shook her head. "Did you forget that's why it's in the shop? The long-range communicator is malfunctioning again."

My shoulders drooped. "Oh. Right. Dad will know we're missing and come back soon. He can't ignore that we're *all* missing, right?"

Waiting here was the right answer. If I just stayed where I was last seen, then they'd come back to find me. But how had he left in the first place without knowing we weren't on the ship? Then again, the droids never left the ship, and Dad probably trusted that I wouldn't leave, either.

It was a perfect series of unfortunate events.

But that had me thinking . . . I turned back to the droids. "How did you get caught by those Jawas anyway?"

The droids exchanged looks. Then Entoo beeped.

"Sadly," Veebee agreed, and heaved a sigh. "And here I thought we were worth more. Apparently not."

I couldn't believe it. "No, Val wouldn't do that."

"Yet he did," Veebee pointed out, and tried to fit her arm back on her shoulder, but it was good and broken and flopped to the ground. The wires were severed, and I'd have to solder it back on with tools I didn't have. She looked down at her arm but didn't bother to pick it up. "He traded us for a blaster pistol."

"What would he want with that?" I mumbled, perplexed.

Sian said, a little distractedly as he eyed a group of men loitering down the street, "Seems like your brother knew the droids would follow him, or he'd already planned to trade them."

"Val wouldn't do that," I insisted again, doing a terrible job of convincing either of us. I watched the men, too, wondering if they had one of those lovely WANTED holopucks, possibly tucked into one of their pockets by Val, but then the group wandered off.

Sian let down his guard, turning his attention back to the matter at hand. "He wouldn't? You're sure?"

No—no, I wasn't sure. Not anymore.

Between our fight in my room, his stealing my master key, and his selling the droids—I wasn't very sure of anything right now except that I needed to get back to the ship to tell Dad. Something was wrong, and it was bigger than just a stowaway.

"We're taking the lander and we're going after the ship," I said.

The three of them all looked at me like I'd just suggested we shoot through an exhaust vent to make a Death Star explode.

I went on: "I know the itinerary like the back of my hand, and I know the hyperspace lanes we use. I've done this route a thousand times. The *Starfarer* has a slow hyperdrive, and *Starstall* is a little faster. We can catch up to them I think."

Veebee said, "Do we get a vote on this?"

"No," I said.

The droid sighed and picked her arm off the ground. "All right. Let's go fly the unreliable, broken, run-down lander back home."

It didn't take much convincing to get the mechanic to release our lander. She had more than enough work to do anyway, and one less thing on her plate for a customer who didn't pay *particularly* well was one less thing she had to worry about.

I took the pilot seat and started the ignition procedure. The coils had to heat up for a few moments. *Starstall* was older than I was and just as finicky as an ornery old widow. You had to boot up the systems in the correct order and talk to it just right before it decided to run properly.

"That's a good girl," I muttered as the console lights flared to life, mostly green systems and mostly ready to go.

I punched the coordinates into the ship's navicomputer. Long distances often required multiple hyperspace lanes, so onboard computers—or droids hooked into the system—calculated accurate jump points to prevent crashing into planetary bodies, space stations, other ships. . . .

I checked the calculations half a dozen times before I keyed them in.

Mom could have closed her eyes and felt how to get home with her wayfinding skills. I wondered if I would ever be brave enough—or lucky enough—to try that. Probably not.

Things were done a certain way for a reason.

The next stop on the tour itinerary was Geonosis, which was fairly close, all things considered, though we had to take three separate hyperspace lanes to get there. The *Starfarer* always made good time, but I hoped we could catch up to them before they took the Corellian Run to the Hydian Way to Yavin 4.

We could make it. I believed we could.

Sian hovered in the doorway to the cockpit.

"Here to say goodbye?" I guessed, rechecking the coordinates again.

Sian shifted on his feet. "Yeah, actually."

Disappointment tasted tinny in my mouth, but I tried not to think about it. I had figured he would be leaving now, but I was still a little afraid to do this without him. "Thank you. For your help with the droids. Did you manage to get your ticket back?"

He shrugged. "I'll get another one."

"They must be expensive."

"Maybe I'll just stow away again. It worked so well the first time," he replied with a bashful grin.

"Yeah. It didn't work out too terribly," I replied jokingly. "Stay safe?"

"Pff, skrunee," he said, and then translated: "Don't count on it." He turned to leave.

"Wait," I said, and he turned back around. Did he look like he hoped I'd say something?

Did *I* hope I'd say something?

But . . . what else was there to say? I didn't have the words, and neither did he. So he simply smiled and said, "See you around, Starlight."

Will I? I wondered.

Or was this the last time I'd ever see him, walking out of *Starstall* and down the ramp, his back to me?

It couldn't be helped, I told myself as I turned back to the cockpit console. There really wasn't another way for this to go, was there? He had somewhere to be, and I was tethered to the *Starfarer.* Not only that, but the longer I thought about Val on that ship, the deeper the stone in my gut sank.

I didn't have time to waste on goodbyes.

Besides, I was used to endings like this. I was just a footnote in people's lives anyway. It was childish to wish this were any different.

The short-range communication relay crackled, and the spaceport's mechanic asked, *"You expecting company, Quay?"*

Company? I replied through the console microphone, "No?"

"Well, you got it."

I glanced up at the viewport. Sian hadn't left the landing pad. Was that who the mechanic was referring to? Why was he just *standing* there, though? I was about to buzz down to him to ask *why* he wasn't leaving—the poor spaceport mechanic was probably all shades of confused—when I saw the *actual* company in question standing in the mouth of the docking bay.

Four Jawas. And about a dozen friends.

And they did *not* look happy.

Their leader pointed to Sian.

I pressed the ship's intercom. "Get in," I instructed.

He didn't have to be told twice and backtracked into the lander, pulling up the ramp as he retreated. The Jawas and their friends had come with blasters.

I did *not* have time for this.

My fingers flew through the start-up procedure. Primary systems were good, life support sufficient, power supply charged. The thrusters hummed to life, rattling the bulkheads. VB-35 flipped down one of the engineer seats—there were two, and obviously she chose the one closest to the emergency exit—and fastened herself in. N2-O rolled themself into a little locking contraption for traveling astromechs, near the back of the cockpit, and buckled in dutifully.

A blaster bolt pinged off the front of the shuttle, leaving a smoldering scorch mark.

"They are *not* happy," said Sian, coming into the cockpit to buckle himself in.

I tapped the gauge slowly filling, waiting to ignite the thrusters. The entire ship shook. "I'm sorry," I said, and I meant it.

He shrugged. "Honestly, I couldn't leave now anyway. I'm too invested."

Was he being genuine? Did I care as long as he helped? "Thank you," I said.

He winked. "I'm just hitching a ride to the next stop, Starlight. But, uh, we should probably leave now."

"Almost."

"We don't have *almost*."

"Almoooooost," I sang. Another blaster bolt pinged off the

viewport. I initiated the sequence to start up the engine and called back to the droids, "You two buckled in?"

Veebee replied, "Regrettably."

Entoo blooped.

Sian swallowed thickly. "What does she mean? *Regrettably?* You can fly this, right? She's done it before, right?" he added, looking back at the droids, but when neither of them answered, he whirled his attention to me. *"Right?"*

I sucked in a breath between my teeth and looked at the console panel in mock confusion. "Oh, stars, how do I take off again?"

Through the shuttle comm, the port master said, "Starstall, *you're not clear to take off yet. Maintain position."*

I buzzed back. "No can do, sorry!"

Veebee told Entoo, "We've had a good run, old friend. I am glad you were my partner."

"Bloop," Entoo agreed.

Sian shook his head. "No, *no—no*!"

Or at least I thought he said no, but I really couldn't tell if it was that or a scream, because at the same moment, the lights on the console blinked green. Our Jawa friends were *way* too close for comfort, and if I put another scratch on the lander, then Dad was *really* going to kill me, so I took hold of the controls and pulled *Starstall* off the ground. The ship banked into the air, quick and sharp, toward the impossibly wide sky.

CHAPTER TWENTY-FOUR

THE INHERITANCE

The first time Dad let me pilot the *Starfarer*, he had sat me on his lap, because I couldn't yet reach the controls, and folded his arms around me, his chin resting on my head. I remembered how incredibly large the galaxy had looked outside the viewport, how frozen with indecision I felt bombarded by the idea—the poetry—of *everywhere*.

Come to think of it, looking out into the wide and impossible galaxy felt a little like looking into Sian's eyes. I should've been frightened, or at least a little discombobulated, faced with such *bigness*, but . . .

I never feared the expanse of darkness and the light of distant stars.

"It's big, isn't it?" Dad had whispered.

Mom was in the copilot seat, humming softly to herself as she made small tweaks to the navicomputer, hypotheses for shorter routes, faster ways to get places, safer lanes. She was always working, always flicking her eyes from the wide sky to the navicomputer and back again.

She said in her soft, patient way, "But don't let that scare you."

"Are all those stars places?"

"A lot of them," Dad replied. "We can go there, if you want."

"We can find a route," Mom agreed.

Sitting at the back of the flight deck, my brother flicked through a holobook about Jedi and other fairy tales. He was nine, I was six, and that was the happiest we'd ever be. "Let's go somewhere cool. I wanna fight some monsters!"

Mom laughed. "How about you, love? Where do you want to go?" she asked me.

I didn't have a specific answer. "Everywhere."

Places I didn't know the names of yet, places I hadn't even dreamed of. If I opened my eyes wide enough, I imagined I could see branching paths, glimmering and twisting and turning, knitting together like threads of string, taking me anyplace I wanted. I used to think that if I chased those strings in the galaxy, I'd find a path that, to anyone else, didn't exist.

Dad had scrubbed my head with a laugh. "Then let's go everywhere."

But we never did go everywhere, especially not after

Mom died. No, we stuck to the safe planets, the well-treaded routes.

The memory filled my heart with heaviness as I looked out at the countless stars, the feeling anchoring me to my chair. My eyes caught glimmers in the darkness. I felt an incessant pull in my middle. Like gravity. But every time I tried to fall, the promise of uncharted places pulled away from me like I didn't belong anymore.

Unchosen.

I eased the shuttle out of the atmosphere, and after a brief check of the systems, I punched in the coordinates for Geonosis, and the navigation did the rest. Once we were clear of the shipping lanes and past the two closest moons, I pushed us into hyperspace, flipped on the autopilot, and unbuckled my seat belt.

We'd catch up to the *Starfarer* in a few hours. I had to believe that.

All the while I piloted, Sian hadn't looked outside—not once. Come to think of it, the only time I remembered him doing so was to watch Naboo, and at that point we weren't moving. Maybe it wasn't space he was afraid of but travel.

Starstall was an RY-280 that had been almost completely gutted and refitted to hold twenty or so passengers comfortably in its main hold, forty *un*comfortably. It was composed of a single large seating area with seat belts, along with booths in the corners for holochess and other games, and three rooms in the back for storage, a kitchenette, and a three-stall refresher with a single shower. The storage room was packed full of essentials and a single flat cot.

"I'm sorry you're still stuck with me," I commented, getting out of my seat, and he followed me back into the ship. I was *starving*. There had to be some sort of emergency snacks in the bins, so I busied myself looking in them.

"Eh, Noola and I have been through worse."

His creature, curled up on a chair, crooned in agreement.

"How long until we reach the ship?" he asked, looking over my shoulder as I took out a rations tin and shuffled through it. Freeze-dried jerky, fruit snacks, some crisps . . . He took a leaf of jerky and sat beside Noola, breaking off a piece to feed her. "Where *are* we meeting them?"

"Geonosis," I replied. "It's a few hours, and we have to transfer at least two lanes, but it's pretty straightforward." I sniffed the fruit snacks, wrinkled my nose at the smell, and decided on the crisps instead. "We'll catch up."

"*If* we don't run into pirates," Veebee said.

Sian sighed. "Pirates, mercenaries, the First Order . . ."

"They only care about the Unknown Regions," I said. "They wouldn't come this far in. The guys on Coruscant excluded. That reminds me, though." I sat down on the other side of Noola and opened the dense crisps. "The story you gave those Jawas about the saber . . ."

Sian fed Noola another strip of jerky, trying to act cool. "Yeah?"

"Was it true?"

He tilted his head. "Which part? About the people who died for it? Or how important it is?"

"All of it," I admitted. "Did your mentor . . . ?"

He let out a hard breath. "Yeah. First Order scum killed her. Some hotshot junior officer was after us—she saw him, I didn't—and she told me to split up. She said we'd meet on Coruscant. At Baelor's . . . but of course nothing went to plan. Nothing ever did, you know? So I didn't expect the *best*, but I also didn't think . . ." He frowned. "I didn't know she'd died until those First Order assholes showed up in that shop instead of her. I'm sure they report to the officer who killed her."

I thought back to my first meeting with him. That was when he found out his mentor had died? I felt sick to my stomach. "How evil."

"A lot of things are evil in this galaxy, Starlight," he replied gently.

Still. "I'm sorry."

He seemed amused. "Why?"

"Because you haven't gotten the chance to mourn."

His eyebrows rose a fraction, as if he hadn't even thought to give himself that sort of grace, and he tore off a piece of jerky and chewed it slowly. "S'fine," he mumbled.

"I don't really know what you're feeling, but I sort of know what it's like," I ventured, glancing at Veebee and Entoo. They'd shuffled through the bins for something to do and gotten out a deck of sabacc cards.

Veebee shrugged. "She'd hate for you never to talk about her, you know."

Sian inclined his head, curious. "Who?"

"My mom," I replied. "She died when I was eight. Do you know the story of my family? The Quays?"

"Can't say I do," he replied, which was one of the many things I was beginning to like about him. Everyone I'd ever met knew about the Quays, so to find someone who had no expectations? It was refreshing.

"Well, we come from a long and storied line of hyperspace cartographers and navigators," I began, "so much so that my mom's side developed a strange sort of *sense*—astrogating. But we call it wayfinding. My mom could pick a point in the galaxy and close her eyes and know exactly how to get there. And coupled with a navicomputer, she could go anywhere. She knew which rare lanes to take, which unexplored ones to discover. She found *new* ones. A lot of people called it luck, and maybe it was, but I like to think it was something deeper."

His eyebrows furrowed in thought. "Your mom's side? So is it inherited? Do *you* have it?"

I shrugged. "I think I do? Mom died, like I said, while trying to get home. She took a new lane to make it home for my birthday and . . ." My voice trailed off, my mouth wobbling. I pressed my lips together tightly to collect myself and tried again. "She never made it home. So afterward, Dad refused to let me practice, and Val left before I had ever worked up the courage to ask him to teach me what he learned from Mom."

Sian cocked his head. "Val knows how to, too?"

"Yeah. He's three years older than me, so Mom taught him a lot more. He was the one we assumed would inherit the ship, but then he left." I lowered my gaze to my hands, picking at my nails. "Val was always the better choice."

"Except he just sold your droids for a blaster," Sian deadpanned.

I sighed. "Yeah, there's that."

"What's his deal, anyway? He just left three years

ago, never sent a message? Never told you where he was? *Nothing?*"

I shrugged, still picking at my cuticles. "No."

Sian's silvery eyebrows drew together, creating a crease between them. "That's mean—to you and your dad and everyone else, too."

"He just wanted a clean start—"

"That doesn't matter, Starlight. That was irresponsible. I would have given anything to have what he just—just—*ignored*. A family. A home. Somewhere he belonged and people who loved him. And it's absolutely *immature* to show up again and expect everything to just . . . go back to normal! *Skootah!*" he cursed.

He was so angry about it, he shoved himself to his feet and started to pace the length of the room. I was surprised, honestly, that he'd had such a visceral reaction. It bolstered my own feelings about the issue, because for three years Dad had just *ignored* the fact that Val left without a note, without contact information—without anything—and had expected everyone else to hang their feelings on a shelf, too. My mouth wobbled a little with emotion, because now here was someone who didn't know me very well, and certainly didn't know Val or my family, but was angry on my behalf anyway.

It *was* mean, wasn't it? And entitled. And unfair.

"Sorry," he muttered, and took a deep breath to calm down. "I know you love him, but—"

"No, you're right," I said, because I didn't want him to take back any of his vitriol. "It's nice to hear, even if I can't say it myself. Thank you."

In surprise he replied, "Erm, you're welcome, I guess."

The navicomputer made a series of beeps that let me know we were approaching Geonosis, so I pushed myself to my feet, too. "We should get to cleaning up. We'll be home soon."

"Oh, good. I was worried this would be an overnight thing," he joked.

I glanced at him while picking up my wrappers. "Why?"

He thumbed back to the alcove beside the storage crates, blankets, and a spare power cell, where the single cot sat with a single threadbare pillow.

"Ah," I replied, nodding knowingly. "That would be a problem."

Sian rubbed his chin thoughtfully. "I guess, if push came to shove, I could be the big spoon. . . ."

N2-O, in the corner of the shuttle, flicked out their small blowtorch. They gave a dangerous bloop.

He raised his hands in surrender. "I was joking!"

Veebee stared at him, unwavering. "So was Entoo," she deadpanned as she laid down a sabacc card without even looking at it.

I rolled my eyes. Why did they have to be so *dramatic*? I'd rather sleep inside a sarlacc gut anyway, even though my ears felt hot just thinking about lying anywhere with him for any amount of time.

But if push came to shove . . . would I really mind it that much?

After we switched to the final stretch of travel, Sian began pacing the length of the main hold, blowing into his hands and rubbing at his arms as if he was cold. It *had* gotten a little chilly, but I was used to it by now. The *Starfarer* was always a bit drafty, so my fingertips were always cold. He finally resorted to popping open the storage crates in the back and rifling through them for a blanket, which he wrapped himself up in warmly. It was coarse and dusty-smelling, but he didn't seem to care as he bundled himself tight.

"Cold?" I asked rhetorically.

"Oh, no. I'm pleasantly warm now." He pulled the blanket around himself tighter for emphasis, looking like a snowy head of hair in a cocoon of starchy beige.

Veebee said, "You should see my poor pantry. He basically made himself a *nest* in there." She'd lost her sabacc game and was currently cleaning up the mess from knocking all the cards on the floor. It was a bit hard to do with one arm. I'd tried to solder it back on with the engineering kit I'd found in the supplies, but the tools were too big. So instead, she'd tied a rope to her dislocated arm's wrist and shoulder insert, and wore it cross-body like a pack.

Sian clicked his tongue in admonishment. "Vee, I thought you promised not to say anything? You know a *nest* costs extra for a stowaway."

I snorted. "We charge by the meter of blanket."

He jabbed a finger at me. "See? I can't even afford to be a stowaway," he lamented as he sank to the floor in a cross-legged position, blanket puddling around him, watching as Veebee shuffled to a seat against one of the outer bulkheads and started straightening out the card deck quietly. Sian turned to me again and asked, "Where would you go? If you could go anywhere in the galaxy?"

Surprised at the question, I turned around in my chair in the cockpit, where I'd taken my post for the last leg of the journey. You never knew what could go wrong. "Anywhere?"

"Anywhere," he confirmed.

That was a loaded question, one I'd thought about a thousand times but could only count a handful of times I'd actually been *asked*. No one really thinks to ask that of people who work on tour ships.

I thought about the beautiful planets I'd seen from the viewports of the *Starfarer*, the stories from all the tourists who'd come through its doors, the languages, the foods. . . . Apart from the handful of planets I'd visited over and over and over again, everything I knew about the galaxy I knew from stories. I knew them, but I hadn't experienced them.

Lived them.

And whenever I thought about those far-flung places, something in my bones spurred me on with the wanderlust of a people who had ferried themselves across uncharted space. And when the galaxy was this wide, and space this quiet, I could hear them calling.

"Everywhere," I decided, answering the same way I had when I was little, because truly nothing had changed. It was the easiest answer and a terribly vague one, but I really meant it. I turned my chair back to look at the swirling blue of hyperspace, each light a place, an adventure. "I want to see it all."

"That would be quite impossible," he said matter-of-factly.

"I know," I agreed, watching the tunnel. "But I'd like to try."

There was a map of stars in my blood, just waiting for me to unfurl it.

I knew I never could, even though I had this deep, *deep* ache in my middle that wanted to take a ship and just *go*. Everywhere—anywhere. But what about Dad? What about the *Starfarer*? The family business? I couldn't abandon it all.

Not like Val had.

So I ignored that deep ache. It'd go away.

It always did.

"Where would you go?" I asked to distract myself, pushing the pain down. I turned back around to him, away from the swirl of hyperspace.

He was quiet for a long moment, his impossibly black eyes studying me. Finally, he closed them and said, "Home."

It was such a simple answer, I marveled at it with a smile. Of all the places—he'd choose *home*? It must have been quite the place. "And where's home?"

He opened his eyes again, black expanses of galaxy staring back at me. "It doesn't exist anymore."

The grin on my face dropped immediately.

He turned away self-consciously and said, "Don't

give me that look. You wanted the truth. It's just gone." He pulled the blanket tighter around himself, as if he wanted to keep out more than just the cold. "I don't remember where I was born, and when I was four I was torn away from my parents and sent to a"—he paused to search for the right word—"an *academy* of sorts. With a bunch of other kids kidnapped from their families."

"What kind of academy was it?"

"The shitty kind," he replied nonchalantly, and busied himself picking at a thread on the blanket. "I hated it. Spent ten years there, and then I saw an opening and ran away when I was fourteen. I lived off stealing creds on a station for, stars, three days? Before the place tracked me down. I wasn't going back, though. I'd sooner die, and I made it everyone's problem. Then my mentor stepped up and said I was her apprentice, and that they had the wrong boy." He smiled as he said it, as if it was a fond memory. "I'd picked her pockets the first day I arrived at the station, and she had been keeping an eye on me ever since."

"So they just . . . let you go?"

He scoffed. "No. We made a break for it and managed to escape, and I went back to Bakura to find my parents—that's where my mentor said I probably came from—but . . ." He shook his head. "I never found them. Maybe I didn't come from Bakura. Maybe I came from somewhere else, so I searched everywhere. Places so muggy you can cut the air with a knife, and continents overrun with vermin and people and flesh-eating plants. Old temples and city slums and spaceports ruled by pirates. Would you believe me if I said I've even been to the edges of Wild Space, where it's impossible to sleep because you are so afraid of what lurks in the darkness between the stars? So I know for certain that it doesn't exist." He shrugged. "Not anymore, anyway. But . . . while on your ship, I got to see what it looks like when someone does have a home, and people who love them. That was nice." And he smiled at that, the corners of his eyes crinkling. "For a few days, I could pretend I belonged somewhere."

I couldn't imagine what it felt like—being unmoored, adrift in the galaxy without anyone to pull you back to port.

But . . .

"I think you're wrong," I said.

He looked amused. "About which part? About home not existing or . . . ?"

"That you don't belong anywhere," I replied. When he looked at me in confusion, I made sure the ship was on autopilot again and sat down beside him, our legs brushing as I pulled mine cross-legged, too. "You do."

"That's very kind of you to say, Starlight."

"Despite what you think, I'm not saying it to be kind, Sian." I hesitantly reached up to brush his silver-white hair out of his eyes. There was the discoloration of a burn along his hairline, and other remnants of old wounds—a ropy scar on the side of his neck, another on his ear, probably others all along his torso and arms, playing the same melody as the moon-kissed freckles across his cheeks. "My dad always told me, after Mom died, that you're made of everyone you meet, and everything you go through. It all becomes a part of you. The bad things, the good ones, the ones you can't remember . . ." My fingers gently brushed the ropy scar on the side of his neck. "You carry home wherever you go."

He shivered under my touch, my words settling on him in a way that made him inhale a heavy breath. His jaw trembled, and then he grabbed my hand that had traced his scar and kissed my knuckles. "How do you do it?" he murmured to them.

I blinked. "Do what?"

"Say the exact thing I need to hear."

I laughed, suddenly very self-conscious, and pulled my hand away. "Oh, I absolutely don't. You're just easy to talk to."

He slid a sly look my way. "Because I'm so charming?"

"Well . . ."

His eyebrows jerked up. "I'm *not* charming?"

I huffed, rubbing the hand he had kissed, because it tingled where his lips had touched my skin, and my heart still fluttered from the contact. "Being charming has *nothing* to do with it."

"So I *am* charming."

I rolled my eyes. "You're impossible."

"You don't mind it," he admonished warmly as I forced myself to my feet again and returned to the pilot's chair. I was glad, at least, that he couldn't see how flustered I felt, my heart stuttering for the first time in—well . . .

Ever, really.

Because no—no, I didn't mind it at all.

From her perch in the corner of the main hold, as she finished straightening the cards, Veebee said to her partner, "You're right, this *is* better than that holonet drama."

"Bleep-boop."

I threw them a murderous glare.

Wordlessly, Veebee turned her back to me, then asked Entoo if they'd fancy another game.

GEONOSIS

CHAPTER TWENTY-FIVE

THE ONES LEFT BEHIND

Geonosis was a sight for sore eyes.

Floating in the distance, the size of a ripe fruit, was the red planet in question, spinning with a skirt of yellow and orange rings. And we'd arrived without running into a single pirate or mercenary or First Order ship, and right on time. Finally, *something* had gone according to plan.

I had been half afraid I was cursed.

Behind me, in the engineering seat, I heard VB-35 make a noise of relief. "Oh, thank the stars. We did not get lost."

Of *course* we hadn't gotten lost. I was, in fact, good at a few things.

I pushed the lander faster, searching the rings for a glint of silver and blue, for a familiar shape among the debris. Where was the *Starfarer*? I looked at the radar, but none of the ships were mine.

"Dad, where *are* you?" I muttered, because I knew the itinerary.

The ship should've been here by now, halfway through its night cycle and well on its way to an early breakfast before touring the battlegrounds of Geonosis. It was one of Dad's favorite spots because a famous battle of the Clone Wars had taken place there, and the Civil War Buffs, though it was before their favorite war, would've been loath to miss it.

Sian leaned against the copilot console, toward the viewport, squinting out at the planet's rings. His eyes reflected the golden glow of the planet, which turned the white specks yellow. He caught sight of something and jabbed a finger toward it. "Found her."

I followed the direction of his finger, and—there, hidden in the rings.

The *Starfarer.*

Home.

Relief flooded through me. The scanners hadn't picked it up, but I pushed the worry aside as I scooted to the edge of my seat. "Veebee!" I told the droid. "The short-range comms!"

Veebee, from her seat, punched herself into the communication terminal and activated their short-range transceiver. "Go ahead," she said.

I pressed the button for comms and leaned into the microphone. "Captain? This is *Starstall*."

"Tell him I said there is a rack of shaak defrosting that needs to be put back in the cooler or cooked—" Vee started, but I threw her a look.

"I am *not* doing that."

"Shaak is expensive! And it might already be—oh, what are they doing?" Veebee asked in horror, watching the *Starfarer*'s engines flash brightly.

I gave a start. "That's the hyperdrive!"

The crackly comms parted, and my dad's voice rang out in the cockpit. *"Ardent, love?"*

I scrambled to the transceiver. "Dad! We caught up to you. Let us dock and—"

"Run," he said, sounding urgent and desperate. There was a loud noise, something that fizzled. Then static rushed through the link.

I ordered Vee to radio them again, but the communication went unanswered. Fear clawed up my throat as I grabbed the controls, ready to push the lander back to the ship as quick as I could. The *Starfarer*'s engines flared brighter. "No," I whispered. "No, no, no—"

And in a spark of white, the ship was gone.

Again.

It was gone.

The fear that had crawled into my throat turned into a lump, and I forced myself back into my chair. My hands were shaking, so I clenched them into fists and pressed them still on my thighs.

Veebee looked at me. "Did the captain tell us to run?"

Entoo blooped in confirmation.

He wouldn't do that unless—

I spun back to the navicomputer. "If I know anything, it's that there's only a few routes the *Starfarer* is already preprogrammed to take without a new calculation, and the most likely is Yavin 4—"

"Maybe we should listen to him," Sian advised, interrupting me.

I shot him a look of betrayal. "Seriously? Something is wrong and you want me to—to just run *away*?"

"Yeah, actually," he replied. He looked paler than usual. "That's what your dad told you to do."

"*No!* No, I'm tired of doing what I'm told! I can get us to Yavin 4. I know the way and . . ."

Veebee gently placed her hand on my shoulder and squeezed it comfortingly, but it was Sian who spoke. "We don't have the fuel, Starlight."

My gaze fell on the orange fuel light. *Oh.*

My hands slipped off the controls. The panic in me had turned numb.

I . . . I didn't know what to do.

"If we take the lander down, I'm sure we can find an outpost with some fuel," Veebee said, looking at a map of Geonosis as she waited for my response. "Then we can find somewhere with long-range comms and call someone who can actually help."

We couldn't do anything else. *Starstall*'s long-range comms were junk, and it wasn't like this lander was equipped for anything other than ferrying passengers. There were no guns on it. No armaments. Not enough water to get us through a single week.

I stared down at my fingers. Maybe if we just waited here, the ship would come back?

That's silly, Ardent, I told myself, and I knew it was, but it sounded so much more likely than . . .

"Arie?" Veebee said.

I'd never been this far away from home before, this far away from my *Starfarer.* I didn't know what to do. I'd never had to think about anything outside of the ship, not really. And now . . .

Now . . .

Run, my dad had said. There had been fear in his voice.

What was happening on that ship?

"I think Veebee has a good idea," Sian said for me, pointing to one of the outposts on the map. "Let's try that outpost. With any luck, it might also have a subspace communicator and we can flag the ship down that way."

N2-O bleeped in agreement.

"What do you think, Arie?" Veebee waited a moment longer for my opinion, but when I didn't give one, the droid switched the pilot controls to herself and moved the shuttle through the rings and into the atmosphere.

I was useless, anyway.

We went to three different outposts on Geonosis, but every one of them had been gutted and picked clean by scavengers. At the third one, we began to lose hope and had even less fuel than when we'd first landed. The air was dry and dusty like on Tatooine, but somehow the planet was even *more* desolate-looking, the surface peppered with mesas and buttes. From the ground, even the sky looked red, making it almost impossible to tell the difference between the harsh arid landscape and the stars. Husks of buildings left to decay, vast abandoned droid factories squeezed between pillars of orange rock, half-buried speeders, smears of civilization left to rot.

The third outpost was on one of those outcroppings of rock, nestled so snugly into it that we almost flew right past. At a glance, it was clear that the place had been abandoned a long time ago, too.

Still, it was worth a shot to get out and look around.

"We shouldn't stay here long," Sian said, beginning to fidget. He seemed to have a habit of biting his bottom lip when he worried, so much so that he'd almost bitten it raw by then. "Geonosis is never a good place to end up."

"The Imperials are long gone," Veebee said, dismissing him with a wave. "The New Republic weeded them out. *Again.*"

"I don't just mean people, Vee."

"Alas, I have heard that some of the best honey comes from Geonosian hives. Imagine if I could use it in my cuisine. . . ."

N2-O bleeped, whirling around to her.

VB-35 put her hands on her hips. "Well, that's rude. I know I can't taste it, but that's why I have *him* here." And she jabbed a finger at Sian.

He sighed. "The things I live to regret . . ."

"I hope you don't mean my cooking."

"Never, chef."

Veebee narrowed her eyes at him.

I barely listened as I took a walk through the abandoned outpost. All the technology was picked clean, the wiring and the vent grates. It was just a husk of a building made out of sandstone and dust. On the floor in the main operations room, bleached-white bones were scattered across the ground. Person or animal, I didn't want to look too closely, and the place was too quiet for my nerves.

I kept picking at my nails, digging into my cuticles as I tried to think of something—*anything*. I didn't notice that Sian had come into the outpost after me until he grabbed my hands, separating my worrying fingers and stilling them.

A knot formed in my throat. My mouth wobbled. "I'm sorry, I'm just scared."

He squeezed my hands tightly. He didn't offer consolations. He didn't tell me it was silly to be scared, that being scared was useless. He simply let me feel it and gave me quiet comfort, and in turn I closed my eyes and pressed my face into his chest and listened to him breathe.

In and out.

In and out.

It didn't dampen the worry in my head, which was terrible for morale, but at least I pulled myself back together enough to finally draw away from him. "Thank you."

He nodded and led me back out into the afternoon. The sand in the wind stung my skin, and I winced against the sharpness of it.

The reality was, Dad had told us to run, but I couldn't. Run *where*? Getting back to the *Starfarer* was the only option. The galaxy was too wide, and my home was small enough to get lost in it, I finally realized.

"Okay," I said to Sian and the droids, "anyone got another plan?"

The droids exchanged looks. Veebee shrugged. "I guess another outpost?"

"I'm sure they will all be like this—*chess ko!*" Sian yelped as Noola scrambled up his pant leg and dug under his jacket, hiding herself there. "What the—what's wrong, girl?" He paused suddenly, glanced around. His eyes widened. "Get back to the ship."

I didn't understand. "What?"

"Now!" he cried urgently, grabbing my and Veebee's arms. "Back to the ship!"

We barely got two steps before a hulking shadow darted out from behind one of the outcroppings of rock between us and *Starstall*. It shook itself out, crouching on all fours, its many black eyes glittering in the shade.

It prowled forward, shaking its head.

Veebee said, "I believe that is a massiff."

Sian reeled back, quickly pulling his arm up to block me. "Isn't this place supposed to be sterilized?"

"Apparently they were wr—incoming!" VB-35 cried as the hulking creature jumped toward us. We ducked, scattering away as it clambered onto a rock, lips parting on its long canine muzzle. There were dozens of spines along its back, some chipped, its leathery hide turning gray with age. It opened its mouth wide, a smile filled with long daggerlike teeth.

We backed toward the ship. The creature lowered into another crouch.

We froze.

I heard something behind us, too. Which was odd, because the only thing behind us was the ship, and no one was on the ship. A part of me didn't want to look, but I did anyway. Something slithered out from underneath our ship and into the sunlight. It didn't look like it had a front or a back, and after a moment of looking at the mass of flesh, I realized the creature's eyes and mouth were in the center of its long body. Which was so, *so* gross.

"That," Veebee said, "is a sand worm."

The massiff bared its teeth.

The sand worm coiled tightly as if preparing to strike.

"Do they want to eat us or eat each other?" I wondered aloud. My back met Sian's, and we pressed together tightly, hands finding each other—something to hold on to. On one side was the massiff, on the other the sand worm. The two droids were at our sides.

"I think they want to eat us, but they don't want to share," Sian replied. "The dog's about to pounce."

"So is the worm," I relayed. I began to wonder which one I would rather be eaten by—the weird worm or the canine? They both sounded like terrible options.

"Okay, when I tell you to run, you run, yeah?" He slowly reached into his jacket and pulled out that stun blaster I had seen him use back on Coruscant.

"Yeah," I agreed.

"Okay."

Suddenly, the massiff lunged. Sian aimed his stun blaster and fired off two shots. They hit the creature square in the chest, and with a yelp it bit the dirt. The sand worm dove for it, terrifying mouth open, and bit into its hide, wrapping its body around it.

"Run!" Sian cried, pushing N2-O to go faster. We made a break for *Starstall*. I grabbed N2-O's other side, and we hauled them up the ramp quickly. Veebee followed, stumbling.

"Everyone in?" I called as she came up the ramp, and went to hit the close button.

Veebee gave an anguished yelp. "My *arm*! It fell off!" She jabbed a finger down the ramp at her arm lying in the sun. Just a few meters away from it, the sand worm was trying to constrict the massiff in a mesh of popping bones and painful yelps.

Sian cursed under his breath and sprinted back down the ramp. He snagged the arm.

The massiff kicked, throwing itself to the ground—right between Sian and the ship. The sand worm constricted tighter, and the massiff howled and tore at its belly with its teeth, exposing organs. The worm sagged against it. Then the canine saw Sian. He held up his hands and slowly began to back away.

The massiff prowled toward him, the worm sloughing off like unwanted clothes.

Sian raised his gaze to me. Noola poked out of his jacket, and he hugged her tightly. *Go*, he mouthed to me, and raised Veebee's arm like a weapon.

The creature snapped at him. He thwacked it with Veebee's hand. He wouldn't be able to fend it off for long.

But I had an idea.

Not even bothering to close the ramp, I raced to the cockpit, where I forwent every preflight check and started the engine. The ship rattled, controls jolting, but I kept a tight grip on them, pushing the ship into the air.

Then I turned it around.

Outside the viewport, the creature had backed Sian up against the abandoned outpost, Veebee's arm in its mouth.

Don't move, I thought to Sian.

The predator dropped the metal arm and lunged at Sian—

I landed the ship on top of it. The front landing leg

smashed it with a sharp crack. Dust and debris flew into the air as Sian threw his arms over his face to protect it, then looked up at me in the cockpit with wide, wondering eyes.

I buzzed down over the intercom, "No one gets left behind on Hyperlight Tours."

He was about to shout something back when a howl came from nearby, and he quickly abandoned whatever banter he'd thought up to snatch Veebee's arm from the ground and hurry up the ramp and into the ship. Once I got the signal that he was inside and the ramp was closed, I took the ship into the sky again, just as half a dozen more massiffs slinked out from the outcropping of rock. There must have been a cave nearby with a den.

Sian limped into the cockpit, clutching Veebee's arm. "That was a close one," he said haggardly, and painfully lowered himself into the copilot's seat.

I looked at him. He looked at me.

And then I started to laugh. I couldn't help it.

"We almost died!" I cried, tears coming to my eyes. I pushed them back as the ship rose through the sky. "Oh, my stars, did you *see* that worm? It was so gross!"

"I think I have some of the massiff in my hair." He giggled, pulling his hand through a dark spot at his temple, raking out a bit of gristle.

I wiped my eyes with the back of my hand. "But you're okay, right?"

He looked down at the blood on his jacket. "Yeah, this isn't mine. I can't believe we survived that," he added, his laughter finally dying.

Mine did, too. "I don't think I'll ever get that sound out of my head."

"At least it's not all over you," he replied.

I winced.

"Not that I'm complaining! I'd rather smell like a corpse than actually be one," he added, and Noola finally poked her head out of his jacket and chirped. "She agrees."

"I've never killed anything before," I realized as I brought *Starstall* up through the atmo toward space. There was nothing left on Geonosis anyway, and I really didn't feel like dealing with more wildlife somewhere else. "I hated it."

"But I'd be dead if it weren't for you," he replied, and nodded to the droids as they finally made their way into the cockpit. Veebee sat in her seat and buckled in, and Entoo went to their docking station.

"We might be dead anyway." I tapped the almost-empty fuel gauge.

He handed Veebee back her arm, and she clutched it tightly. "Could we make it back to Tatooine?"

I doubted it, but I tried the calculations anyway on the navicomputer. It beeped angrily at me. "No. We'll run out of fuel halfway there, and all we have is a short-range transceiver, so it would not be a good idea to get stranded in the middle of nowhere."

But if there wasn't fuel *here*, what other options were there? I knew all the well-traveled lanes. They were imprinted in my memory like lifelines on my palms, and none of them could get us to the *Starfarer* with the fuel we currently had.

"Wait." Sian suddenly sat up straight, as if remembering something. "Can't you do that wayfinding thing you were talking about? Get us a shorter route?"

He sounded so hopeful, and that sound curdled in my ears. "No," I said. "I can't."

"But you said—"

"I've never tried. I don't know how."

He sank into quiet again, and then pulled up a map of the galaxy.

I held tight to the controls as the ship rattled one last time in atmo and then, with a sigh, broke into space. "I wish I could, Sian. I can't make hyperspace routes out of thin air."

"Technically," Veebee said, "neither could your mom. She found the lane, the clear path safe from the noise and chaos of the galaxy, by wayfinding."

"Not helping, Vee," I mumbled. "We can't go anywhere with the fuel we have. We're stranded, and once the fuel goes out, the power goes out, and then the oxygen recycler goes out, and we die."

"Well, that is quite dark," said Veebee, and N2-O agreed.

Sian mumbled something to the map and then asked, "Do we have enough fuel to make one jump? A small one?"

"How small?"

"*Small.* Here," and he motioned for me to come over and look, so I engaged autopilot. He enlarged the map of where we were and pointed to a planet I hadn't heard of. "Alakor. The planet's deserted, but I remember there being an old research facility there. Maybe also some fuel and a long-distance transceiver . . . ? But I'm not sure." He sighed in frustration. "It's a gamble."

Veebee considered it. "And if you're wrong, we become stranded in space. Where there is a hundred percent chance you two will suffocate and die and I will waste away my life's potential alone."

N2-O gave an accusing bloop.

Veebee said, "I'm *not* discounting you. I'm just being realistic. You're old, I'm young, they're fleshy. Besides, how do we know this Alakor isn't picked clean like all the outposts on Geonosis?"

"I'm sure we'll find at least fuel," he insisted. "The research facility was basically untouched."

It was either be stranded here on Geonosis or somewhere else. At least *there* flickered a spark of hope. "You're sure?"

He nodded. "I don't particularly have a death wish, Starlight."

I took a deep, steadying breath. "Okay. Punch in the coordinates. Let's go to this *Alakor*."

CHAPTER TWENTY-SIX

THE LOST

When I was little, I had a lot of nightmares. Even before Mom died, they plagued me more often than not. My parents said I had an overactive imagination, and maybe I did. But often, when I'd wake up from one, I'd run to the bridge, snot dribbling down my face, to find my parents. Dad would snatch me up in his big arms and hold me tightly and tell me that nothing in my dreams was real.

There was one night, however, when I ran to get comfort from my parents and I found Mom at the helm. Dad had snatched me up, like he always did, and put a finger to his lips. "Shhh, watch," he said in a secretive whisper, his eyes glittering. "You'll see magic."

The viewport was so bright it rendered her in complete shadow, her curling auburn hair catching the light of a thousand stars in strands of silver. She sat perfectly still at the helm, eyes closed, mouth buttoned, as she ferried the ship between worlds faster than the speed of light.

"Isn't she impossible?" Dad had said in wonder.

She was.

Impossible in the way the galaxy always tended to be—impossible moments strung together by impossible people doing impossible things.

I feared I would never be impossible.

Hyperspace was quiet, but the anxiety in my head was so loud as I watched the fuel gauge get emptier and emptier. My palms were sweating, and my palms *never* sweated. What if I'd done the calculations wrong?

And what if this planet didn't have the fuel we desperately needed?

I had a lot of time to worry, since Sian had excused himself to take a short shower in the refresher and get the massiff off himself and his clothes. I should've washed the dust off, but I told myself I'd do it after we made it to this uncharted planet.

Veebee asked if I wanted to play a game of cards with her, but how could I concentrate on anything other than flying right now? Besides, too many things were bouncing around in my head.

What if we failed to get home and something bad *did* happen to the *Starfarer*? Something we could've stopped? I couldn't ignore the very real possibility that Val had something to do with it. There were only a few reasons why he would need a blaster on the *Starfarer*, and that coupled with his adamant search for Sian and my dad's warning . . .

What if he hadn't been concerned with Sian being a stowaway? I had figured the WANTED holopuck had tipped Val off about Sian, because it wasn't like the guy was *subtle* in his meanderings around the ship.

But maybe I was wrong.

What if he was looking for the lightsaber, too? Though, if he knew about the lightsaber, I was aware of only one other group who knew about that.

Beneath my fingers, the flight controls jerked.

Then—alarms. Everywhere. Lighting up every panel on the dash. Loud, screeching, they tore me out of my thoughts. I knew those alarms. They were connected to sensors warning of close celestial bodies. And if they were going haywire, then that meant—

"Sungrazers," I whispered like a curse, and pulled the lever to shut down the hyperdrive.

Starstall careened out of hyperspace like a pebble from a slingshot hitting water. It slammed into realspace with enough force to knock the wind out of me. I barely had time to brace myself and prevent my face being imprinted in the console. While Veebee was strapped in, Entoo wasn't so lucky, their restraints snapping as they were flung toward the front of the ship and rebounded off the bulkhead with an anguished cry.

I hadn't even thought to look out for meteor showers. They were rare, anyway, and most were tracked with navigation systems. Others, however, were sporadic like solar flares.

Of course this was our luck. Of *course* it was.

I scrambled to wrestle back control.

Suddenly, something loud and large slammed into the side of the ship, spinning it sideways. I grappled with the controls again, panicked and clumsy. We should've stayed on Tatooine. We should've waited. We should've—

A warm hand enveloped mine on the controls, and Sian, hair still dripping wet from the shower, squeezed it tightly. He didn't say anything, but he didn't have to.

His steady gaze was enough.

It grounded me.

Then he sat down in the copilot's chair and buckled himself in.

Behind us, Veebee tried to reroute power from the damaged section. "We need to get out of here!"

Didn't need to tell me twice.

I snapped back to my senses, planting my feet, Sian's

hand squeezing mine on the controls again. He glanced at me, and I nodded back. I was okay. I had this. *Starstall* whined as I forced it out of its spin. "Veebee, how much power do we have?"

"Enough!"

That was all I needed to know. I slammed my fist on the button to stop the alarms and shouted, "Hang on!"

Then I throttled it.

The ship whipped around, dodging another asteroid, and ducked under the next one. It was a small field of sungrazers—I could already see the end of them. *Easy*, I told myself.

This was easy.

Veebee shouted, "Ahead of us!"

"I see it!"

"Left! Go left! *Port!*" The droid went on. "And there's one on your right! Go *faster*!"

I snapped, "Stop backseat flying!"

Entoo blooped, but Veebee shot back, "*You* are a worse flier, trust me!"

Which was quite a low bar.

Another meteor sailed toward us, and I spun away from it. Then another, popping between the celestial bodies like a skipping stone.

If I drove a speeder well, I flew a ship better.

"Do you have this?" Sian asked tightly.

"Just watch," I whispered. My heartbeat slowed. My muscles relaxed.

There were few things I excelled in more, and even with this tragic bout of luck, I *wasn't* going to die here.

Sian never once took his eyes off me. Not for all the things racing toward us, spiraling in bright clumps of stone. Not for all the near-death misses, or the saves. He never once looked away. Like there was nothing else in the galaxy more impossible.

I didn't see any of that at the time, though. I was simply making sure we didn't explode into the side of a sungrazer. I concentrated on the feel of the ship. It was a little too sensitive when banking, and the thrusters reacted *way* too slowly. I cursed myself for not getting better acquainted with the controls when we first left Tatooine.

Then again, I hadn't thought we'd run into an *asteroid field*.

It was fine.

We were almost out of it.

By the radar, the big ones were behind us, and it was fine if some of the smaller bits of debris plinked off the exterior of the lander. The ship had gone through worse.

When we were finally free of the asteroids, space went silent again. I gently pried my fingers off the controls, finally beginning to realize what I'd just done:

pulled us out of hyperspace, stranded us somewhere in the galaxy, and—

I quickly pulled up the fuel levels, and my stomach dropped into my toes.

Red, all the way across. Almost on empty. And certainly too low to make another jump.

No, I thought, panic eating at my edges, *no, no, no—*

"There!" Sian cried in relief. "See? I told you it was there."

I glanced up, eyes watery.

And just as he'd said, in the distance was a planet.

ALAKOR

CHAPTER TWENTY-SEVEN

THE FUEL

The planet was a pink-and-green marble, no bigger than a moon, in a dense black pocket of space.

I checked the map, searching for anything else nearby, but it really *was* in the middle of nowhere.

Veebee noted, "It is smaller than I would have imagined."

Sian shifted to the edge of his seat, looking out the viewport at the strange-colored marble. "It hasn't changed," he said hesitantly, as if the place were a mirage and could disappear at any moment. "Take us down over there, toward the middle of the continent. There will be a ravine with a river cutting through the middle. The research outpost should be on the west side."

"*If* it is still there," VB-35 said.

I took hold of the flight controls. My hands were clammy. "Let's hope it is."

As the lander entered the atmosphere, we sank into the pillowy pinkish clouds. The wings began to rattle, and the controls shook. I held them tighter, planted my feet, and eased the ship down through the atmosphere. The asteroids had knocked a few things loose after all. For a brief moment, all I could see was pinkish cotton, and then the ship broke through the clouds. The sun blazed, bright and golden, across a landscape of deep orange and cider rocks, the soil a rich purple.

Sian pointed to the ravine in question and the line of bright blue water cutting through the middle, and I followed it as he'd instructed. After a few minutes of flying, the shuttle shuddered again. The left side dipped.

I quickly pulled it back level, adjusting the thrusters, and checked the console.

"I guess we got hit harder than I thought," I said, tapping a warning light just to make sure it wasn't malfunctioning.

Sian grabbed ahold of a handle above him. His knuckles were white. "Is it bad?"

"Nothing worse than the trouble we're already in," I supplied, flipping two switches to divert power. At least, nothing I couldn't handle for *now*. When we landed, N2-O needed to check on the ion accelerator. "Where's the facility?"

"It should be coming up soon—there. Over there, the building with the glass dome," he said, pointing toward a rather small building eaten almost completely by the yellow-and-green foliage around it. The research facility looked more than just a few years abandoned, and a sinking feeling tugged at my gut.

It didn't seem like anything was left here, either.

I circled the building to find somewhere to land and then eased the shuttle down at the edge of the ravine.

I hoped I was wrong.

Sian was the first one out of the ship. The droids ambled down the ramp after him, both appalled that he hadn't even *checked* the atmosphere. It could have been poison for all we knew, but I wasn't concerned about that. Sian wouldn't take us somewhere without breathable air, and Noola *absolutely* would not have gone running out if she couldn't breathe. Poor thing. She was stir-crazy.

I rifled through the crates for a flare gun and tucked it into my belt. It wasn't a blaster or anything, but it'd do in a pinch, and I *wasn't* going to get caught empty-handed again if the wildlife decided to eat us. Even though the planet was deserted, there were still creatures and plants and other dangerous things. Deserted didn't mean *dead* and definitely didn't mean safe.

"Arie, are you coming?" Veebee called from outside.

"Right behind you!" I hurried out of the shuttle and closed the ramp behind me.

The air smelled sweet and fresh, mixed with the crispness of salt water that blew up from the ravine below. The atmosphere was so different from the arid plains of Tatooine and Geonosis, not just in smell but also color and sound. It was a breath of fresh air to be somewhere *not* dusty for once. Nature had overtaken most of the research building, covering it in creeping vines of yellow and green, the underbelly of the leaves a deep shade of indigo. There was forest as far as the eye could see, spotted like fungus on the purple dirt.

The planet was beautiful—*breathtaking.*

"How could a place like this be abandoned?" I asked, feeling the ground. Even the *soil* was soft and smelled sweet.

Veebee replied, "For good reason. We just have not found it yet." As Sian went to work prying the strange flowering vines away from the door, she turned to me and said a little quieter, "I do not trust this."

"This planet or . . ." I shifted my gaze to Sian.

Veebee shook her head. "None of it."

I sighed. "I know. Well, if we die, then it's your job to make sure someone writes a very smutty version of my story someday. I want it steaming. I'm talking the kind of smut that'll make *Daaric* blush."

"Daaric cannot bl—oh, I see. Well, now I kind of want you dead so I can read that smutty version." Then the droid paused. "Would these scenes be with Sian?"

My mouth dropped open. *Oh.* "Well—I—um . . ."

"Ah."

"Are you two talking about me?" Sian called, and with a grunt, jimmied open the door. "Because that's rude."

"No!" I quickly replied while Veebee—the traitor—said, "Yes."

I glared at her. She shrugged.

He stuck his head inside. "Well, let's all talk about me in here, yeah?"

"We weren't—fine," I mumbled, begrudgingly grabbing a glow rod from my belt and shining a light into the dark building. "I hope something's in here."

He let me go first and then followed me inside. "You and me both, Starlight."

Inside, the air smelled stale but still somehow sweet. My glow rod caught the motes of dust, and they glittered strangely. Vines grew between the cracks in the walls, letting in strokes of golden light where small pink flowers sat, basking in it. A thin line of dust coated everything—the desks, the consoles, the strange research contraptions in the center of the room. The technology was all clearly dated by at least fifty years, but amid all the obsolete junk were other things much more recent—

Two cots, a spent cooktop, wrappers from ready-meals.

"My mentor and I came here once in search of an

artifact," Sian said by way of excusing the wrappers. "We found this place and set up camp for a few nights. We didn't want to stay longer, though."

I turned my glow rod to him. "Why?"

His eyes were caught in the light, black sclera glimmering with pinpricks of quickly shrinking white irises. "It's nothing dangerous."

"I'd still like to know."

He shrugged and slipped up beside me, between the beams of sunlight. I shuffled back, my heart jumping into my throat, until I bumped up against one of the dead consoles. The droids hadn't followed us in here, I realized. We were alone. The vines tickled the back of my neck.

He raised his hand toward me, and my heart quickened—

He plucked a pink flower from the vine by my head and twirled it between his fingers. "The pollen from these flowers was used as a truth-telling drug once."

It took a moment for the words to sink in. Then with a gasp, I covered my mouth with my free hand. "That's not *not* dangerous!"

"We'll be fine," he went on, stepping away from me with a shrug. "Maybe a little too blunt for each other's comfort, but I'm sure we don't have any deep dark secrets, do we?"

"Depends on what you count as deep and dark."

He shrugged. "We'll find out. The bad part about the pollen is not the truth-telling. It's the fact that it corrodes most metals very quickly, so your droids can't stay planetside long. Neither can the ship, honestly."

"And that's why this place is deserted," I realized.

"Exactly. See? Not dangerous."

Except truth was very dangerous in certain situations—and so were lies. And lies weren't tools we had at our disposal at the moment.

"But if the pollen corrodes metal," I said, following him deeper into the building, "how are we supposed to find fuel here?"

"Fuel isn't metal, as far as I know." He shrugged, and instead of getting rid of that awful flower, he tucked it behind his ear. Like a madman. "My mentor and I almost didn't make it off this planet. We realized a little too late that it almost ate through our entire fuselage. This way." He motioned through another doorway, following thick tubes on the ground.

I stepped carefully after him. "You were after an artifact here?"

"The opposite, actually."

"But aren't you studying to be an archeologist?" I asked, confused.

"I *am* an archeologist," he stated.

"Well, then—*ah!*" My foot caught on a vine. With a yelp, I stumbled, but Sian planted a hand on my shoulder to steady me. Blushing, I righted myself. "Sorry. I'm usually not this clumsy."

"It's because of me, isn't it?"

"Yes," I said before I could stop myself, and gasped, slapping my hand over my mouth. "I mean—because you brought us down here! To this planet! Not because—because . . ."

"Mm-hmm," he purred, letting his hand fall slowly from my shoulder, his calloused fingers trailing down my arm as he snaked deeper into the building, his touch begging me to follow. "I know what you meant."

And if he had to tell the truth, like me, then what did he think I meant? That I was distracted by him or that it was because of the planet or—

Stop thinking about it, I scolded myself, glad that the building was dark so he couldn't see the blush raging across my cheeks.

"With my mentor, we studied long-dead places and people and committed them to memory. And sometimes, when we could, we returned artifacts to the places they were supposed to be."

I carefully worked my way across a rather thick section of vines on the floor, refusing to trip over them again. "So you steal things?"

"Is it really stealing when it's not theirs to begin with?"

"That's a fair point," I acknowledged. "Is that how you got the lightsaber?"

He cocked his head. "Yeah, actually. My mentor wanted to deliver it back to where it belonged, and we just got caught up in something too big." He sounded regretful, and I wanted to reach for him and pull him into a hug.

And what a strange thought *that* was.

Did the pollen also affect my emotions?

We ventured through another room, where the tubes ended. Encased power cables were hooked up to a generator of sorts, and beside that were large red barrels of fuel stacked beside smaller silver ones.

"Ah!" he said in relief. "Here we go."

My eyes widened. "Are you *mad*? That's *rhydonium*!"

He didn't see an issue. "It's fuel."

"Sure, if you want this entire planet blown to bits! And didn't you just say that the pollen eats through *metal*?"

"These barrels aren't metal, for one, and both that and the coaxium seem to be stable," he added, glancing at the smaller cylinders. "We shouldn't take it all, but one barrel should be good, yeah?"

My eye twitched. But then I squeezed my eyelids shut

and breathed out through my mouth. It wasn't like any of us had weapons that could ignite the fuel anyway.

Except for the lightsaber and my flare gun, I reminded myself. Neither of which would be used within a billion meters of this place.

"Let's go tell Veebee and Entoo," I said, because the canisters looked heavy. "They'll make quicker work of refueling than we will."

"Good, I didn't want to suddenly and mysteriously hurt my back . . ." He dramatically rubbed the lower part of his back for show, and I rolled my eyes.

"Do you think this generator panel still works?" I asked, motioning to the switches. "I think I saw a communication console in the first room. Should we try it?"

"I don't see why not," he replied, and blew the dust off the panel. The labels were scratched into the metal beside the switches. "We can put some fuel in one of the generators and see if anything comes on."

"Didn't you say you hurt your back?" I mused. My nose had grown used to the sweet smell of the flowers. They weren't so bad. Telling the truth wasn't *awful*, even though I really, really didn't like some of the things I'd admitted to.

He feigned surprise. "You really do care about me!"

"Of course I do." I followed one of the cables to the generator in question. To my surprise, there was still fuel inside, so I returned to the panel. "Why would you think I didn't care?"

"Because the only other person who ever has died—*aaaaah*, and there's the truth pollen working," he added with a nervous laugh. "Forget I said anything?"

"I don't want to—*argh*." I winced. "Sorry."

He massaged the bridge of his nose. "You need to stop being so nice. It makes me think you want something, Starlight."

"I don't want anything," I replied, puzzled, and then realized with a strange sort of relief that I had to tell the truth.

He hissed air out through his teeth. "Except I don't believe you."

"I can't lie."

"I know! And yet I still feel like a gullible *wermo* whenever you say it. Because everyone in the galaxy wants something, Starlight. Everyone. I feel like you don't trust me. I feel like I can't trust myself. Everyone I've ever gotten close to, anyone I've ever *liked*, has died, and why do I think *you'll* be any different—oh, void take me, please tell me to *shut up*—"

I grabbed his face with my hands so he could look at nothing but me. The flower tucked behind his ear fell away. "Hey, stowaway. Shut up."

His tense shoulders slowly unwound.

But I didn't let him off the hook, not by a long shot. "You just admitted that you like me," I said.

His eyes widened. "I did."

I couldn't help smiling as I let go of his face. "What else were you saying? I can't remember."

He huffed a laugh. "You're too good for someone like me."

In reply, I reached around him to flick a random switch. "I know."

Suddenly, the generator hummed to life, the long tubular lights above us blinking on. They popped on one by one, back the way we'd come, and from the front room we heard the tell-tale sound of computers booting up, their processors sounding like chewed-up nails in a blender.

I shrugged. "Lucky guess. C'mon, I need to get some air." And without thinking too much about it, I took his hand and led him out of the building. He let go of my hand the moment we got outside, in sight of the droids, and I tried not to think too much about that, either.

"There's a transceiver in there that we're going to try," he told them, thumbing back toward the facility.

Try was doing a lot of heavy lifting, sadly, because the transceiver console was so old it took two swipes to get enough dust off the display for me to read it at all, but somehow the console itself still worked. Hope rose in me like fizzy soda, and I quickly keyed in the prompt for the ship's calling code.

Veebee and Entoo came into the building on the way to the fuel and stopped beside me instead. Sian leaned against the doorway, tapping his fingers on the frame nervously.

The astromech droid gave a series of beeps.

I sighed. "I *know*, but I have to try to reach them again anyway."

Even though the last time we'd tried, Dad had told me to run. Of course he should know I wouldn't. And maybe it was a miscommunication. Whatever it was, either they would answer me—a random ping from a defunct research facility in the middle of nowhere—or they wouldn't.

So I adjusted the mic and switched on the broadcast. The sound crackled. "*Starfarer*, this is Ardent Quay. Please answer."

For a long moment there was nothing.

"*Starfarer*," I repeated, "this is Ardent. Pick up."

From the doorway, Sian said, "What if something *is* wrong?"

Helplessly, I shrugged. "I don't know, but—"

The comm crackled, and a garbled voice replied, *"Arie?"* It was Val.

Sian pulled his hands through his hair and nervously paced.

"Arie, where are you?" He sounded genuinely worried. *"Why did you leave the ship? We've been looking everywhere for you."*

But that couldn't be true, because Dad *knew* I wasn't on the ship. And Val hadn't asked about the droids, or if I knew where they were—because *he* knew. Or at least he thought he did.

"It's a long story. Where's Daaric?" I asked. "Doesn't he usually man the comms in flight?"

"He's preoccupied for the moment looking for you," Val replied, sounding annoyed. Then, a little quieter, *"Did that criminal kidnap you? Tell me where you are. You don't need to protect him."*

I locked eyes with Sian. "I don't?"

Sian looked wounded.

"Look, Arie, he's dangerous. I don't know what lies he told you—but he's no good. Where are you? Send me your coordinates," he said. *"You trust me, don't you?"*

I realized then that the flowers of this place wouldn't let me lie. *I did,* I could say. *I want to.* But I couldn't lie and tell him what he wanted to hear, because the simple fact was that I *didn't* trust him. I hadn't since he'd returned to the ship, and I couldn't figure out why. Because I should. He was my *brother.*

I curled my hands into fists. "Okay."

And I gave him the coordinates.

The next moments happened so quickly. Sian lurched over to me and slammed his hand down on the end-communication button. His face was livid. "What did you *do*?"

Coolly, I stepped away from the console. "I'm bringing them here."

"This is *not* the time to give him the benefit of the doubt, Starlight."

Veebee agreed in her deadpan way: "He sold me for a blaster."

Entoo blooped angrily, flicking out their blowtorch.

"I know," I replied, digging into my jacket. "But it makes more sense for the *Starfarer* to come here than for us to try to catch up with her. Our lander is pretty beat-up from the sungrazers. It could make one jump, maybe two? But beyond that . . ."

Veebee and Entoo exchanged looks.

I asked, "Aren't you going to say this is a bad idea?"

"No," Veebee said simply, and the astromech agreed with a bleep. "Something is very wrong, and if I don't cook the shaak I defrosted soon, then it will ruin, and I spent good money on that shaak."

Sian studied me, and his shoulders rounded in release. Noola scurried up to sit on one, munching on another piece of jerky she'd stolen from our stash. "You don't trust him," he realized.

"Of course I don't. He's my brother. I know him better than anyone," I replied, finally finding what I was looking for in my pockets. One of the few good things about not changing out of my ship uniform: I still had Lady Sosha's contact card. I showed it to them. "I also know when I'm in way over my head."

If I survived this, I'd read that last installment of *Under the Tan-Tan Sun*. It felt silly now to have put it off for so long, especially when life seemed to jump out at me at lightspeed.

CHAPTER TWENTY-EIGHT

THE ELDERELS

The plan was simple: refuel the lander and wait for the *Starfarer* to grace the skies of Alakor. By my calculations, if they were near Yavin 4 when we contacted them, it'd take quite a few hours for them to come all the way back to this side of the galaxy. Val *could* astrogate here quicker, but I doubted he would.

Until then, we waited.

I tried not to look like a bundle of anxiety, so I took myself out to the edge of the ravine to pace. My fingernails were almost bitten down to the quick already.

After Yavin 4, the itinerary took the ship to quite a few stops before ending on Endor's forest moon. I'd been truthful when I said that catching up to the *Starfarer* would be impossible, so this *was* the right choice. It had to be. I'd rather something happen in the middle of nowhere than above a planet full of people.

Not that anything will happen, I told myself. There were hundreds of guests on board. Dad wouldn't let anything happen to them. He'd give his life to protect them—the entire crew would.

That was what worried me.

That and the blaster now in Val's possession.

"Hey." Sian drew me out of my thoughts. He stood a few meters away, hands in his pockets. He nudged his head away from the facility. "Want to take a walk?"

"You go ahead."

"It'll take your mind off things."

"I doubt that."

"Fine, then will you take a walk with me so I can show you something?" he asked. "My mentor and I found it last time we were here. I think you would appreciate it."

"What is it?"

He put a finger to his lips. "Why don't you come with me to find out?"

Infuriating—he was infuriating and . . . I probably *did* need to take a walk. At least it would be different scenery than a sheer drop to my death. So I caved and told him to let me grab my satchel and tell the droids. They had holed up in the lander with the air ventilation on to keep themselves from corroding too heavily. I glanced into one of the reflective sheet metal surfaces of the bulkheads, my face distorting like a ripple in water, and quickly looked away.

It didn't matter what I looked like—why should I care if my hair was frizzy or my eyeliner running? I didn't.

The droids were on the deck, playing a game of sabacc when I found them.

"Sian and I are going for a walk," I told them, grabbing my cross-body satchel from the pilot's chair and pulling it over my head. "So, if I never come back, look for my body at the bottom of the ravine."

"Hilarious," Veebee said, shuffling the cards. "Just . . . be careful. That sounds like a lot of work on my part. Especially with only one arm."

"I'll help you reattach it when we get back," I promised.

"No, Entoo can reattach it."

I hesitated, because she always wanted me to. "Are you sure?"

"I can't rely on you for *everything*. Besides, it is my fault we are in this mess," the droid went on, her gaze flickering to me. "I was not paying attention to your brother when he sold us. I was looking at spices. If I would've taken you seriously, we wouldn't be here. I feel like I failed you."

I knelt beside her and put a hand on her shoulder. "I shouldn't have asked you to go. It was reckless."

"Perhaps," she agreed, "but it is in my programming

to want to be useful. Though I feel like I have never been that to you, not since you saved me from the junkyard. You are the first person I remember, asking me every question I couldn't answer yet. Who was I, what was my name, did I want to come with you." She tilted her head, thoughtful. Then she closed her card hand, set it face down on the deck, and turned to me. "Ardent, I am an amalgamation of dozens of different droids pieced together. Not quite one type, not quite another. I am finicky. I am peculiar. I am testy. I am very likely to explode. And you did not care. You *do* not care," she corrected, her bright eyes studying me. "You are my family."

"Vee . . ."

"So do not take this apology away from me," she said pointedly.

I barked a laugh. "I love you," I said as I hugged her around the middle.

"Ah. Yes. Touchy-feely." Veebee awkwardly patted my head. "But would be remiss not to say: This is a terrible plan, Ardent. The statistical odds that the *Starfarer* is perfectly fine and we simply missed them on Tatooine *and* misheard your father are low. Very low."

"I know."

"Then you know that either Sian is lying or Val is."

My throat tightened. "Yeah."

Entoo beeped and picked up their cards nonchalantly.

"You're right," Vee agreed. "We *can* kill them both if we need to. Now go have your walk and your fresh air, and we'll attempt to not corrode while you're gone."

So I left the lander to walk into the sweet-smelling air again. I noticed the strange sharpness in my head after I'd breathed it in a few times. These flowers really were menaces. I followed Sian back to the edge of the ravine and down a narrow path cut into the side of it. The drop was steep, so I trained my eyes on his back so the height wouldn't make me dizzy.

It did still make me nervous.

"So, where are we going?" I asked, pressing as close to the ravine wall as I could.

"To a temple of sorts. I figured, since you like stories, you might like this one."

That *did* intrigue me. "A story?" But then a piece of the path by my boot crumbled, and all I could see was—

Down.

"We've got time, if you want to hear it," he replied, glancing over his shoulder only to find me frozen in my footsteps, staring down the cliffside at what I knew was my doom. He backtracked to me and offered his hand. "Hey," he ventured gently.

All I saw was rushing water far, far below.

So he took my hand and squeezed it tightly. The touch startled me, and I finally tore my gaze up to his.

Rushing river was replaced by infinite night sky, and my fear settled again. "Just keep your eyes on me," he said quietly. "I promise it'll be worth it."

I'm not used to taking chances, I wanted to say, but I was embarrassed to admit it. I wondered what he'd say if he knew that the first time he met me on Coruscant was the first time I'd ever left the ship on my own. And the first time I'd lied to my dad about it. The first time I had managed to squirrel myself out from under his watchful eye.

If I'd been more like Val, maybe I could've fallen into a thousand adventures by now. What kinds of stories would I have found out there in the stars? What kinds of people would I have met, secrets learned, mysteries solved?

I mourned that girl who didn't exist.

I would've liked her very much. A girl like her would've been perfect for someone like Sian.

Not me.

"I'm fine," I whispered, dropping his hand. If he looked disappointed, I decided not to notice as I kept my hands firmly on the rock face, feeling the smooth stone beneath my fingertips, and waited for him to descend. "But I'd like to hear the story."

So he led me down the ravine and told the story.

Thousands of years ago, this planet was inhabited by a people his mentor called the Elderels. Not much was known about them—their great libraries were burned, their records scattered—but of the few facts that remained, his mentor knew that they were a fierce and protective species who excelled in the arts—

"Watch your step," he added, motioning to a gap in the path, and helped me over it. His fingers brushed the small of my back, featherlight.

I let go of his hand again, though I didn't want to. The farther down we went, toward the calm aquamarine river below, the darker the stone walls became.

He told me the Elderels excelled in music. They spoke in songs, but not like the ones we knew. They communicated through some sort of aeolian notes.

"Aeolian?"

"It's the sound you hear when the wind whispers across the rocks, over the sands, through the trees—my mentor said it was the sound of the galaxy in motion."

"I always thought the galaxy sounded like the hum of a ship," I mused.

He glanced over his shoulder at me. "You really did grow up on that ship, didn't you."

I shrugged. "What does the galaxy sound like to you?"

He gave it some thought while helping me down the last switchback that led to the bottom of the ravine. Beside the rushing water was a small path that snaked into an alcove that couldn't be seen from the top of the cliff, hidden away. Secret. "I don't think I remember thinking it sounded like anything. Silence, probably. Yeah, a lot of silence."

"That sounds lonely."

"So does the galaxy sounding like a ship," he replied, and then winced. "Sorry—*sorry*. The flowers . . . that was rude."

"True though," I admitted. It wasn't like he was *wrong*.

He helped me down the last bit of rock, hand in mine, but when our feet were on solid ground, I decided not to let go again. I folded my fingers through his, as if to tell him that I wasn't alone now, and neither was he. He squeezed my hand back.

My heart did a funny flip in my chest.

"What happened to the Elderels?" I asked, trying to ignore the feeling as he angled his head toward the alcove.

"Why don't we see for ourselves?"

Cut into the rock was a temple of swirling stone chiseled to look like waves of water or waves of hair—I couldn't quite tell. The pillars stretched twenty meters high, framing a stone door that had cracked centuries ago and was now broken on the ground. There were patterns carved into the door, but they were so faded I couldn't tell what they'd once been.

Sian led me to them and into the temple ruins.

The air inside was cooler and strangely dry. But stranger still, the sweet scent of the flowers was gone. I felt like I could finally breathe again.

And lie again, I thought, though that meant he could, too. I didn't realize how comfortable I'd gotten simply telling the truth.

I'd spent so much of the past few years lying—small lies, about how I was feeling, what I wanted in life, being satisfied on the *Starfarer,* happy on the *Starfarer,* enough on the *Starfarer—*

I wasn't at all.

The salt from the river must have absorbed the smell, and it didn't look like the flowers could grow in darkness—they had only been in the shafts of light in the research facility—so it made sense that there weren't any down here.

Then Sian inclined his head, and we walked on.

The walls of the ruins were decorated with faded murals and chiseled reliefs, some barely recognizable. Others were completely desecrated. There were blue streaks of stone on the ground and the walls, growing denser the farther we traveled. I had to step lightly over them so I wouldn't trip.

"Did they move to a different planet? Did their food run out? Did they destroy themselves?" I wondered aloud, studying the murals of beautiful humanoids with spindly arms and legs, dancing across the stone like they were made of air.

Sian glanced up at one of the faded murals, studying it with his starshine eyes. "Yes. They did. An entire people killed instantly, most of them where they stood." Then he stopped just before one of the blue streaks of stone, and I came up beside him. He motioned to it.

But now that I looked at it, something was off. A face, and a head—arms and fingers and legs and toes, all curled around a smaller bundle—

I lurched back. "Stars! It's a grave! You brought me to a *grave*?"

He gave me a strange look. "You take people to a grave every tour."

Alderaan. I squared my shoulders and rooted myself to the spot, determined not to desecrate any more. "That's different, Sian."

"How?"

"Because we help the station—we pay respect to those we lost. What are we doing *here*?"

In reply, he sighed and put his hands back in his pockets. "Paying respects, too. C'mon, a little farther." He started into the darkness again, but I lingered behind, debating whether to turn and leave this hollow place. How was I any different than Val had been all those years ago when he'd snuck away to break into an

Imperial walker and see the bones of Imperial soldiers?

Sian called over his shoulder, "The whole galaxy's a graveyard, Starlight. We're all made from the dust of things that came before us."

"I know that . . ." I mumbled, and gently stepped around the blue stone to reach him, folding my fingers into his again. Though this time I knew when my heart jumped, it wasn't from the sweet-smelling flowers. "I just don't want to dishonor them."

"And we aren't, trust me on that. You told me I wasn't alone in the galaxy. So I wanted to return the sentiment." A soft wind swept through the corridor. Suddenly, he perked up. "Oh, it's time! Quick, close your eyes. Do you hear that?"

I closed my eyes.

And there, in the quiet of the temple, came the faintest of sounds—of wind whispering through the cracks in the ruins, of the river rushing through the ravine, the world breathing in groans and cracks.

The Elderels' song persisting.

It grew louder, giving way to popping crackles, like wood burning. I opened my eyes—

And gasped.

The temple flickered with light. The petrified remains began to shift, sprigs of algae blossoming over their limbs, glowing effervescent blue in the dark. Then they broke off their stems, like leaves in the wind, and floated into the air.

"This way," he whispered, as if anything louder would disturb the sight, and pulled me through a narrow passageway that led to a set of spiraling stairs. We climbed, and climbed. My lungs burned, but I followed him up. The darkness slowly grew lighter and lighter, until windows began to light our way, and still we climbed, the ground getting farther and farther below.

We were in one of the spires, I realized. They weren't just sheaves of rock—they were towers.

As we climbed, the floating tufts of algae caught up with us, pouring out of the windows, and lit our way to the top of the tower, glowing a soft and welcoming blue.

When we finally got there, the algae swarmed up and around us, drifting higher and higher into the evening sky like lanterns. The foliage and sweet flowers far below had shriveled, closing their buds for the night and leaving the air salty and fresh and cool. Dusk colored the landscape in hues of orange and cream as the twin suns sank below the horizon.

And pulled us into darkness.

Far below, the lander's warm light spilled across the landing platform in front of the research facility, *Starstall* looking like little more than a toy from this distance.

Above us, the stars were impossibly bright.

A bubbling laugh escaped me—I couldn't help it. "It's beautiful!" I marveled. "I've never seen anything like this before in my life."

"I hadn't, either," Sian agreed. "The algae can only grow on the petrified bodies of the Elderels." He caught a lantern of algae in his hand, and the light leaked out between his fingers. "They believed that when you die, you don't simply cease to exist. You are still of and part of the galaxy. Bits of you stay. They just change a little."

He let it go, and the lantern algae drifted up, and up, and up.

"I like that thought. That pieces of us stay when we die. My mentor's teachings are in me, and the love of your mom is in you, and those things can only grow in us. It's our job to remember them, and nurture the pieces that stayed."

Tears burned at the edges of my eyes. I pushed them away quickly. "Oh."

"Oh, no, no, I didn't mean to make you cry," he said, cupping my face in his hands and using his thumbs to brush away the tears that kept spilling. "I just wanted to thank you."

My bottom lip wobbled. "My dad never talks about her—like he wants to forget she ever existed, and I'm always so afraid that whenever he looks at me, all he sees is her. I'm afraid I'll never be enough like her. I'm afraid I'm too much like her. I don't know which is worse."

"You are Ardent Quay. You said I was made up of all the people and all the places and all the stories I've met and been to and heard. Why won't you believe that about yourself? You're incredible, Ardent—"

I leaned forward and pressed my lips against his.

He went rigid with surprise, and I thought I'd made a mistake, but then, like a desert plant finding a drop of water, he came alive under my kiss. He angled his head down for a better approach, his eyelids falling shut, drinking me in like sunlight. His fingers found their way into my hair as he gently pushed me against the pillar, and I tried to place the way he smelled—there were a billion stars, but I was sure that given enough time, enough taste, I could find where.

Everything was quiet, save for the song that hummed through the tower. I'd been kissed before—only a handful of times, but enough to know that this was different.

This felt rare.

He tasted like dust and licorice—the taste of the flower, perhaps?—and I melted into it gladly. I curled my hands against his shirt, wanting to be close to him, closer still. So close I ached. Dad had once said that when he met Mom, he knew the moment he kissed her, he was found—

Found in a way that was indescribable. Found in a way that you only were when someone saw you, truly saw you, and didn't want to look away.

And even so far away from the *Starfarer*, I felt found.

My fingers traced the collar of his shirt to the hooks. I undid the top one, and then another, slipping my warm fingers beneath to his cool chest. He gave a quick gasp against my lips. It tasted sweet.

I opened my eyes and met his heated gaze. "Is this . . ." I murmured, embarrassed. "Is this okay?"

"Okay?" he asked gruffly, searching my face. "This is perfect. You are perfect."

I bit my bottom lip, not quite sure I believed *that*.

He made a noise in his throat and kissed my mouth again. "Whenever you do that, it drives me mad."

"When I what?" I asked between kisses.

"Bite your lip." He planted another kiss on my jawline and then the side of my neck. "When you get that little crease between your brows, too. When you stick your tongue into the corner of your mouth when you're thinking."

That surprised me. "I do that?"

"All the time." His mouth navigated its way back up the other side of my neck. "I can't look away. You're made up of all the things I'm not—a constellation I've never seen before." He kissed the sharp edge of my jaw. "I want to chart it all. Every smile, every grimace, every freckle across your nose . . ." Then he kissed my mouth again, hungrier this time, deeper. His tongue played against my lips, asking for entrance, and I gave it so willingly it wasn't even a question. My belly burned for him. "I want to know them all," he whispered, his gaze heated and sharp. "Intimately."

Dizzy from his kisses, my heart thrumming so loud in my ears it overtook the song on the wind, becoming one in my body instead—loud and bright and wanting—I pressed my forehead against his. And in the loudness of ourselves, we studied each other's gazes.

"I want to know yours, too," I admitted.

The lantern algae emptied into the nighttime sky as we slid down the pillar, hidden in the warm blanket of night. I leaned against him and felt the lightsaber jab at me. He laughed and took it out of his jacket, when something small and disk-shaped slipped out of his pocket and rolled onto the ground.

A hexagonal pin with an inverse of a black sun in the middle.

I picked it up. I knew that symbol.

The First Order.

CHAPTER TWENTY-NINE

THE TRUTH

The danger the *Starfarer* faced wasn't on the ship. It was here—with me.

My stomach turned.

Stars, I'd *kissed* him. Shared deep feelings with him. Started to fall in *love* with him—

I felt sick.

Because Val was right.

Sian's voice interrupted my thoughts, a deep and quiet murmur of "Starlight?" as he set the lightsaber down and shrugged out of his jacket. I'd let down my guard, and now I couldn't even look at him, afraid my face would betray my horror.

The glint of the pin was harsh in the shine from the night sky. My hands began to shake.

He sat up, finally realizing something was wrong. "What's wrong?" And then, with a bolt of fear, he checked his pockets, but I already had what he was looking for.

He turned those strange galaxy eyes back to me, and then to the pin in my hand.

At the same time, my gaze fell on the lightsaber.

The next moment was a blur. I reached for it, and so did he, but he was a moment too late. I grabbed it and lurched away from him to my feet, pointing the saber at him like a weapon I knew how to use, and I most definitely did *not*. The metal was cold against my skin, but my resolve steadied. My hands had stopped shaking.

"Ardent . . ." he started, palm raised toward me as if to calm a wild animal.

Oh, he did *not* know just how wild I was about to be.

"Ardent, I can explain."

So he *was* First Order.

I aimed the mouth of the saber at him and pulled my thumb over the button. It was broken—something I very much knew. We both did. I could do nothing with a broken saber, but he still needed it, so . . . I pulled it behind my head, ready to throw it.

He shot to his feet. *"Chuta,"* he cursed. "Wait a moment—"

I glared at him. "I *trusted* you," I spat, my voice sharp and cold. "The men on Coruscant—you planted that First Order code cylinder, didn't you? You tricked me into thinking they were the bad guys, but it was *you* the whole time."

His eyebrows shot up. "I . . . *what*?"

"You're a monster," I ground out.

His eyes widened with sudden hurt. Then his shoulders slumped, and he suddenly looked very, very tired. "Yeah, I guess I am."

"I *trusted* you," I seethed.

He swallowed thickly. "I know. But . . ." His gaze didn't stray from mine even as I tensed to throw the saber, as if it wasn't as important to him. "I didn't plant anything on those men, Starlight. They were actually First Order."

"Right, and you're going to tell me this *isn't* yours?" I opened my other hand, where the pin had pressed into my palm.

"No, it is." He glanced down at it and then back at me. His white pupils dilated for a moment—an anxious pulse—before he reined them in again. "I just could never bring myself to throw it away."

I tightened my grip around the saber.

"I promise. The academy that I told you about? It was a First Order school. They kidnapped children and took them there to train them to be mindless soldiers. That was my pin."

I gritted my teeth. "Why should I believe you *now*? Why shouldn't I just toss this and then go with Val and leave you stranded here?"

He set his mouth in a thin line. "Because I have nothing to lose."

"Says someone caught red-handed."

"Ardent, I wouldn't—"

"I don't believe you," I announced.

His face flickered with determination. Then he plucked a closed bud from the vine that twined around the tower's pillar and popped it into his mouth and chewed. "I'm not lying," he replied, wincing at the taste. "That's awful."

"Get that out of your mouth!" I yelped in alarm. "You don't know if it's poison!"

"I'm not lying," he repeated, his heated gaze on mine. He tucked the half-chewed flower into the corner of his mouth and talked around it. "I promise I'm not lying, Ardent."

Again, he said my name. Not *Starlight*, but my name. Soft at the front, sweet at the back. Like some sort of tender word, even when he sounded desperate.

My hands curled tightly around the saber again even as I lowered it. "Then whose is this?" I asked. "Why is it so important?"

"I don't know," he admitted. "I just know that my mentor thought it belonged to"—he gritted his teeth and then sucked in a breath—"to Luke Skywalker."

My eyes widened. I looked down at the broken piece

of junk in my hands. I guessed it wasn't so much junk after all.

"Oh," I said faintly. "That would be a reason why people want it."

"Apparently he hasn't been seen in a few years, so"—he shrugged—"I guess it's proof of death?"

"Or proof of life," I argued, because Luke Skywalker, hero of the Republic, wasn't *dead*. He couldn't be. Just . . . missing. Though, if this was *his* saber, then where was he? Those were questions I couldn't think about right now.

He extended his hand to accept the pin back, and so I returned it. He felt the indentations with his fingertips, flipping it over. "What I wouldn't give to live in your world, Starlight." He sighed.

I frowned. "You do."

"Nah, because in your world everything is nice and right and kind," he said, talking more to the pin than to me. "Where the good guys always win, and orphans are reunited with their families, and everyone lives happily into old age—it's a good story."

"I don't think I live in that world," I replied, "but I *want* to. Do you think I don't have to convince myself every single day that the galaxy is good and kind? That it doesn't take *effort*? It does," I declared. "Being angry at the galaxy is easy, but being kind to it? Searching for something good in all of this bad? You should try it sometime, because when you do you'll see how *exhausting* it is."

"Then why do you do it?"

"Because I want to hope that someday it won't be so hard," I told him earnestly. "I'm sorry I didn't believe you. I guess your pessimism rubbed off on me."

"I'm sorry I lied," he replied.

I motioned to his mouth. "You haven't for the last few minutes. Though you might die soon, so I accept your apology."

He barked a laugh and opened his mouth, revealing the flower sitting prettily on his tongue. He then tucked it back into his cheek. "They're not poison, by the way. My mentor experimented with them the last time we were here. You can even ground up the roots to make a powder. It's very fine—ends up looking a bit like sand—but it works the same way as the pollen."

"I don't want to ask how she found that out."

"She was something else." Then he looked back at his pin, rotating it in his fingers. He took a deep breath, turned to face one of the arches of the tower, and threw it away. The metal hexagon arced high into the air, glinting in the starlight, and disappeared into the night. Then he turned back to me. "Look, this saber has cost me so much. I don't apologize for keeping things from you. I just—I didn't want to see anyone else killed. I thought if I kept enough from you, even with you helping, you'd somehow . . ." He closed the distance between us and took my hands again, squeezing them tightly. "You'd get out of this."

"I know."

Which made what I needed to say next even harder, but it was really the only thing to do at this point. The *Starfarer* was coming here, and Val was after the lightsaber. I was sure of that now. I took a deep breath and said, "Take the lander and go."

He gave a start. "What? But—what about you? Your brother? You know he's—"

"Yeah. He's a pretty awful brother, but he's still mine. And if you can get out of the First Order, then he can, too." I was grateful it was nighttime, because the flowers couldn't stop me from saying what I needed to. "I'll be fine. *Go.* Like you said, the saber's important. What it represents is important. As long as stories persist . . ." I added, quoting part of the *Starfarer*'s motto.

Though I wasn't sure how much of that I believed anymore. Because there were some stories that didn't persist, that couldn't.

Some stories were simply forgotten with the last person who'd remembered them.

And I wouldn't let that happen today.

"I'm glad I met you, Sian . . ." And then I laughed,

more at myself than at our predicament. "I just realized I don't know your family name."

"Alakor," he replied.

"After the planet?"

"After my mentor, who named the planet after herself."

I smiled at how much I loved that—and didn't want to dwell too long on that word, on *love,* not now. "I'm glad I met you, Sian Alakor. I hope I see you again. I know that makes me naive—"

He grabbed the back of my head urgently and pulled me close. "It makes you brave, Starlight." Then he kissed me, desperate and crushing. In all the serials I'd read, whenever the author said that a kiss tasted like goodbye, I rolled my eyes, because what did goodbye even taste like? But now I understood. It tasted like salt. It tasted like tears. It tasted tinny with fear.

I decidedly hated the taste.

We broke apart and descended the tower together.

CHAPTER THIRTY

THE ARRIVAL

Sian took *Starstall* and left.

There were no long goodbyes. No more heated kisses. I simply went through the preflight check for him, made sure he had enough fuel to go somewhere far, far away from here, and let him go. Mom always said if you held something too tightly, it'd disintegrate in your arms, but if you let it go? If it was meant to be, it would come back.

I didn't fool myself into thinking Sian would ever come back.

When *Starstall* was a far-off glint in the sky, I sat down on a boulder outside of the facility and watched it disappear. I wasn't sure how I was going to explain the missing lander to Dad, but I hoped once I told him the story, he'd understand.

If I ever got to tell him the story.

"Do you think Lady Sosha got our message?" I asked

the droids, who were sitting in the dust, picking up their sabacc game again.

"I hope so," Veebee replied. Entoo *had* reattached her other arm, and probably did it a lot better than I could have. "I think you're cheating."

Entoo gave a warble of admonishment.

"Yes, I *know* I'm losing, but I do think you're cheating. The odds of me losing this many times are abysmally low."

In reply, Entoo gave another smart beep.

Veebee was quiet for a moment and then set her hand down. "You're right, the odds aren't zero."

I closed my eyes and breathed in the cool night air, listening to the quiet of the planet. The crackle of the fire Veebee had started. The buzz of the cards as she shuffled them between her fingers. The gentle chirp of bugs, the rustle of wind through the vines, billowing dust up. I was sure by the time the ship arrived, I'd be dusted over.

That gave me an idea.

If I already knew what to expect, maybe I could plan a little in advance. I couldn't control what Val would do or what would happen once the *Starfarer* landed, but I could guide a little. Ever since Val had come onto the ship, he'd done nothing but lie to me, and I was sick of it. It was time to even the playing field—and maybe if I did, I'd find my brother somewhere underneath it.

"Vee, what do you think about experimenting while we wait?" I asked, plucking a bud from a vine and twirling it in my hand.

She looked up at me, intrigued. "What kind of experiment?"

"Remember how you made that fine powder from the starblossom?" I asked, and she nodded. "Do you think you can do that with these flowers?"

"I did not actually use the starblossom itself, but its roots," replied the droid.

"That's perfect, actually," I replied. "Do you think you could?"

She looked around at what little Sian had left us with—some rations in a crate and a communicator. "With a will and a dream, I can do anything. And some rocks. I can use rocks. And Entoo's blowtorch."

Excitedly, the astromech popped out their blowtorch. *"Bloop!"*

"But why?" Veebee asked. "Care to fill us in? I can see the cogs in your head turning, and that is never a good sign."

"If Val wants the lightsaber, he's going to tell me why—whether he likes it or not."

That was all either of the droids needed to hear to agree to the plan. So I went about digging up a few roots of the vines and finding rocks that Veebee could use as a mortar and pestle. I hoped this would work.

At what point over the past three years had Val fallen in line with the First Order? At what point had he been so desperate that he joined a fringe group of zealots? I didn't understand it. He'd never liked the Empire—neither of us did, as kids of rebel fighters. We grew up on Mom and Dad's stories of running supplies and dodging firefights, and the terror they still felt whenever they heard the sound of ships breaking out of hyperspace, always expecting an ambush of TIE fighters.

The war had done so much damage to all the people who'd fought in it, and even to the ones who hadn't, who simply existed in the galaxy and found themselves pulled in from the edges.

In the quiet of the planet, I could hear my childhood in the white noise, my brother's bright laughter as we played rebels and fought imaginary foes.

"Pow-pow!" my brother cried, aiming his makeshift blaster at boxes stacked up and wrapped in white like stormtroopers, ducking behind a crate in the storage room of the *Starfarer*.

"Throw!" I cried, throwing out my hands. "I will send them flying with the Force!"

He scowled, peeking up from behind the crate. "You *know* the Force doesn't work like that, Arie!"

"I don't know how the Force works, so it can do whatever *I* want it to do," I replied indignantly.

"No, it can't!"

"Yes, it can."

"Whatever. Pow!" he added, miming shooting the sheet-clad enemy. "They're dead, anyway. Blaster bolt between the eyes."

Of course he always had to have the last say. I hated that. So I gasped and cried, "Oh no, they're taking over my mind!"

"What is?"

"Eeeevil! Terrible! The daaaaark side! It's implanted nano-droids in my miiiind!" I cried, convulsing, and dropped to the floor. Then I gasped, reaching out for him. "Go! Save . . . yourself!"

But Val set his mouth in a thin line and pretended to reload his blaster. "Never! I'll save you, Arie! I'll always be on your side."

In the end, he destroyed the "control box" that had taken over my mind, just in time for the *Starfarer* to kick out of hyperspace near Corellia, where the next tour would begin. When we finally walked into the mess hall for dinner, Dad came up to us and took us by our shoulders urgently.

"Where have you *been*?" he asked, face red with anger. "I've been looking everywhere!"

"We were in the cargo hold," Val said.

I added, "We were playing!"

"Don't ever do that again. I didn't know where you were," Dad said. "You can't go down into the cargo hold again. It's dangerous."

"It's on the *ship*, Dad," Val argued, wrenching his shoulder out of Dad's grip. "Where do you think we'd go?"

Dad shook his head. "This isn't an argument."

"It's not fair! Mom would let us," he added, storming out of the mess hall. He didn't have dinner that evening.

Dad looked at me. Mom had been gone for two years at that point, and Dad hated having us out of his sight. I shifted on my feet. "I'm sorry, Daddy. We won't do it again," I added, because I knew that was what he wanted to hear.

He gave a relieved sigh and pulled me into a hug. "You two are all I have left, love," he whispered into my hair. I looked past him, over his shoulder at the other crew members, some of them hired for only six months or a year, some permanent like Daaric and Maeve. *But what about them?* I wanted to ask, but I never did, and Daaric and Maeve pretended nothing had ever happened.

The *Starfarer* was my home, but as I opened my eyes and looked out at the wide sky, I knew it was also my cage.

Nothing bad ever happened as long as I was on the *Starfarer*. That was what Dad had taught me. It was a lie, because bad things happened whether or not I was on the ship. He couldn't protect me from everything—he *shouldn't*.

I could protect myself, too.

Veebee had ground the roots into a powder. I began to dust it over myself, the grains so fine they were almost translucent. It made me shimmer a little more than usual, but I didn't mind.

Like starlight on my skin. Maybe Sian's nickname really did suit me.

I had nothing to hide anymore, nothing I *wanted* to hide.

Far above us, the only home I'd ever known pulled out of hyperspace, materializing in the sky like magic. My heart hurt in my chest as I looked up at the metal bird, feeling equal parts homesickness and dread. I stood and took a deep breath. The powder on my skin smelled sharp and sweet like the flower itself.

All this for a lightsaber.

Behind me, Vee told her partner, "You were the greatest pain in my ass, Entoo. If we don't survive this, I will miss you. And our holochess matches. And our sabacc games."

"Bleep-bleep-bloop."

"I'm sorry. You cheated *how many times*?"

With a deep and calming breath, I said, "I guess I should radio up to them. It's time to get off this planet."

N2-0 tilted their cylindrical body forward with a dismayed chirp, and I couldn't agree more. I *really* hoped the Force was with us, too.

CHAPTER THIRTY-ONE

THE LAST CHANCE

The *Starfarer* landed on the indigo soil with a sigh.

I had told the droids to duck into the research facility and behind cover in case anything happened. If bad came to worse, they could send out a distress call from the communication console.

I hoped Lady Sosha had gotten my message.

I hoped, if she'd gotten it, she wasn't too late.

The gangway to the *Starfarer* lowered and settled on the ground with a hard thunk. I hoped to see Dad on the ramp, arms wide, telling me how worried he'd been, how I should never get separated again—a scolding I would have killed to hear.

Instead, it was my brother framed in the open cargo hull. Behind him, the Civil War Buffs stood like good little soldiers. Of course they did. Val raised his blaster at me—the one he'd sold the droids for.

I didn't even need to feign hurt and confusion, because my brother had never pointed a blaster at me before, and even after everything, I could have sworn he never would. But there he was in the doorway, dressed in a crisp dark uniform, a matching hat with the First Order insignia pulled low on his brow.

"What's this?" I asked, my voice wavering.

His disappointed gaze turned cold as he moved down the gangway, flanked by Spectacles and all his friends. And to think, I'd actually thought they were just guests. They sure fooled me. Had they boarded the ship because of Val? It seemed like it, the way they fell in line behind him. They were each dressed in a similar dark uniform.

The sight of them sent my stomach turning.

"Where's Dad?" I asked as he came down the ramp. "Where's the crew? The guests?"

"They're alive—safe, for the most part," he added, and with his free hand dug into his uniform pocket and produced my master key. "I locked everyone in their rooms. Well, with the exception of a few people. Dad just can't seem to take orders, you know?"

I tensed. "What did you do?"

He replaced the master key in his pocket. "What I'm asked to. Where're the others, Arie?"

"Others?" I echoed.

He motioned to the facility. "Check in there," he instructed his troops, who of course found the droids and forced them out at blaster point.

Veebee muttered, "Compensating much?" as she shuffled out with N2-O.

Val's face pinched. "I sold them."

"They're worth a little more than a blaster," I replied, eyeing the other weapons. "Or a *few* blasters, apparently. So I got a refund—ow!" I hissed as he grabbed me by the arm so tightly I'd bruise and dragged me in close.

"This isn't a *game*, Arie." I searched his face for any sign of the brother I'd known. He was in there somewhere, beneath this awful uniform. "There are powerful people who want powerful things."

"So you turned to the *First Order*—"

"Do you think I *wanted* this?" he hissed, and his eyes widened. He let go of me quickly, his jaw muscles feathering. The dust—it was working. He just didn't know what it was, why he was compelled to tell the truth, if he talked at all. He shook his head. "You could have done the right thing. But then our stupid *father* sent you that message—he's always ruining everything."

My face hardened. He really didn't know me at all. "I'm not going to abandon the people I love."

"And look where that got you! Locked up on a *ship*. You can't even tell Dad about your cute little stowaway you met out in the city. You have to lie about it, Arie!"

I steeled myself. "So you left and joined a few zealots who can't just let the past go?"

He gritted his teeth. At least I still knew how to get under his skin. It was a little harder now, but all I had to do was dig. "The First Order is everywhere," he hissed. "If we're going to survive, we can't be on the losing side. The galaxy isn't like in your silly little holonovels. Love isn't going to save us, Arie. We have to save ourselves." Then he turned back to his men and waved them inside. "Take the droids. Scan their memory banks. I'm sure they know where that stowaway went."

His men began to drag the droids away. I fought to get out of Val's grip, but his fingers just dug into my arm harder. "Don't you dare hurt them!" I snarled, glaring at my brother.

He scowled. "Don't look at me like that. They're just droids. Unless *you* want to tell me where that stowaway went."

"What stowaway? Ow! You're hurting me," I added with a wince.

His grip loosened a little. A muscle in his jaw twitched. "You helped him on Coruscant. My men told me. And you helped hide him on this ship." My eyes widened. So the men who had chased us in the city—*he* had ordered them? Then . . . the junior officer Sian talked about . . .

I felt sick to my stomach.

"Now *where is he*?" he pressed, and began to raise his blaster. "Don't make me regret this, Arie—"

Suddenly, and with an enraged cry, Veebee threw off the two men who held her. They tumbled down the ramp. She roared, "You are the architect of your own misery!"

N2-0 blipped in concern, trying to get free, but they couldn't.

Val, startled, turned his blaster on Veebee. "Stay where you are!"

VB-35 stalked down the ramp. Her eyes were bright, twin moons boring into him. "If I am *just* a droid," she snarled, "then you are *just* a slab of meat!"

He commanded the droid to halt, but she'd never been very good at obeying orders—not mine and certainly not anyone else's. He shot at her shoulder and then her leg, blowing off bits of metal, but it didn't even faze her.

Veebee was terrifying.

She shot her hand out and grabbed ahold of Valor's neck. And she started to squeeze. He choked out a gasp. His fingers slid off my arm. I backed away as quickly as I could.

"Run, Ardent," she said, holding my brother by his neck. "Onto the ship. Take it out of here. You're fast.

And if any of you try to stop her, he dies," she went on to Val's men, who weren't quite sure what to do.

Val gasped. "Let—go—you defective—"

"Vee," I said, "don't do this."

Because we knew the only way it would end. If I left on that ship, she wouldn't be going with me. And neither would Val.

This was not what we'd planned at all.

She pinned me with her bright starlike gaze and said matter-of-factly, "Your brother will never destroy me."

The next moment, a blaster bolt tore through the side of her face.

CHAPTER THIRTY-TWO

THE FIRST ORDER

I screamed.

Vee's hand went limp, and then she dropped like dead weight to the ground. He'd shot her. He'd actually killed her. I fell to my knees, but there was nothing to be done. One entire side of her processor was blasted through, sparks hissing out in angry static gasps. I hadn't thought I had any more tears left, that I could ever cry when I felt so frightened, but they came out in hot, choking gasps anyway.

Val found his footing again, rubbing his throat, which was now red, and turned his blaster on me. He said hoarsely, "I'm sorry, Arie. It was her fault."

I caught a sob in my throat, pushed it back down. *Her fault?* "B-but you are the o-one with the weapon," I stuttered, gulping down another sob, refusing to give him the sight of me coming unraveled. "*You* shot her."

He motioned to his men to take the other droid up. Entoo was screaming, ramming into every shin they could, but the men managed to immobilize them. "See if that droid knows anything about the criminal. He has something the First Order wants—"

"A lightsaber," I interrupted, and I relished his look of surprise. I curled my fingers into fists. I wasn't useless. I wasn't just a bird trapped in a cage. "Do you really think I don't know what comes on and off that ship? You keep underestimating me."

That must have done it, whittled so far down it cracked his composure. He snapped, "We *will* get that weapon—with or *without* you alive. Unlike your droid, I'll let you choose."

The words that left his mouth seemed to surprise him, too. Veebee's powder had worked. And this was how he really felt. It was sobering and solidified something that had been soft in me. Her last words were fresh in my memory—

Your brother will never destroy me.

He also would never threaten me. He would never point a blaster at me. He loved me. But while his face was familiar, a foreign malice had settled in his cold gaze. It was something I hadn't been able to put a name to until just now. Hatred. The brother who had left three years ago was gone, buried somewhere deep beneath that cruel-cut uniform. I wondered if, this past week, I'd seen the real him at all.

I wondered if that brother of mine was even still alive.

"You won't find it," I finally told him, which was the truth.

He gritted his teeth. "That's not what I want to hear. He's going to be angry. He's going to *kill* you, Ardent."

I inclined my head. "*Who* is?"

Suddenly, there was a flash of silver above us as another ship came out of hyperspace, and in the night sky a ship of darkness and dread appeared, all angles and corners. It wasn't a ship I'd ever seen before, and I had seen so many in spaceports across the galaxy.

Not a single one of them had made me feel as terrified as I did then.

"Him," Val whispered.

Above us, a terrible capital ship loomed.

One of the soldiers—Spectacles; I was so disappointed in him—said, "General Hux has arrived, sir."

Val's face pinched. He massaged the bridge of his nose, and I noticed that the palm of his hand where he had touched me glittered like fine sand. "I *tried* to protect you. It's all my fault what happens next. I mean—it's n—*not*. . . ." He touched his mouth with his fingers.

Confusion flickered across his brow.

I smirked. "You're truthful for once."

He shot an imploring look down at me, but I just said, "Maybe your conscience is catching up to you."

His eyes widened.

From the imposing ship came a command shuttle, and it shot straight toward us, kicking up wind and leaves and dust as it descended. My throat stung. The dirt in the air made my eyes water as the command shuttle landed a hundred meters away.

Over the roar of its engines, Val snarled at his men, "Bring out the captain and crew!"

His men jumped at the chance to do just that—*gleefully*, in fact. I wondered, at first, how five men could have commandeered an entire ship from under my father, but it turned out to have been rather easy in the end.

All Val had to do was threaten my life, and the entire crew folded like a bad sabacc hand.

The men brought my family out and lined them up like prisoners in front of a firing squad. They stood, handcuffed together, looking worse than I'd ever seen them. Kotti and the seasonal crew members were dragged out in their pajamas. Daaric was missing his eye patch, Maeve was missing her front right tooth, and Telly was missing altogether. My heart began to squeeze with panic, and then I saw my dad. He went slowly, clutching a wound on his side.

A scream tore out of my throat. I lurched toward him, but Val grabbed me by my jacket and pulled me back. He shoved his blaster into my side.

"He's *fine*," Val snapped. "He got into a bit of trouble when trying to warn you."

When I had called the *Starfarer* near Geonosis, when Dad had told me to run. My knees felt weak with the horror of it. Val would do this? *Val?*

Dad lifted his head to me. Dried blood coated his pristine blue uniform where he clutched his side. His eyes flicked to the corpse of VB-35 at my feet, and anguish crinkled his brow. He mouthed, *Love you.*

I wanted to cry, but I bit the inside of my cheek to steel myself. I wasn't going to give Val the satisfaction. I'd already let my emotions get the better of me.

Someone I loved had already died.

From the shuttle came half a dozen stormtroopers, blasters at the ready. At the center of them was a tall figure clad in black, a nightmarish mask concealing his face. A chill shivered down my spine at the sight of him. Beside him walked a redheaded officer in a military uniform, with a jacket and cap, all as black as night. He pulled at his cuffs in a fussy sort of way, clearly knowing how important he looked flanked by men in armor.

"What backwater planet did you bring us to, Officer Quay?" the redhead asked in an unmistakable and insufferably snide voice. It was the same voice I'd heard outside Val's room that night on the *Starfarer*. I guessed this was his commanding officer. "I hope, for your sake, you have what we need?"

"General Hux." Val greeted him with a salute, fist to his chest—the salute of the Empire. "This girl knows where it is. We'll tear apart the whole ship if we must."

This girl—he hadn't even called me his sister. Maybe that was for the best.

Daaric, from his spot in the lineup, barked a laugh. "And you know what you'll find? Suitcases, scared guests, and commemorative Pieces of Alderaan, but you folks refuse to learn from history, don't you?" Just as he finished the question, one of Val's men slammed the butt of his blaster against Daaric's mouth and told him to shut up.

I gave a start. "Stop! Don't hurt them!"

The redheaded general—*Hux*, was it?—bristled. "And who are *you* to order us?"

Beside him, the tall figure held up a hand in silence, then turned his abysmal gaze on me. *"Let the girl speak."*

The voice was deep and terrifying, not quite organic, not quite mechanical, either. I wondered what was beneath that mask—a droid? Some sort of sentient monster? The coldness, the flatness of his tone, made me want to run—as far and as fast as I could—but I was frozen to the spot in petrifying fear.

"I warned you," Val hissed.

Daaric silently implored me not to, while Kotti and Maeve ducked their heads, afraid to watch. They all saw VB-35 at my feet. They all knew the danger was very, very real. Dad kept his silence, his stony face all I needed to see. He knew stories like I knew stories, and despite telling Sian that I looked for the good in everything, I knew that not every story ended well.

Not every one of them could.

But just as I was about to tell Dad how sorry I was, a glint in the distance caught my eye. Metal? But metals corroded and turned to dust from this planet's pollen, so it couldn't be part of a ruin. And the only other metal objects here were the droids, the *Starfarer*, the *Upsilon*-class command shuttle, and—

Starstall.

I faced the warlord and raised my chin high.

I was my father's child, after all: rebel scum.

CHAPTER THIRTY-THREE

THE MONSTER

"I know where the lightsaber is," I said. Cold sweat slid down my back. I tried to look calm, but I was staring down death and I knew it.

But what would happen if this strange fringe group got their way? Solidified their lie about Luke Skywalker and how he'd abandoned the galaxy—and how everyone else would abandon them, too? Because stories, who told them, and who heard them mattered, woven together in a tapestry called history.

Maybe Luke Skywalker had abandoned the galaxy, but it didn't mean everyone would.

Good wasn't always easy. It wasn't always safe. It meant that sometimes the people you loved died in terrible, awful ways.

Good, as it turned out, was the hard choice.

Good was the long way around.

Tears burned at the edges of my eyes.

It wasn't fair—it wasn't fair.

But I knew that. Good wasn't fair. Good did not grow from nothing, just as evil did not bloom unattended. But even as I repeated that—*It's not fair, it's not fair, it's not fair*—I knew what I had to do.

I just hoped I had the courage to do it.

"The lightsaber's not here," I said, my voice strangely calm to my ears. Was this how I sounded before I died? Unafraid of death?

The general narrowed his eyes.

Val spun to me as if I'd just betrayed him. Well, probably so. *"What?"*

"The saber. It's not here with me. How did you think I got the droids back, *Brother*?" I asked him sarcastically. "That I stole them? That I killed the Jawas for them?" I met his gaze in a challenge. "I didn't know how important it was. I'm just a poor naive girl on a ship, after all."

He turned back to his superiors. This time *he* looked panicked. "She's lying about something, sir. She has to be."

The lander was getting closer, moving faster and faster, but they'd notice it soon if I didn't do something.

I wished I could tell Dad how much I loved him.

I took a deep breath and faced the terrible tall man in black armor. He really did look like a nightmare—some warped version of pictures I'd seen of Darth Vader. "And I'm sorry to tell you this, sir," I said to him, "but that mask is ugly, and probably so are y—"

The warlord snapped out his hand, fingers splayed.

I felt an invisible force grab me by the throat. I couldn't move. I couldn't breathe. I couldn't—I couldn't—

His power was so overwhelming, it was crushing. It hurt. Everything hurt. He dragged me closer, my feet brushing the ground. The planet around me grew faint—like a holo playing in another room. All I could do was stare into that terrible mask. Beneath his helmet was nothing but seething hatred. I could feel it—thorns spiking off of him like lacerations in the galaxy.

"Then I'll just look in your mind to see where it went," he said—

Or I thought he said. I wasn't sure. His voice was everywhere; it was in my ears, in my head, in my *bones*. A sharp stab of pain cut through my thoughts, a dull knife splitting apart flesh as it burrowed through my head. It hurt—it hurt so much I forgot to breathe.

He pulled away memories of Mom. Memories of sitting with Dad in the cockpit. Memories of playing pretend with Val. Fixing up Veebee. Laughing around the table in the mess hall with the crew. Guests—countless guests, so many guests, faces that bobbed in and out of the darkness, half remembered.

How unremarkable, I heard.

My life. He was referring to my life.

Itineraries and places and star charts and finding Mom's copies of *Under the Tan-Tan Sun* in a crate in the storage room, kicking my feet as I read them secretly late at night, finding the last installment in a shop on Coruscant—

No, I thought, trying to shove him away, but I was helpless. Powerless.

He really was a monster.

He saw the firefight. He saw Sian and me hiding in the alley. The lightsaber. Sian stowing away. The night we talked on the flight deck. Personal things—*private* things. Tatooine. Bartering with the lightsaber. Keeping it.

There was a thread of satisfaction when he saw that.

Geonosis. Alakor. *Kissing.* He lingered on that. Strange. Revolting. Then Sian taking the lander to leave. The *Starfarer* arriving. Val killing Veebee. The agony in that moment. He paused there. Relished it. Then he inspected my memory of seeing him for the first time, this awful monster, this warlord of nightmares, this—

Kylo Ren, he said.

I would remember that.

And then he saw the glint of metal in my memory. The lander—

Suddenly, there was a noise, so loud it made my head ring. He wrenched out of my thoughts, dropped me to the ground. I puddled there. If I had bones and skin and blood, I didn't know it anymore. He turned, raising both hands—

The lander, meters away, came to a dead halt.

I gasped for air, curling into myself on the ground, the feeling coming back like a needle of pain in my spine. My eyes were blurry. My throat burned.

With a cry, Kylo Ren threw the lander away like it was a children's toy. The ship flipped over and rolled to a stop against the facility. Smoke sighed from the engines. No—Sian. *Sian!* I clawed at the ground. It was spinning too much.

"Bold," remarked Kylo Ren.

I heard the lander door open. Through my blurry vision I watched someone stumble out.

The warlord took something from his belt. His own lightsaber. He activated it. The blade was as red as blood, a shorter blade on either side hissing, seething. I felt the heat burning my skin. He held it so close to my neck, I began to blister. I smelled my hair singeing.

He was going to kill me. There was no reason for him not to—

"Stop. Let her go," said Sian, stumbling toward us. The troopers raised their blasters at him, but the warlord motioned for them to stand down. "I have it—I have it here. Just let her go."

"You are bartering with me?" This Kylo Ren sounded angry now.

Sian took the saber out of his pocket. He held it up. "I'm pleading—"

The lightsaber was snatched from Sian's hand like it was on an invisible string. It flew into the warlord's grip. His shoulders hitched up in elation—

A moment passed in silence.

And then he yelled in anger—loud, frustrated, raw. He crushed the hilt in his hand like it was made of tin.

"This isn't the one!" he roared.

The pieces of the saber clattered to the ground, the strange yellow crystal inside cracked in two.

He turned his attention back to me, raising his red saber. Sian shouted. My family pleaded. I squeezed my eyes closed, until suddenly, I heard a familiar sound.

I knew that sound. I knew it well. It was the sound of a ship approaching in the atmosphere. The sky filled with the scream of ships. I glanced up. Three sleek, elegant fighters with chrome finishes soared toward us, firing bolts at the stormtroopers. The men scattered like herd creatures.

Kylo Ren deflected a blast. It careened into the research facility, where it met the fuel there and exploded, knocking everyone off their feet.

Everyone except him.

"Kill them," the warlord spat as he spun on his heel and returned to the shuttle. *"You've wasted enough of my time."*

When Val tried to follow, the general aimed his blaster at him. "No, *you* stay here with your mess."

My brother gave a start, his eyes wide. "But I *found* the lightsaber for you!"

"I'm glad you understand," the redhead spat, and turned his blaster on me.

Sian positioned himself between me and the general. Though I couldn't see what was happening, I imagined that the general had looked into Sian's eyes.

General Hux snarled, "A *Lucem*?"

"In the flesh," Sian replied, opening his arms wide with a mock bow. "I wonder, what do your dull eyes see?"

Then General Hux vomited. Two of his men grabbed him and ushered him quickly away toward the shuttle. Halfway there, he recovered enough to snarl into his communicator in a hoarse, cracked voice, "Fire on the ship when we've evacuated!"

The three fighter ships were coming back for a second round. They fired on the command shuttle, distracting the bigger ship in the sky, too.

For a moment, the planet was quiet.

For a moment, I sat on the ground, clutching my neck,

gasping for breath, Sian picking up the shattered pieces of the saber, while Telly and Maz stole out of the ship to undo the cuffs on the other crew members.

For a moment, everything stilled as my father slowly got to his feet.

For a moment, we were alive.

But not for long.

The command shuttle took to the sky.

From the communicator tucked into my jacket, I heard Lady Sosha yell, *"We'll hold them off while you go! Go!"*

Val wordlessly turned back to face us. There was a terrible dark shadow across his face. His hand still gripped the blaster, finger on the trigger. "You ruin everything," he snarled, storming toward me, stepping over the corpse of my friend. "You—"

Suddenly, he was pulled to the ground. He whirled back to see what it was—

Veebee's hand gripped his ankle. Half her face was melted, and her remaining eye flickered with life, but as she silently turned her gaze to me, I knew she wouldn't let him go. What had that Rodian said an eternity ago? *Always check for a pulse.*

We were still alive. Our deaths weren't foregone conclusions—not until we stopped fighting.

The hyperdrive engines weren't primed. The navicomputer wasn't programmed. It would take too long for

Dad to get the *Starfarer* into hyperspace before that terrible big ship above us shot us down.

But I wasn't Dad.

And this wasn't a normal ship.

This was *my* ship.

"Get on the ship!" I shouted, shoving myself to my feet. My stomach heaved. My entire body hurt. I couldn't think about that. "Hurry—Sian! Hurry!" I cried, sprinting up the ramp and through the cargo hold, glancing back to make sure everyone was making their way inside. They just had to get to the ramp. That was it.

Val struggled to get to his feet, having dropped his blaster, but Veebee kept her hold.

She was giving us a gift. I better not squander it.

I raced onto the bridge and fell into the pilot's seat, firing up the hyperspace engines. They yelled in warning, but I ignored them. The light for the airlock turned off a moment later and then—

"Everyone's inside," Dad reported from a comm station by the door. *"Except . . ."*

"I know, Dad. But he's . . ."

"I know, love. We have a responsibility."

We did.

I didn't have time to boot up the navicomputer. I didn't have time to run any preflight checks. I hoped everything worked. The ship had never failed me yet.

Warning lights flashed as the First Order's capital ship locked on to its target, but Sian dismissed them as he sat down beside me in the copilot's chair. I didn't know where to go, where we would be *safe*—

The three fighters banked toward the First Order's capital ship, swirling around it like gnats.

I flipped on the thrusters and pulled the ship off the ground. I had to at least get to the atmosphere before we jumped. I had to find a lane. I had to figure out where to *go*—

Through the communicator, Lady Sosha said, *"We'll meet you back at Endor,* Starfarer."

Endor it was.

Sian took my hand and squeezed it tightly. "Trust yourself, Starlight."

Glaring red lights lit up the console, alarms whirred, and then—

Trust yourself, I thought, and squeezed my eyes tightly closed.

I slammed down the hyperspace lever. The stars blurred. The thrusters glowed white. And suddenly I found myself in the space between spaces, where time swirled around us instead of sitting still. My wrists tilted the controls—nudged them, ever so slightly—left and then right and then left again. I couldn't *see* the celestial bodies we passed, the ships in the lanes around us, but

I could feel them. I understood them. Where they were going. Where they'd been.

Mom was right: Wayfinding was as easy as breathing.

The universe unfurled in front of me like a tapestry of lanes not yet taken, impossibly wide and beautiful, and I understood now—

I understood why my Mom had loved this so much.

The stars stretched onward. For one breathless second. Two. Three.

Ten minutes. Thirty. An hour—I didn't know. I couldn't tell. *This* was why Mom had liked to have someone she trusted in the cockpit while she astrogated. Because while I did, I wasn't in the cockpit. I wasn't in my body.

I was the product of time and motion.

All I knew was when it was time to disembark. It felt like delicately extracting myself from a tapestry, knitting myself back into my body. I pushed the hyperspace lever back up.

The *Starfarer* came out of lightspeed with a pop.

Through the viewport, Endor's forest moon sat peacefully in a pocket of safe space. No ships were waiting for us. No firefight. A few moments later, the three chrome ships that had helped us left hyperspace at our side. We had made it. We had escaped—*somehow*.

And the First Order didn't follow.

ENDOR

CHAPTER THIRTY-FOUR

THE RESISTANCE

Everything was quiet.

I sat back in the pilot's chair. My fingers shook. My chest hurt every time I breathed. And it was only after a few breaths that I realized my cheeks were wet. That my eyes were blurred—

That I was crying.

I felt like I'd cried enough in the past day to last a lifetime.

Without hesitation, Sian pulled me against him and pressed my head into his shoulder and held on so tight I didn't fear coming apart, because even if I did he was there to keep me together. At least for the most part. There was a piece of me still in hyperspace. A piece of me I'd never get back, forever lost wandering the lanes between time.

There was the me from before.

And there was the person I was now.

The tears helped ground me, and the circles Sian

rubbed on my back gave me something to think about, and finally, finally, I settled again. If this was how stories felt, being in the middle of them, I had told them all wrong since the beginning. I'd told only about the wonder, the exhilaration, the elegance of it all—even the bad things, even the moments that changed people forever.

There was nothing elegant about any of this. Nothing wonderful. Nothing exhilarating.

It was raw and painful and frightening. It made me want to bury my head in fiction and never come out again. This was horrid. This was disappointing.

And yet Sian's embrace was warm, and the words he muttered—"We're safe, we're safe now, we're okay"—felt true even if I knew they had never been true and would never be true. Veebee was gone, and my brother was a traitor.

But for the moment, his arms around me were nice. I burrowed my face into his shoulder and inhaled his scent of dusty otherwhere and complimentary shampoo.

It was a comfort.

There was a knock on the door to the flight deck, and then it opened for my father. He had an arm slung around Daaric to stay upright, his other clutching his side. When they saw me, relief washed over both their faces.

"Daughter," he sighed as I lurched out of the pilot's

chair. He abandoned Daaric and stumbled toward me, and we wrapped each other in a hug. He smelled like blaster emissions, pungent and tart. "Daughter, Daughter," he murmured into my hair.

Sian slipped off the flight deck with Daaric, who wanted to treat Sian's wounds from his tumble in the lander. They closed the door behind them.

"I was so worried," I said, hot tears still spilling down my cheeks. "I'm sorry."

"Hey, hey, none of that, love," he replied, kissing my cheek. His beard, rough and familiar, scratched my skin. "You did good. I'm so proud of you."

"Is e-everyone okay?" I asked, sobbing.

"Yeah," he replied, also sobbing. "We're alive. We're alive because of you."

But not all of us. Just most of us.

"I didn't want to leave her," I cried into his shoulder. "I didn't want to leave her." The words came out of me like a broken record. VB-35 had been with me through everything. She'd been my first friend and the first person who'd found me crying after Mom died, the first person to tell me it was okay to be a little messy and a little off-kilter. She'd always made sure I ate, and she'd always made sure I never worked too hard and never sat too long in my own feelings alone—

I'd spent so much of my life wondering what it would

be like to still have a mom that I hadn't realized I'd had one the entire time. Veebee had been there for me, and I'd never thanked her.

And now I couldn't.

I didn't know how long I'd cried into my dad's shoulder, and I wasn't sure how much longer I would have if the comms hadn't crackled, startling us from our tears.

A soft, melodic voice hummed through the speakers: *"This is Sosha Soruna checking in. Ha-ha! I haven't had a thrill like that in twenty years! May we guide you in to land on Endor,* Starfarer?*"*

We landed in a clearing beside a beautiful dark blue lake. After seeing so much dust and sand over the past few days, even after Alakor, the green grass and lush trees were a welcome sight. I disembarked from the ship with Dad and walked toward Lady Sosha and her two pilots on a beautiful flower-filled patch. I tried to tell him to sit down and let me greet her alone, but he refused.

He was still the captain, after all, and he said, "If I stop moving, that's when the pain'll catch up to me."

"That's because you're running on adrenaline, old man."

"Bah! This is just what it's like to be alive!" he crowed, and kissed me one more time on the forehead as Lady

Sosha slid out of her fighter ship, tossed off her helmet, and walked to us.

She threw up her arms. "What an *exquisite* getaway!" she cried. "Hansifred, you truly outdid yourself. Especially with that injury of yours. Are you sure you should be up and about?"

"Ah, well," Dad drawled, "it actually wasn't my flying. It was my daughter's."

"What a gift," the ex-ruler of Naboo complimented, smiling at me. I think she'd already known. "You must be proud."

"Incredibly," he replied, his voice breaking a little in the center of the word, as if it didn't quite encompass how much.

"Thank you for saving us," I told her. "I was afraid you wouldn't get the message."

The older woman shook her head. "You saved yourself, Ardent. We just helped however we could. It was quick thinking to send a message to us from Alakor. I'll admit that I didn't expect it. I'm sorry it took us so long to reach you. I was hoping we'd get there before the *Starfarer*, but hyperspace travel can be unpredictable."

"At least you arrived," I pointed out. "I was worried the console was too old to work."

"It worked well enough. But now we have a problem

and, ah, I hope you don't mind, but I invited a friend to help solve it," Lady Sosha said, glancing up at the sky as a sleek-looking ship entered the atmosphere.

It was Senator Leia Organa.

She wasn't a senator anymore. Her insistence that the First Order was a real threat, as well as some other overblown scandals, had made her retreat from New Republic office. But I didn't know how else to think of her. If not a senator, then . . .

I wasn't sure what to call her.

I had seen Leia Organa on holovids before, but much like everyone else, they rarely did her justice. The woman who strode across the green grass of the valley toward the *Starfarer* had a rigid spine and kindness hidden in the laughter lines around her eyes. She wore her gray hair in a practical bun behind her head, matching the rest of her uniform—a soft shirt with a utility vest over the top and coarse dark pants tucked into impeccably shined boots. The only signifier that she had once been a princess was the way she held herself, her shoulders back and her chin high, as if not even gravity could defy her.

I had never met a story before, but Leia Organa was everything I had imagined she would be.

Lady Sosha told us that Leia Organa knew what had

happened—Lady Sosha had called her just after receiving my message—and called the crew down to meet with her. The guests had begun to filter out of the ship, as well, stretching their legs and wandering about the meadow. So Dad gathered everyone to introduce them.

"Senator Organa," he greeted.

She clasped his hand in a strong shake. "It's General now," she said, and surveyed us all. "Right—I believe in getting to the point. It's apparent that the First Order knows your ship, and most of your faces. You will be in danger because of that. Also," she added, turning to me, "I have taken the liberty of buying out your and your friend's warrant. Since it was unlawful to begin with, I had some say. However, I can't do that again in the future."

Dad gave a start, turning to me. *"Warrant?"*

"For a crime she didn't commit, I assure you," General Organa said.

Telly stroked her whiskers and muttered, "If the First Order knows our ship now, it'll be too dangerous for tours in the future."

"I was thinking about retiring anyway," Dad mused, to the astonishment of everyone in the group.

I gaped. *"Retire?"*

Daaric put a hand on his shoulder. "Sweetheart, you'd sooner die."

"I almost died today," Dad pointed out.

General Organa smiled at that. "I think you're made of sterner stuff, Hansifred Quay. I've a better idea. You should look into changing careers. I've a few friends who could use an old, reliable ship like the *Starfarer*, and an old, reliable captain like you. I can't guarantee exotic locales or safe missions, but we are making a difference. You saw firsthand the terror of what still lurks out there. Something is stirring. We need to be ready."

My dad scratched his beard. "Erm. I'm not too keen on wars anymore, General. How's the pay?"

"Abysmal," she replied.

"Holidays?"

"None."

"Any perks at all?"

"The safeguarding of our freedoms and Republic. What do you say?" And she reached out her hand.

The captain looked around at his crew. Daaric said, "We follow you, Captain," and the sentiment was echoed by everyone else.

So my dad turned back to the general and said, "Well, when you put it that way, how can I refuse?" And he clasped her hand in a firm shake. "You've got us."

General Organa smiled. "Welcome back to the fight, Hansifred."

CHAPTER THIRTY-FIVE

THE STARFARER

That evening, Dad decided to throw a party.

If it was the last night he'd be the captain of the touring ship the *Starfarer*, he wanted to celebrate it. It was decided that the passengers—who were all safe and accounted for—would be taken back to Coruscant on a separate ship, with Lady Sosha's and General Organa's help. Everyone was promised refunds, and I knew we didn't have the creds for that. It would wipe out what little funds we had.

Though I suppose it didn't really matter. The First Order knew the ship. They knew our faces. General Organa stressed that the *Starfarer* needed protection, if nothing else. It couldn't operate as a civilian vessel any longer, not without a whole host of paranoia. But in the Resistance, my dad could continue flying. He didn't know anything else. But still, everything that I knew—everything that I'd grown up with—was gone.

Just thinking about it made my stomach churn.

Ironically, no one asked where the Civil War Buffs had gone, but a few lovelorn guests did come around to ask after Valor.

Lady Sosha had sent a rescue party to Alakor to pick him up, but apparently no one was there. No Val.

And no VB-35.

Wherever they were, we couldn't find them.

That sparked a little hope in my chest. It was an addicting feeling. I could see how entire wars might be won on it.

Dad had ordered Telly to break out all the best casks of wine and wheel out all the food that was about to spoil, and we'd have a party like no party ever before. (Telly had been locked in the galley until they'd reached Alakor and Maz found her. She'd gone down for a caf before her night shift, and when she found that the droids were missing, Val sealed her inside and then locked down the rest of the ship.) A large brilliant bonfire crackled in the middle of the meadow, reflected in soft hues of orange and yellow in the *Starfarer*'s metal skin. Guests danced and drank and sang while a volunteer spun music that was loud and bright. Entoo didn't have the heart tonight, and we couldn't blame them.

At the beginning of the celebration, Dad had—against *everyone's* better judgment—climbed onto a log and cried,

"To Veebee-Thirty-Five! A storied life and a storied memory!"

"To Veebee-Thirty-Five!" everyone cheered.

Veebee would've hated it.

Beside me, Entoo beeped.

I patted them gently on their dome. "I know, friend. I miss her, too."

Together, we watched the party, them just beside me while I sat on an overturned log. I didn't really feel like dancing, and my body was sore from, well, *everything*. I wasn't sure I could dance anyway, with all the bandages Daaric had stuck on me. Every little cut needed one, apparently. But I'd showered and dressed in clean clothes—not my uniform, just normal trousers and a starched shirt and my mom's worn leather jacket—and grabbed the last installment of the serial to read out by the fire.

I connected the datatape to my datapad to transfer the story over and lounged back on the log, but my brain wouldn't concentrate on the words. It was ironic that I had the time to read it now but I couldn't.

There was so much to do, so much on the *Starfarer* to fix. At least there *had* been, until I reminded myself that there would be no next tour. No next itinerary. This was it.

And then . . . *anything*.

Anything at all.

Would I have to go with Dad into the Resistance? I wasn't sure I could. I wanted to help the galaxy, obviously, but I needed to find my own way to do good. Dad's life was the *Starfarer*, and I wasn't sure I wanted mine to be anymore. It wasn't a cage like Val said, but it wasn't really *home*, either. I didn't think it ever really *had* been home.

Home wasn't a place to me.

It was Dad at the helm, and Daaric beside him. It was Entoo's favorite tunes and Veebs's terrible kitchen concoctions and Telly's once-in-a-decade laugh and Maeve's fathier winnings and Kotti's larger-than-life hugs. It was the taste of freshly brewed caf in the mornings and the smell of recycled air and the thrilling shake of a ship as it breached atmo.

Stars—home was *everywhere*.

It just took me losing sight of the *Starfarer* to realize it.

I wanted to do good. I *would* do good. But like wayfinding, I just needed to find my own lane there, through all this chaos.

After a while, Entoo beeped a goodbye and wandered off to chase the DJ away with their blowtorch and take up their mantle as the real DJ. The music got a lot better after that.

I hid a smile as I watched the party unfurl: Maeve

flirting with a burly Houk, Kotti dancing with two very beautiful people, and Telly drinking a mug of wine across the way. She found me looking and lifted her mug.

I lifted my datapad in reply.

Once, there had been soirees and holochess tournaments and dances and birthday parties under the motto my Dad had carved in the main chamber, and this was what was left.

I was sad to see it go, but . . .

The possibility of the future made my heart ache, like a serial leaving off on a cliffhanger. No heading. No map.

No idea what came next.

How thrilling, how new, how *novel*.

I didn't have to know what came next to trust myself that whatever did, I could figure it out. I had surprised myself so often over the past few days, I was sure I could do anything.

The party spun on, the din of guests sweet with laughter, returning the galaxy to some off-kilter semblance of normal. I was glad for the soundtrack. It broke up the tension that had settled between my shoulder blades. Over at a table, Dad was leaning against Daaric, and they were laughing and smiling at each other, thinking no one was paying attention.

Things were changing. Things had already changed and would continue to change. *I* had changed. I felt it deep in my bones.

"So, is that him?" asked Lady Sosha, startling me out of my thoughts. She sat beside me on the log and pointed her chin toward Sian, who was sitting on a tree stump over by the lake, inspecting the pitiful remains of the lightsaber. He looked hopelessly lost staring at it.

"I didn't—he's not—we're not—how do you know?" I sputtered, turning red.

She laughed. "Relax. Your father told me about him. The stowaway and his lightsaber."

My shoulders slumped. "All of this over a lightsaber," I murmured. "It's so silly."

"You think so?" she asked, tilting her head. "I don't think it was about the lightsaber at all, but what the lightsaber meant. A man felled an empire with a lightsaber. You know how stories go. They become bigger than the people in them. They become symbols."

"But it was the wrong lightsaber. It was all for nothing."

"Imagine if it hadn't been. Or imagine if the First Order had a little more imagination." She snorted. "Too bad they never will. Fear is the death of creativity." Then she took a deep breath. "I hope the First Order stays on the fringes. I hope they die in the darkness they came from. I don't think I can live through another war. One is enough for a lifetime."

Then she patted me on the shoulder and excused herself to save General Organa from a rather intoxicated man who looked to be coming onto her a little too strong, which she was about to make everyone's problem.

I stowed my datapad in my leather jacket and pushed myself to my feet with a slow groan. My entire body hurt, and the meds hadn't even touched some of the soreness. Dad said I'd probably be hobbling for a few days. How did people *live* like this?

When I reached Sian, Noola was sitting on his shoulder, snacking on a fresh grape and purring.

The creature chirped, and I scratched her under the chin as I sat down.

He gave a start. "Oh," he said, realizing, "it's just you."

"*Just* me? I'm offended," I remarked, and knocked my shoulder against his. We settled into a comfortable silence. After a while I asked, "How do you do it?"

Confusion flickered across his face, but soon it melted into understanding. I had meant how did he exist knowing there were monsters like—like that *Kylo Ren*. That anyone could turn to the dark side, even people he loved—people *I* loved, like Valor. That evil wasn't defeated—that it was still here. Still festering. Still thriving like an infection under an already-stitched wound while we slept off the fever, hoping it would go away.

He brushed the curls out of my face and kissed my forehead. "By meeting people like you who tell me good is worth the fight, and that's how we survive."

My throat felt tight. "It was all luck, Sian."

"What do you think hope is, if not a little luck and hard work and sacrifice? And that doesn't mean that what you did wasn't extraordinary. Never apologize for hoping, Starlight. We need that in this galaxy—people like you. People who teach pessimistic nerf herders like me that if we didn't have at least a little of that, we'd be lost." He threaded his fingers through mine and kissed the back of my hand. "*I'd* be lost."

I leaned toward him and pressed my lips to his. They were dry and cracked, and he no longer tasted like dust and mystery and spices but blood and salt and sweat. "Thank you for coming back," I whispered against his mouth, because he could have left—he could have taken the lander and fled.

But he hadn't.

He'd come back.

He held my hands for a long time, tracing my

knuckles with his thumbs. "Enough people have died for this saber, Starlight. I didn't want you to be another."

I leaned my head against his shoulder and studied his fingers laced through mine. "Still," I whispered, "it was brave."

Just like Mom had said—even when you let them go, the things that were meant to return did.

And it was more than I could put into words, but luckily I didn't have to, because he understood and kissed me again in reply, as if to say, *Of course I came back.* It was the kind of kiss that was soft and comforting and languid, the kind of kiss that took its time because he wasn't going anywhere.

He was staying right here.

The kiss filled my heart so full, the encroaching fear dissipated like an echo in a cave, and what remained was what always remained—the parts of me that were knitted together from all the years I'd lived on the *Starfarer.* The parts of me that couldn't diminish, couldn't die, even when faced with things so dark they smothered everything else they touched.

Home.

"Honestly," he murmured against my mouth, "I learned it from you—"

"Ah! Is that the saber I've heard so much about?" Maz

came up to us and picked up one half of the crystal. She inspected it in the light. Sian and I immediately sat up and separated, and she slid a sly look between us. "Don't get uncomfortable on my account."

A blush ate across my cheeks. The tips of Sian's ears went red.

She grinned, eyes dancing. "Vek told me you were a good egg, my boy."

Sian's embarrassment washed away in a wave of surprise, and he looked like an orphan boy who'd just heard someone say his parent's name. "You knew my mentor?"

"Crossed paths a few times," Maz replied, setting the broken crystal back on the stump. "We agreed a lot on the *reclamation* bit of her work. The galaxy is worse off without her in it."

He swallowed thickly. "Yeah."

Maz hummed. "You know, I haven't seen this saber in years. It's a pity that that warlord destroyed it."

"He didn't care," Sian replied. "He thought it wasn't Luke Skywalker's."

"It is."

Sian gave a start. "What?"

Maz hummed, putting her hands behind her back. "Heroes are never as stagnant as their stories. They're just people, even if they are called to greater things, and in their different seasons they take up many different weapons. In the end, some are lost, some await new owners, and some find themselves in the precarious hands of new stories."

I looked down at the bits of the broken one, its crystal soft and golden. New stories? I liked the possibility of that.

"So my mentor was right," Sian whispered. He blinked, tears at the edges of his eyes. "She . . . always knew. She *knew* it was his. She just didn't know where it belonged, with Luke Skywalker missing."

The old woman leaned in close, as if to whisper a secret. "There is a Jedi temple on Tempes. It belongs there."

He sat up straight, excited, until he realized—"Oh. I can't return it in pieces."

Maz clicked her tongue in thought. Then she snapped her fingers. "*Ah!* I think I know someone who can help. At the Black Spire Outpost on Batuu."

He snorted. "Can they fix lightsabers?"

Maz grinned and replied, "I'll tell Savi to expect you."

So Sian would be leaving. *Really* leaving this time. Sosha's people had given him a ship—it was a clunker, but it'd get him where he needed to go as long as he didn't need to get there fast. And now he had a heading, a destination: Batuu. And then he'd be gone—forever gone—out of my life just as suddenly as he came into it. The thought pulled at something in my chest, deep and yearning and as old as I was. Something that had as much to do with Sian as it did with the going. There was a whole galaxy out there, and for a moment I'd glimpsed it, and it was beautiful.

"Maybe the Force be with you," she said with a playful wink, squeezing his shoulder, and walked away from the party into the darkness of the woods, like a ghost dissipating in mist.

I never saw her again.

Daaric *really* owed me a better story about his time before the *Starfarer.* With a boss like that? There was no way it wasn't full of at least two near-death experiences.

"Oh! That reminds me." I took the celestialabe out of my pocket and handed it to Sian. I'd snatched it from my dresser drawer when I got the datatape earlier. "Can you tell me what this is?"

He turned it over, inspecting the letters carved into it and the different star charts. "Aaaah, is this the infamous celestialabe you wanted to return?"

I stuck out my tongue at him. "Imagine if I *hadn't.*"

He grinned. "I can't. You're not the stealing type."

I mocked a gasp. "I steal *some* things!"

"Sure, and what do you steal?"

"This," and I kissed him quick on the mouth and

won that argument immediately. I decided that I liked winning arguments with kisses. "So is it real? The celestialabe?"

His attention dropped to my lips, and then he cleared his throat. "Sadly not. It's a tourist trinket from the Corellian Engineering Corporation. Before the Galactic Civil War, they gave these out to kids who aced a navigation quiz." He handed it back to me. "You're more authentic than this thing."

I slipped it back into my pocket. Maybe it was just a trinket, but it had given me some good luck, I thought, so why not keep it. "Well then, this authentic celestial-abe would like a dance." I pushed myself to my feet and offered him my hand.

He accepted it without a moment of hesitation. "I thought you'd never ask."

CHAPTER THIRTY-SIX

THE STARLIGHT

We danced so long, laughing and trying not to hurt ourselves more than we already had, that I didn't notice until Entoo put on a slower song that it was almost morning. Already? It had been barely dusk an hour ago, it felt like. And soon it would be tomorrow, and I didn't know what sort of tomorrow that would be.

"You look lost in thought." Sian's voice drew me out of my head. We swayed slowly, at the edge of the party.

"Everything is going to change now," I said.

"I guess so."

"And I guess you'll be going, too?" I went on, because it couldn't be helped. The tour had come to an end, and like every other one, I was expected to say goodbye. To become barely a passing footnote in the lives of everyone else.

He clicked his tongue, pondering the question. "Maz gave me a lead to get this lightsaber fixed, so I think I'm going to figure out how to get to Batuu."

I pressed on a smile. "Maz won't steer you wrong."

"No, I don't think she will. But—Ardent." He swallowed thickly and stopped dancing, his face serious. He squeezed my hand. If he wanted to say something else, he didn't say it, or didn't know how to, and I couldn't make him, either. I didn't know what I wanted him to say, anyway. I just knew that the galaxy was quiet, and my heart sounded so loud, screaming for him to ask me to come along.

But he never asked.

And I never answered.

So we stood in the quiet a moment longer until Dad wandered over, leaning heavily on a cane. His wound had been bandaged up, and he'd dressed down for the party, though he looked so odd in just a linen shirt, trousers, and well-worn boots. Like it was a disguise that didn't fit him. "Aaaaah, Daughter! Look at you! Still dancing away," he said warmly. "I was wondering where you two had wandered off to."

Sian quickly lurched away from me, hands in the air. "I—um—I don't think we've met. Sian." And he extended a hand.

Dad regarded the hand silently and then took it, maybe a *little* too hard. "Quay. I hear you stowed away on my ship."

"Um, it was a mutual stowing. Ardent knew about it—and the droids."

"You stayed in the pantry."

"It was very cozy."

"And you helped save the *Starfarer* and all its passengers."

"Just a little," he said hesitantly, clearly worrying that he'd never get his hand back.

Finally, Dad let go, eyebrows set into a serious line.

I rolled my eyes and punched Dad in the shoulder. "*Stop* it. You're scaring him."

Dad cracked and grinned. "*Ha!* I've always wanted to do that." Then he put a hand on Sian's shoulder and squeezed it tightly. "Thank you, m'boy. You did good."

That caught Sian off guard. "Um . . . it—it was nothing."

"It was *not* nothing. You helped my daughter. I'll never forget that. If you ever need a home, you have it here." And then he pulled Sian into a one-armed hug, something the boy *absolutely* had not expected, but he melted into it like a child not knowing how much he'd needed it. Then he pulled away quickly and cleared his throat. "I—thank you. Excuse me," he mumbled, and with one last lingering look at me, he departed from the party and went into the ship, Noola following.

"He's a good kid," Dad said. "A bit rough around the edges. But good. I can see what you like in him. Is that how you did it? You trusted him to have your back while you looked at the sky?"

My throat tightened a little, and I swallowed the lump in my throat. Of course Dad knew that I'd astrogated without my having to tell him. I gave a single nod. "It felt—*amazing*. Like something in me had finally come alive."

"Because a part of you probably did," he admitted. "You're so much like her, it scares me sometimes."

Tears came to my eyes, and I scrubbed them back. I leaned my head on his shoulder, and we faded into silence again, the soft whisper of the wind through the trees and grass cool on our skin. The *Starfarer* sat so peacefully in the meadow, tinged green from the reflection of nature around it. The ship had ferried us through so much.

I closed my eyes. There were so many memories on that ship. Happy, buoyant ones. *Good* ones. Bittersweet ones, too, of Mom in the cockpit, or Mom making caf in the mornings in the galley, or Mom humming as she braided my hair in my room.

"I miss her," I whispered.

"I do, too, love."

"But . . ." I swallowed the trepidation that bubbled up in my throat. I knew what I had to say—and it was a decision I had made somewhere between Coruscant and here. "I can't stay, Dad. I know you're afraid that I'll go off and never come back, too, but . . . I want to see things. Experience them." My voice broke, and I bit my bottom lip to keep myself grounded and blinked away the tears. I had thought by now I wouldn't have any left, but I kept surprising myself in more ways than one. "I want to go out and see if I am made of the same star stuff my mom was."

"Oh, love." Dad kissed the top of my head. "I know. I've been thinking about that, too. I think she'd want you to go out and see the galaxy. Find out what you're missing." He took a deep breath. "As a parent, I want to protect you from everything . . . but I have to trust that I've given you the tools to protect yourself, too. It's just hard."

"You have to let me try," I begged.

He nodded. "I will. And I'll always be here when you're missing home. You've got stars in your blood. No matter where you are, you'll always find your way."

"Even to you? Will I always find a way back to you?"

He hummed, soft and gentle. "I'll never be far, love. Never."

But somehow, this felt like a goodbye. Not a bad one. The kind you whispered at night before you turned off the lights.

It felt like an invitation to try something new.

When I had finally astrogated, the sky itself had

cracked open for me, wide and impossible and exhilarating, beckoning me with a thousand stars, a thousand stories, and a thousand different beginnings.

And I knew exactly where I wanted to start.

"I should probably go find him before he disappears, huh?" I asked.

"Yeah, I think that was his plan," Dad replied.

I kissed him on the cheek and hurried across the party and up the ramp into the *Starfarer*. I went to my room, where I shoved a few clothes into a bag, then hurried down to Kotti's door. I knocked on it urgently.

A moment later, her sleepy face appeared in the doorway. "Best friend," she slurred, pulling me into a tight hug. She smelled like a cask of wine. "I'm glad you aren't dead."

I hugged her tightly. "I'll see you later. I'll write often," I promised.

"Go chase those stars, Arie."

And so I did. I turned on my heel and hurried down the corridor again, toward the galley. Veebee wouldn't be there, but I knew who would. Rations were expensive, after all, especially for a stowaway. He'd finished shoving his pack full of supplies when I caught him. I was breathless, my muscles sore and aching.

"I hope you weren't leaving without saying goodbye," I started.

He had the gall to look bashful about it and pulled his long fingers through his silvery hair. "I'm bad at goodbyes."

"So am I," I admitted. I took a deep breath and added, "So let's not say goodbye. I want to go with you." If I was going to start taking charge of my future, I needed to start here, with the small things. Maybe the big things would be easier in time. "You'll need a good navigator. I'm the best."

"Are you now," he replied. Noola purred and poked her head out of his pack, but he shushed her. "Do you have references?"

"I do. His name is Sian. He thinks I'm impossible."

"Does he," he said. His ears were turning a lovely shade of pink, making his eyes look all the blacker.

I liked them—both his ears and his eyes—very, very much. But more than that, I liked the way he saw me through them. I liked the way he held my hand, and the way he asked if I was okay, and the way he *had given up escaping a terrifying warlord to ram a lander into him instead*. All of him, really.

I liked all of him very, very much. Maybe enough to love—*was* this love? A feeling bigger than any one part of me. Bright and hopeful and shining, like a star.

He said, "Well, I guess I can't argue with him. You do seem quite impossible. One of a kind." He held out his hand and asked, "Would you want to go on an adventure with a stowaway?"

I was already accepting his hand as I asked, "Will it be dangerous?"

"Probably." He tugged me out of the galley and down the corridor.

"Will I need to rescue you?"

"More than once," he confirmed.

I closed the space between us, and there in the dull halogens of a starship made of stories that persisted long after the people in them, I kissed a stowaway made of star stuff and faraway things, and he tasted like hope and adventure and impossibly wide skies.

Then I led him down the ramp and into the meadow, where sunlight broke across a purpling sky, catching in the dew on the grass and in the trees. They sparkled like stars, and the morning was cool and quiet, and the sky was wide.

And with his hand in mine, we decided to get lost.

ACKNOWLEDGMENTS

When I was little, I used to play *Star Wars* with the neighborhood kids. We would pretend to be Sith and Jedi, fighting epic lightsaber battles on our front lawns. I never imagined that twenty-five years later I would be weaving a story in a galaxy far, far away. How amazing, how rare, how *lucky* to be able to create in this space with other passionate people.

To the team at Lucasfilm Publishing and Story Group—Michael Siglain, Jennifer Heddle, Kelsey Sharpe, Pablo Hidalgo, and Matt Martin: thank you for being my unending encyclopedias, my cheerleaders, and my North Stars.

To my copy editor, Meg Speer-Levi, for catching all my discrepancies and keeping my timeline in check.

To my cover designers, Madison Ackerman and Kurt Hartman, and artist Ombretta Tavano: thank you for bringing Ardent and Sian to life on such a beautiful cover.

To interior design, managing ed, marketing, and publicity: thank you so much for working on this novel. I appreciate you very much, your passion and your dedication. Thank you for making this book look hella good, and for getting the word out about it.

But most of all, this book would still be a distant dream without the hard work and determination of Emeli Juhlin, the mastermind behind this entire endeavor. I remember when she first asked me to be a part of this initiative. We were having lunch, and she leaned in with a glimmer in her eyes and asked, "Do you want to write a romance?"

I couldn't say no.

So thank you, Emeli, for giving me the keys to a galaxy far, far away for a little while. I had the best time playing on the front lawn, exploring the lovely and impossible places *Star Wars* has gone, and has yet to go.